AF751635

Affirm press

Sonia Orchard is the author of *Something More Wonderful* and *The Virtuoso*, which won the Indie Award for Best Debut Fiction of 2009. She has a PhD in Creative Writing and lives in the Macedon Ranges (Victoria) with her husband and three children.

PRAISE FOR *INTO THE FIRE*

'Delicious, dark, smouldering — Sonia Orchard's *Into the Fire* is an unflinching post-mortem of a once life-giving friendship, swirled with the doubts, guilt and shame that every woman under patriarchy recognises, lying alone in the belly of night.'

Feminartsy

'From the outset, Into the Fire is never less than riveting, compelling drama... a superbly crafted novel...'

Fairfax

'Orchard is a superb storyteller. Her writing is intimate and animated, with a lullaby quality. Part homage to motherhood, part critique of third-wave feminism, *Into the Fire* is a powerful discernment of the complexity and fragility of human behaviour.'

Australian Book Review

'A literary trend I'm enjoying very much is the novel focusing on the tribulations of female friendship. Think Elena Ferrante's *Neapolitan Quartet; Marlena* by Julie Buntin; *The Burning Girl* by Claire Messud and *Give Me Your Hand* by Megan Abbott...'

Readings February Book of the Month

'...what's most intriguing about this story is the sharp commentary on gender politics, comparing our university-age selves to our mid-career selves, and the subtle power of gaslighting. *Into the Fire* will appeal to fans of Emily Maguire, Zoë Heller and Sofie Laguna.'

★★★★ *Books + Publishing*

'*Into the Fire* explores what Lessing demonstrates: how even the best-intentioned women, even feminists, might fail one another simply for not appreciating the many reasons – hidden, silent, structural – that their sisters end up thwarted, or in the most tragic circumstances, dead.'

Sydney Review of Books

'*Into the Fire*'s honesty in looking at often ugly behaviour, and its ability to knuckle down into the core of its characters' complexities, make it hard to put down...'
The Saturday Paper

An 'attractive, intelligent and steadfastly feminist novel...'
The Adelaide Advertiser

'A perceptive, provoking story of friendship and intimacy, which examines the conundrum where the personal and political collide. *Into the Fire* raises a timely question: what stories are we willing to believe about our own and other people's lives? I loved it.'
Rosalie Ham

'In this taut and thoughtful novel, Sonia Orchard deftly steers us through the twists and turns of female friendship, love and motherhood, and past the multiple hazards of the male gaze. *Into the Fire* is a smart, heartbreaking and richly rewarding read.'
Jacinta Halloran

'Orchard is an astute observer of long friendships, their binds, their blind loyalties, their casual betrayals. Alice, Crow and Lara will stay with me a long time.'
Kristina Olsson

'A compelling and affecting novel that cuts to the heart of what it means to live a meaningful life, especially in the midst of an acutely narcissistic culture. Orchard's portrait of her flawed, deeply human protagonist is sometimes hard to bear witness to. This is a beautifully controlled novel from a writer who shows us the power of fiction to engage both empathy and intellect. A reader can't help but come away powerfully changed. A timely and necessary book.'
Julienne van Loon

'Heartbreaking: long after the final pages, Orchard had me sifting through the embers to find what was left of friendship and loyalty. Forced to review her past through the lens of a tragedy, Orchard's narrator is a woman wrestling with just how much blame she can apportion, and how much she herself has to shoulder.'
Cassandra Austin

Into the Fire

This exclusive Booktopia Book Club edition is not for resale has been published under licence in Australia and New Zealand by:

Booktopia Publishing, a division of Booktopia Pty Ltd
Unit E1, 3-29 Birnie Avenue
Lidcombe, NSW 2141, Australia
www.booktopia.com.au

First published by Affirm Press in 2019
This edition published in 2021
28 Thistlethwaite Street, South Melbourne,
Boonwurrung Country, VIC 3205
www.affirmpress.com.au

Text and copyright © Sonia Orchard, 2019
All rights reserved. No part of this publication may be reproduced without prior permission of the publisher.

Title: Into the Fire / Sonia Orchard, author.
ISBN: 9781925995916 (paperback)

Cover design by Lisa White
Typeset in Garamond Premier Pro by J&M Typesetting
Proudly printed in Australia by McPhersons Printing Group

FSC www.fsc.org MIX Paper from responsible sources FSC® C001695

This project is supported by the Victorian Government through Creative Victoria.

CREATIVE VICTORIA

UNESCO United Nations Educational, Scientific and Cultural Organization
Melbourne City of Literature

Into the Fire

Sonia Orchard

booktopia book club

For Sunday, Leo and Remy xxx

Enough ink has been spilled in quarrelling over feminism, and perhaps we should say no more about it.

Simone de Beauvoir, 1949

I will not be silenced.

Rebecca Walker, 2007

1

Driving up the hill near the back of their property, I can't help thinking about the many years I've spent heading up and down these quiet bush roads, visiting Alice, Crow and the kids, and how strange it will be to stay down there now that she's gone.

None of us handled Alice's death very well. Crow's been the most peculiar, but that's understandable. I'd have thought he'd turn to his friends, though; keep us close. I've heard him mention her death in interviews, and there was everything that came up during the police investigation, but he's never spoken about any of it with me. The past – myself included – has been shed like old skin. He's made it difficult to visit, always coming up with excuses, saying how busy he is. But he knows this will be the last time I'm able to get down for a while. Plus, I don't want to shy away any longer, which is what I've been doing, happy to go along with his recalcitrance.

The moon is not yet visible in the sky; I can't see more than a metre off the side of the road, just the poa grasses lining the edge of the dirt and the palsied limbs of the stringybarks jutting overhead, bleached white in the headlights. Just like that night. I'd driven in the back way so missed all the traffic that would have been hurtling back and forth along their street. Horrific to think of me careering along, unwittingly, towards them: music blaring, a stubby of cider wedged between my knees.

I've just gone over the rise and down to hit their street. It was about here, about to turn right onto their road, that I first noticed anything. It looked like small snowflakes feathering down from the sky, but not many of them; not enough to cause alarm.

Something jumps out up ahead – my foot slams on the brake. Out of the blackness, and straight in front of my car's glare, appear a mob – no, a family – of grey kangaroos. The mum, strong but slight, stands side-on, turning her head to stare accusingly at me from the middle of the road, indifferent to the screech of my tyres. She turns, unhurriedly, and hops away, her tweens dutifully following. My car's stalled. I sit and watch them bound silently along the road in my spotlight, across the T-intersection, and into the bush on the other side of the road. Thank God, I say and close my eyes. I'm in no state to be hitting a roo.

It must have taken a couple of hours for them to put the fire out. Once the water pumps had been switched off, the quiet of the night was frightening. The other onlookers had left by that stage, and slowly, sometime after, sound returned: the trilling crickets and marsh frogs, the *roh-roh* of a barking owl, the police talking as they cordoned off the area, and the firefighters packing up to leave.

I start the ignition and crawl along so slowly that I can hear the crunch of gravel under my tyres.

It will be a year next week. I was driving down on a night just like this: the air the same viscid warmth as my skin, the sweet straw and dung reek of the earth, and the trees, still like cutouts against an unsuspecting deep violet sky.

I think about that night often. I dream about it too, always waking with the same feeling, irrational as I know it to be: that I could have done something. That it was, somehow, all my fault.

2

It's hard to get the measure of the house when I drive up in the darkness. The driveway is the same, with some new growth – leggy acacias, a brilliant olive green under the car's high beam – sprouting up where the old ones have been felled, a few blackened trunks visible in the mix. The front light is on, and I can make out an igloo-type building, rendered in the same mustard brown as the road. My first thought is that it looks like some crazy minority religion headquarters from an American Midwest desert. I helped construct these walls, filled the chicken wire with tyres and all manner of rubbish. But that was not long after Alice died, and it had felt like a kind of macabre art therapy. And now here it is, Crow's new house. I don't think I was prepared for the shock of seeing it here at the end of the driveway. Back to the present, Lara. Move on.

Crow is already standing at the front door with hands in his pockets, head to one side. As I waddle towards him he smiles, amused, then leans in to give me a hug. It's uncomfortable, the pressure of him on my abdomen, the jar of bones against organs, pushing up into my lungs. 'Ha,' he says, 'the ol' A-frame.' He relaxes for a moment then gives me another squeeze, his cheek resting on my head, then slowly exhales. 'It's good to see you, Lars,' he says, then grabs my bag, ushers me inside and closes the door behind us.

He puts down my bag and walks towards the kitchen area, switches on the kettle then pulls out two beers. 'You drinking?'

The kitchen is just a few water pipes, exposed within the chicken-wire walls, and a sink that runs into a bucket – with some vintage cupboards, an old benchtop oven and gas burners on a trestle table, and a large butchers' block.

'I said, you drinking?'

'Have you got a light?'

He scoffs. 'Me? Just drink half.' He pops a beer and lands it on the bench next to me.

'So. Look at *you*!' He grins. 'Yummy mummy!'

I smile, knowing this not to be true. I'm fluid-filled and puffy. I walk like a penguin and look like I'm about to birth triplets. But of course, Crow's looking good – always does. It's jarring next to my transformation. He has one of those rugged Irish faces and rangy builds that age well. His hair is a little longer, nearing shoulder length; he's always been proud of his thick black locks, with not a grey in sight. And his eyes remain a shrill blue, almost unnerving in their clarity. Dorian Gray, we used to call him.

'Well, what do you think?' he says, waving his hand about. 'Impressive, isn't it? See what I mean I've been busy?' He gives me a long gaze and one of those toying smiles of his – hitching up one side of his mouth – making his brusqueness seem playful.

Adjoining the kitchen area is a living room, a circular space with a cushioned pit in the centre. There's a Moorish influence: the round rooms, arched doorways, curved rendered walls and domed ceilings; also the deep blues, greens and maroons of the tapestry saddlebags, and of the glass bottles he's embedded into the walls. I feel as though I'll look outside in the morning to see camels sauntering by on the sand, rather than the smoky blue-green of the bush.

'It's beautiful,' I have to admit. But she's not here and there's nothing of their old house. Nothing for my eyes to rest upon – no 'ah yes, *that*' – the soothing furnishings of the familiar. And yet there's Crow, at the bench, drinking a beer, pointing to the door behind which their three children lie sleeping.

'Alice would love it,' I say, stumbling with my tenses. I don't know why I say this: nerves, struggling to be polite. I'm not even entirely sure it's true.

He presses his lips together for a moment, takes his time. 'Yeah, well, it was for her.' He crosses his arms then uncrosses them, rubs the bridge of his nose. 'It was always going to be for her. All of it was.'

A moment passes before I remember what to say. 'So show me around!'

Crow hands me my beer, then walks from the bench, his free hand brushing the air like a tour guide, pointing out various features and acquisitions – a pair of Tibetan prayer bells and an Eocene fossilised bird feather that were sent to him by sympathetic fans. Naturally, Crow is filling the house with his fancy fittings before finishing off the necessities. Despite there being no proper oven or stove, there's a metre-long French iron pot rack, which he tells me he bought at a local auction, leaning against a wall and almost obstructing the way to the back door.

After going from room to room – poking our heads into the darkness where the kids sleep – we return to the pit and sit with our beers. Crow reclines with his arms resting along the top of the cushions, his feet elevated on a black-and-white leather ottoman. He grins. 'So I've run out of money. But did I tell you? I've got an admirer who's going to help me out.'

I shake my head as I take a sip. He hasn't asked me about the birth, the mental-health series I've just finished post-production on, Christian. And Alice – he hasn't spoken about her either.

'Thinks my contribution to music and modern architecture makes me a good recipient for her excess cashflow. So she's funding the album I've got coming out in April.'

'Great news.'

'I'll let you have a sneak preview.'

He gets up to fetch another beer for himself and switches the kettle on for me; returns, puts his beer down on the slab table in front of us, along with his rolling tobacco, then gets his guitar. I think about saying something, asking how the kids are coping without her, but I'm too tired. Easier to let him talk.

'In fact, you can be one of the first to hear my new song.' He sits down and starts picking at the strings. It's a new tune but the same old Crow, with his rasping lilt and the familiar modulations, achingly simple and sad. I've read about studies that have used MRI scans to show that evocative music maps onto the same part of the brain as salient memory, creating a kind of soundtrack for parts of your life. That's what it feels like when Crow sings.

He finishes his song, lays his guitar next to him on the couch. 'Might roll a spliff.' He looks over at me, hands on thighs, about to get up. 'Oh Jesus, should have known. Invite a pregnant woman into your house, of course there's going to be tears.' He shifts over to sit next to me, puts his arm around my back, pulling me in.

'I just think about her all the time. I think about what happened.' I wipe away tears with my sleeve. 'I still can't believe it. And I can't help feeling, y'know – I just wonder if I could have—' I stop, remembering that I've never told Crow what happened between Alice and me, that last time she came to visit. His arm stiffens then drops to the couch. 'I don't know, just – been a better friend.'

He leans forward to put his elbows on his knees then shifts away a little so he can turn to face me. 'Lara. She was really unwell, you know that. I mean, you can ask her doctor. You heard about the toxicology report, yeah? She was off her bloody nut. Jesus, I can show you the coroner's report if you like, it's all there.'

'I know, I just,' I pause, thrown by his mention of the coroner's report. It hadn't occurred to me until now that there would be one. The silky smooth scar tissue from that time. And my immediate thought: *Am I in it?* 'I just keep thinking about it ...'

He doesn't respond, just looks off to the side.

'Don't you?'

He flicks his gaze back towards me, head cocked, squinting. 'What do you bloody well think?'

'I'm sorry.' I dry my face with my sleeve.

He stands and walks to the old kitchen dresser against the wall behind me, opens a drawer.

'I'm really sorry,' I say again as I stand. 'Hormones. And I'm tired, really tired.'

He's walking back towards the pit, holding the vintage Log Cabin tobacco tin he's always kept his pot in, and I'm just standing there, awkwardly, unsure whether to kiss him goodnight, or even how pleased he is to have me here. I put my arm around him, burying my head low, and give him a light squeeze. 'Goodnight.'

'You probably needed to get that out.' He lets me go, then goes to the door and picks up my bags. 'You can sleep in Caleb's room.'

3

It's so humid and still, even the cotton sheet over my legs feels clammy. And dark – I'd forgotten the molasses black of the bush on a moonless night.

Above the steady sound of the crickets outside, Crow's strumming starts up from the living room. It's an old tune, one he used to play with the band in the early days. It sounds different played acoustically; I can't quite remember the title.

Lisa – the counsellor I started seeing after Alice died – told me I'm very prone to guilt. At the time, I'd started pre-production on the mental-health series I was filming for the ABC, so I was rereading all my old psych books. When I mentioned to Lisa I'd been dipping into a bit of Freud, we gave his theories a good workout: how guilt stems from a fear of losing love – it's a kind of social anxiety – so in order to feel guilt, you don't just need an understanding of right and wrong, but also a strong sense of your place in the tribe. Yes, I admitted, I did indeed feel all these things. And yes, Lisa, guilt is a healthy human emotion, evidence that we care about the wellbeing of others. It's antisocial – narcissistic – to feel no empathy, no guilt. Yes, yes, yes, Lisa, but – and this is where I kept tripping up – there's guilt, and there's guilty. Freud's feelings of transgression versus actual culpability.

'Do you believe it should have been you that died in that fire?' Lisa asked me once. That threw me. In fact, if I recall, I didn't answer. I just started crying. She put a lot of my feelings down to survivor guilt and kept telling me that I needed to stop dwelling on the problems in my friendship with Alice. Besides, she said, Alice was clearly a troubled person, and she was under professional care. Her wellbeing was not my responsibility. I stopped seeing Lisa after a couple of months; I didn't actually want to hear that I was blameless, virtuous, and that all accountability lay with Alice. Or maybe I did want to hear these things, I just didn't want to hear them from her. No, I needed to know what state Alice was in on the day of the fire and how she felt about me coming down to see her. I needed to hear these things from Crow.

My scalp starts prickling and my chest tightening. I take some deep breaths. Ground yourself in the present – that's what Lisa used to say to me. Obediently, I wriggle my toes and wedge my hand under my bulbous belly, cradling my baby, feeling for any movement. I listen for the upcoming modulations in Crow's strumming and the quiet percussion of the crickets.

But that's the thing. The past wasn't all bad – quite the opposite. For the first few years, we were the most important person in one another's life. I'd never met anyone like her. She was everything I could have wanted in a friend; everything, in fact, that I – myself – wanted to be.

It was first-year university, 1990. We were both taking Women's Studies, in Ms Horsfall's tutorial – or Horseface as we imaginatively renamed her, even though she was more hawkish than equine in appearance. Her serious, makeup-free face suggested to us she was gay, as that's what everyone said back then about women like her. 'What she needs is a good root,' we'd say, laughing (and gifted by some red-blooded, hetero man, naturally). We also wore no makeup, and had hairy underarms, but we were supple-skinned and flirtatious. That made us immune from the kinds of taunts we slung at Horsfall.

As eager as I was to find my new uni tribe, Alice didn't hit my radar straight away. Perhaps it was her purring Canadian accent that initially deterred me. I'd recently moved down to Melbourne from Sydney with my parents, so while scouting about for a suitable scene, I dismissed those from overseas or the country. I pictured two-minute noodle dinners in sharehouses filled with other out-of-towners, piling into university buses to comedy nights with three-dollar jugs of beer. I thought they'd all behave like drunk, horny backpackers. And I'm afraid Canada meant little more to me than Celine Dion and mountaineers: *nice* Americans.

But then, in week three, the infamous separatist feminist Harriet de Silva was a guest speaker in our Women's Studies lecture.

De Silva – nudging six foot tall, spiky grey hair, steel-blue eyes – marched into the hall, leered at us like a rearing cobra, then spat out the notion of a matriarchal society where men were kept like animals, farmed for their semen and then killed at adolescence. 'Men start the wars!' she declared. 'They're responsible for the violence! There isn't a single crime that women commit more often than men!'

The room was dead quiet, without even the ubiquitous cough that usually managed to fill those moments. Then, from up front, Alice's hand shot to the ceiling. 'How about infanticide?' she called out. I looked over. She looked sweet as pie with her long blonde plaits, sitting tall in the middle of the front row, with her hand still in the air.

De Silva, who'd walked to the far wall, spun around to locate the voice, her eyes narrowed.

Alice continued, 'Infanticide is the single crime that women commit more often than men.'

De Silva disputed her claim and dismissed the statistics Alice served up. The two of them argued for a solid five minutes before de Silva, standing centre-stage, cut Alice off and announced with a smirk to the rest of us: 'No one has come here today for a criminology lecture.'

Alice sat back in her seat, arms crossed, quietly triumphant, for the remainder of the lecture. I was seated several rows behind her, leaning up against the grey besser block wall. I looked towards her several times, wanting to signal my approval, but never managed to catch her eye.

At the end of the lecture, I gathered my books and ran to catch up with her at the top of the stairs. 'Great what you said to de Silva,' I said, arriving by her side.

She shrugged as she looked at me. 'She might be a celebrity around here, but she's still got to stick to the facts.' She looked up ahead as she trotted down the vinyl steps.

'Sure,' I said, catching a closer look at some of the badges crowding her denim jacket: 'Racism Sux', 'Nuclear-free zone', a colourful mandala, and one with heavily scrolled pink lettering, bejewelled with sparkles and flowers, which I only just managed to decipher as the word 'Cunt'.

'Back home, you're encouraged to debate ideas. You're not supposed to just sit there, dumb, sucking it all up like people do here.'

I nodded, unsure what to say, whether I was being implicated in her critique. We stepped outside – it was late summer, another bright, hot, breezeless day – and walked towards the lawn, which was covered with students: picnicking, throwing Frisbees, playing hacky sack, kicking a footy, or canoodling. To my right, I saw two policemen walking up the alleyway in our direction.

'I didn't think the pigs were allowed on campus,' I said, appealing to her clearly rebellious nature.

'They're not,' she said with a frown, removing her jacket.

We stopped and watched as the two men strode past.

'Oh thank God!' Alice called out, loud enough for them to hear. 'The police are here! I feel so *safe* now!'

I looked to her, hand over my mouth, laughing. She was grinning, her eyes alight as she waited for a reaction.

'I gotta go.' She turned back to me, still smiling; she'd clearly enjoyed herself. 'Got a job interview at the radio station. See you Wednesday.'

'See you Wednesday. Good luck with the job.'

'Thanks, chica.' She held up her hand in an 'okay' signal, made a clicking sound between her tongue and teeth, and winked. When she jogged towards the large yellow-brick union building, I noticed that the floral cotton top she was wearing was backless – just a front piece held on with a few ties across her back. And below her long Rajasthani skirt and silver anklets, she wasn't wearing any shoes.

Alice and I started chatting before class. I even found myself getting in early and leaning against the corridor wall, waiting for her to arrive and tell me her latest story: how her housemate had got stoned, left chips cooking in a frypan and set the kitchen on fire; or how she'd lost a dare with a friend on the weekend and had to steal a bottle of Stollies from behind a nightclub bar. I did my best to match her with my tales of living at home with my parents, told with eye-rolling weariness. 'So my dad, right, is a total dick, and my mum had just had it with him. She got up and left for Tassie to stay with her sister for a fortnight. We ate takeaway every night and, seriously, one day I found my dad at the kitchen sink scrubbing his business shirts with dishwasher powder and steel wool, and he had his socks and jocks soaking in the lettuce spinner.'

'Oh my God, that's hilarious.' She heaved with that deep, masculine laugh of hers.

I leaned back against the wall, flushed with pride.

Then one day in tutorials, while we were having the handout for a test explained, two mousy girls who'd never said a word all term crept in late. Horsfall continued her explanation without pausing to acknowledge them so, after a few minutes, Alice slid her handout to the girls, then shuffled her seat towards mine. I slid my page towards her – unnecessarily so – as a sign of collaboration. To let her know that I'd have done the same, even though I'm sure I wouldn't have. I felt a pang of adoration for her at that moment. That tiny gesture had been the missing ingredient that tied her personality together into a perfect, glorious whole. It turned that lecture-room outrage – on everything from the legal defence of provocation to the percentage of female CEOs – into something real, beyond the intellectual aerobics of banging lofty ideas into one-thousand-word essays. I knew she was clever, ballsy and fun. But now I also saw she was kind. I decided, right then, that I would endeavour to be her friend.

One of our first nights out together was to a warehouse party in Collingwood, where one of Alice's obscenely cool friends from the radio station lived. Approaching, I could hear the *doof doof doof* from the far end of the cobblestone laneway, and see a group of five or six, smoking and chatting around the heavy wooden doorway and stairwell entrance. The party was up three flights, in a large gutted warehouse, choking with bodies crushed together in a haze of dry ice, cigarette smoke and sweat. There must have been several hundred people in there, mostly visible only as silhouettes against the murky kaleidoscopic-coloured smoke: fur collars and top hats, with the occasional flash of sequins or spandex under the theatre lights. Giant inflatable insects hung from the ceiling among the tonnage of lighting and speakers that were bolted along the scaffolding. The music was so loud it was barely audible, just a techno throb that seemed to pulse up through the floorboards. We stood there near the entrance until Mikey, a friend of Alice's from the radio station, appeared – God knows how he could have seen us. He and Alice were locked in an embrace as they spoke. His pony-tailed friend pulled me in, in the same manner, his lips glancing my ear, but I couldn't make out a word. He pulled away and held up, in his palm, a tiny ziplock bag with several white pills inside. I raised my eyebrows at Alice. She shook her head, grabbed my hand and pulled me through the crowd to the bar, where she ordered two vodkas.

As we clinked our plastic cups she said with a grin, 'Can't believe you wanted to do ecstasy with *him*.' She took a sip. 'I mean, can you imagine?'

I joined in her laughter. Suddenly it did seem the most absurd idea – this thing she imagined, whatever it was. And I realised, for the first time, that I didn't actually care what I did, as long as I did it with her.

'I'd love a cigarette though,' Alice said as we walked through a room where a group of men were playing pool; they seemed an anomaly at this party, with their flannel shirts and surfie hair. I caught the gaze of one of them, who leaned against the white pitted concrete wall, watching the game. As we passed, he turned from the pool table and looked straight into my eyes while he lit a cigarette. I waited for the tip of the cigarette to glow, then plucked it from his chapped lips, mouthed 'thanks', and handed it to Alice. After the brief moment it took for him to comprehend what had happened, he smiled and gave a little nod, as if *he* were the one to be thankful.

I can't remember much beyond that: taking his cigarette, his eyes – so azure when the spinning lights flashed across his face – his grateful nod, and Alice squinting at me through her smoke, giving me a wink. I can't remember what happened, because it was the feeling that was important. It was the moment I announced to myself, to the world, that the rules in my life had radically changed.

I'm embarrassed thinking about all this now, though I have to remind myself that my brazen self-conceit was all a part of this new image of womanhood I was awkwardly trying on. Because back then it had been made quite plain to us – the educated white women of my generation – that we were the women who would have it all. We were the fortunate ones, born at precisely the right time and place to ride the wave created by those before us. Women had the vote, the pill, had earned the right to equal pay and no-fault divorce; we could be politicians, CEOs, anything we pleased; there was nothing to stop us. It felt so terribly auspicious that just as Alice and I were on the cusp of adulthood, the gates were swinging wide open for the very first time. All we needed to do was to file in and claim our space. It's little wonder I acted as I did.

That night Alice and I danced for hours among a sweaty, strobe-lit crowd, then ended up ensconced in beanbags in the chill-out room with a dozen others. The ultraviolet light made everyone's teeth and eyes glow luminously; dust particles floated like bioluminescence. The music was a slow, liquid organ with a metronomic snare that seemed to roll on forever, and that Alice started to rap to.

'You'll have to come back to Canada with me sometime,' she suddenly announced. 'You can kayak with orcas off Vancouver. And the mountains – my God, the mountains!'

'I'd love to.'

And with that, a plan had been hatched; our futures, that easily imagined. Nothing was out of our reach.

We lay in the luxurious quicksand of the beanbags with a dozen other warm, languid bodies around us, all smelling and feeling delicious. It felt heady and precarious, and I remember thinking that this was what being an adult was about: being poised at the edge of some magnificent gorge, about to take flight. How glorious it was to be us at that intoxicated, deluded moment. The music was smooth and syrupy, and under the galactic glow of the lights I felt an intensity of love for Alice – and for everyone around me – and a feeling that my life had finally begun.

Alice spent most of her time outside of uni waitressing at Gianni's Pizza on Lygon Street, volunteering at the university radio station and helping raise money for Malawian women and children affected by the AIDS epidemic, through events she organised at the university union. I was living at home and working most nights behind the bar at Cafe Clicquot. Sometime later on (influenced, I might add, by Alice), I started working for the campus Environment Society, making limp gestures with negligible impact, such as organising screenings of *Koyaanisqatsi* for the dreadlocked patchouli crowd to smoke joints in front of. In the early days, before we started living together, we'd mainly catch up over lunch at the cafe, on the lawn, or occasionally at Jimmy Watson's on Lygon Street for a carafe of dry-and-dry and a plate of meatballs and olives. We discussed writers from Tim Winton to Adrienne Rich, and filmmakers from Kubrick to Tarkovsky. We argued about feminism: I was a small 'l' liberal, a firm believer in affirmative action, and fighting for equal pay and rights; Alice was more of a radical, demanding an entirely new paradigm. She was fascinated by matriarchal and matrilineal societies, and read everything by Vandana Shiva and other ecofeminists who likened the oppression of women to the oppression of indigenous societies and nature. Despite her earnestness, though, she maintained a sense of humour: her style was lived-in, fun, forthright, epitomised in her act of knitting a giant bright-red uterus and hanging it at the door to the union building women's room. When I questioned the wisdom of this, suggesting that our intention should be for people to take women's issues seriously, she replied,

'Should I knit a giant surfboard instead? Or a fishing rod? People take them seriously.'

I laughed, relieved I hadn't offended her.

Then she added, 'Might knit you some balls to scratch while I'm at it too. You'd love that, wouldn't you?'

We spent a lot of time debating ideas, workshopping notions of what was right, as a way of propelling us towards some imagined but perfectly possible endpoint: a fair and just society, in which all people and the environment could thrive. So our constant jousting was an invigorating part of our friendship. It helped us sharpen our focus and prune away what Alice referred to as 'unhelpful thinking'. I remember one of those times: we were standing in line at the cafe, backs against the bain-marie; I was watching a group of girls – two of them wore barely-there miniskirts, and another wore jeans and a midriff top – standing among all the tables, swinging their hips around, laughing loudly: *attracting attention to themselves*. I turned to Alice, 'I get so pissed off that modern, educated women feel compelled to dress like that. It's just taking us backwards.'

She looked over. 'Do you think they owe you, and your feminism, something better?'

'What?'

'Maybe they're not dressing like that for men, or for *you*. Judging them like that, aren't you doing the same thing we've always criticised men for?'

I turned back towards the open kitchen of the cafe and was grateful to find it was my turn to be served. I ordered a bowl of soup, busied myself collecting cutlery and a napkin, then looked back at Alice to tell her I'd grabbed hers too, all the while trying to understand what it was I was feeling. I experienced this often when discussing ideas with her: it started off with a sting of humiliation, but then quickly transformed into a kind of exhilarated wonder, as if a door in my mind, that I'd never even known existed, had suddenly been unlocked and thrust open.

Every free moment was spent together, trading information from our lives, as if there was some urgency – not so much for each of us to know everything about the other, but for each of us to be known. We gossiped about guys we liked, parties we'd been to and bands we'd heard on the radio. We workshopped our lives, analysing our families with an aloof self-righteousness, congratulating ourselves for having turned out *so normal*.

Alice told me about her father – an English teacher who self-published poetry, she proudly told me – who'd died when she was four; he'd been from Melbourne, which was why she'd come here to study. He'd been an only child, but his elderly mother still lived in a nursing home in Mildura, where Alice would often visit her. Alice's mother, Colette, had remarried when she was eight, to a red-headed bear of a man called Steve. Within two weeks of Steve, a policeman, moving into Alice's house and ordering her to call him 'Dad', he caught her sitting on his side of the bed with the semi-automatic pistol from his bedside drawer in her lap. She'd just wanted a look at it, she said, but as soon as she'd picked it up, she'd been awestruck by how heavy and cold it was; she couldn't stop touching it, and hadn't even noticed Steve enter the room. Her stepfather pulled his belt out of his trousers in one swift move, his flaming skin now matching his hair, commanded she pull down her skirt and lie on the bed, then proceeded to thrash her. 'Needless to say,' Alice told me at the time, '*Steve* and I never really hit it off.'

Alice also said that Colette had been very upset when Alice told her she was leaving to study in Australia. Her mother had a phobia of flying and had accused Alice of moving overseas to punish her, threatening to never visit. And Colette kept her word: Alice only saw her mum when she and Crow flew back to Canada with the kids – something they only managed twice. The only time Colette ever came out to Australia was when Alice was in hospital, after the fire, two days before she died.

I realise now how little she actually told me about her mum, and what scant amount I told Alice of my mother also. My father and her stepfather dominated the childhood tales we told one another. It was a rich vein, and a commonality that cemented our friendship with mutual understanding and care.

The first time Alice came to my house in Balaclava was a warm spring day, and Dad was in the garden wearing only a pair of Hard Yakka shorts, squatting on the ground in the shade of a flowering gum as he sorted through his brown plastic fishing-tackle box. I called across the lawn to introduce her, hoping he'd allow us to pass with his usual greeting, a nod. But he turned and saw her – her long blonde hair down over her shoulders, and wearing those denim cut-off shorts – then rose, rubbed his hands on a towel, came over and shook her hand.

I was appalled that he was standing there with almost nothing on, his gut spilling over his shorts and his chest, grey-haired and glistening with sweat. I grabbed Alice and gave a little tug, hoping she'd follow.

He asked Alice what she was studying, and I wanted to reply that she was doing the same 'Mickey Mouse degree' as me, but she politely told him that we'd met in Women's Studies.

'So she's not going to appreciate your chauvinistic jokes either, okay?' I added.

He raised his eyebrows at her and smiled, eyes pawing at her. 'Well, I'm sure there are some feminists out there with a sense of humour.'

I pulled harder on her arm, took her inside and apologised for my father. Alice turned to me with a look of distaste and said, 'Does he always flirt with your friends?'

I wasn't sure what to say. I was usually the one to tell others how awful my father could be; they were usually charmed. There was a part of me that wanted to stick up for him, as if his behaviour might somehow reflect upon me.

'How gross,' she continued, and I could feel an anger rising in me.

We went up to my room, which contained little more than a double futon, a bookshelf and tallboy, and the desk and chair I'd had throughout childhood, which still had Holly Hobbie stickers on it that I'd tried to scratch off. The floor was strewn with clothes, and books were piled next to the bed. Alice went straight for my record collection, housed in a milk crate under my desk, while I lit incense. She put on Eartha Kitt, then lay back on my bed, hands behind her head on my pillow, while I sat at the desk. I realised I was trembling all over.

'Sorry about my dad,' I said again, trying to shake this feeling, and hoping she might apologise too. But instead she continued.

'He really has no respect for you – or probably all women – does he?'

I felt my eyes start to tear up. I fiddled with the snow dome paperweight on my desk, blinking.

'Why don't you move out with me?' She swung her feet to the floor, sat up and faced me.

It was useless now trying to hide my tears, I let them roll freely, which just made her laugh, jump up and hug me. It was as if the embarrassment and shame had been drained from my body, and the vacuoles they'd filled had been replenished with a smooth warm liquid. A feeling of gratitude and love.

Within a month, Alice and I had moved out together into a small, mushroom-coloured single-fronted terrace in Greeve Street, Fitzroy. The hallway was narrow, and the white peeling walls had giant cracks arching down from the ceiling on the detached side. The floors fell away slightly, and were covered with a cloud-textured carpet of white and every shade of brown. As vomitus as the carpet was, we came to love how well it hid red wine stains. A cup of salt poured on top, then vacuumed up some time over the next few days, was generally enough to convince us we'd get our bond back. The kitchen, at the back, had pale-pink vinyl cabinetry and a fake woodgrain lino floor that curled up at the corners, collecting crud. It was just large enough for us to put a wooden dining table in, so that was where we usually ate dinner. The kitchen was the only room that had a window out onto anything other than the grey paling fence of our western boundary – there we got to look out over the concreted backyard instead. The house was undeniably ugly and smelled like mould, no matter how much Nag Champa incense we burned. But from day one we loved it; it was our home.

The night we moved in, mid-October, was uncharacteristically mild, so we took our takeaway pizza boxes, cask of red wine and jam jar glasses out the front. On our small tiled verandah, we'd put an old mustard velour couch next to the wheelie bin, flanked each side by milk crates covered in lairy floral cloth that Alice had picked up from the op-shop.

Wrapped in a mohair blanket and sunk deep within the bony lap of the couch, my tongue furry and dry from too much cheap wine, I stared out beyond the clematis-covered wire gate, beyond the street and the row of identical worker's cottages on the other side to the puffs of mauve-coloured cloud scattered across the sky. Alice had put on a Nina Simone record, and her jangling piano melded with the sounds of tram bells and car horns from Brunswick Street.

'So what do you want in life? Where do you see yourself in ten or twenty years?' Alice asked.

I'd had too much to drink to consider the question clearly, beyond a general feeling of exhilaration at the possibilities. All I could really grasp was a general sense: I want to do something *different*. When I considered what I meant by this for a moment longer, it distilled it into a single thought: I didn't want to be my mum. Always the one to reach for the bruised apple in a bowl of fruit. I pictured her, the woman of my childhood, shelling peas at the sink, her third gin-and-tonic for the evening sitting on the window ledge next to a drooping cyclamen, and a TattsLotto coupon stuck to the fridge – the golden ticket that might grant her passage out of there. Even at a young age, I was aware that this was not where my mother wanted to be: carving up a roast for an ungrateful husband and kids, then facing a pile of greasy dishes, folding away the washing, preparing the school lunches and finally collapsing into bed half-drunk, only to wake up and start over again the next day. I heard her tell a friend once in passing that growing up she'd always wanted to be an architect. It was the first and only time I heard her mention this, and it was said in such an offhand tone that it was clear that this dream from adolescence, having been deprived of oxygen for thirty years, had taken its last gasp decades earlier. Her resentment of her husband – of her life – was all palpable in my mother's silent performance of her role, duty propping her up like scaffolding. She hosted a great dinner party, my mum: got roaring drunk and told a good yarn. But I wondered whether she hated those dinner parties too, knowing, as everyone did, that Dad had probably slept with half the female guests.

'I want money and independence,' I said, watching the woman across the road – a nurse who worked nightshift – get into her snappy little red car and speed away.

'You don't want a family? Kids?'

'One day, I suppose.' Family sat within some distant blurry picture of the future, but I wasn't about to admit to any romantic or maternal longing, even to Alice. It didn't seem the thing for a modern, ambitious woman to do. 'If I can find myself a good house-husband I'll consider it,' I added with a laugh.

'Well, I suppose with all that money of yours, you can just buy yourself some kids, then roll up a wad of hundred-dollar bills and roger yourself with them.'

We laughed, riffing on this idea for a while, imagining our futures as if brainstorming ideas for a script. She put her arm around me, and I returned the gesture, then leaned over to kiss her on the cheek. Her profile was lit up under the streetlight and it creased into a smile. I snuggled further down into the couch, wishing I could stay right here, feeling this way, forever. I didn't care I only had forty dollars to live on for the rest of the week and a three-thousand-word essay, that I'd yet to start, due on Thursday. I was enjoying the kind of serene benevolence that can settle on you like a mist when everything in life seems to be in a perfect equilibrium.

4

Crow appeared in our lives – for the first time – near the end of second semester. It was a Wednesday morning and we were on our way to our tutorial on Sexuality, Contraception and Reproductive Rights. I'd done none of the reading; Alice had done all of it and was in my ear about Andrea Dworkin, the Marquis de Sade and the societal role of pornography. I walked through the door ahead of her and there he was: Damien Crowley – Crow – tall and pale with limp black hair, watery blue eyes and a wry smile, as though enjoying his own private joke. He was lounging back in his chair, wearing a suede hat and a David Bowie 'Heroes' T-shirt, the short sleeves hiked up in the heat, showing off his sinewy arms and Celtic cross tattoo.

I took my usual seat beside Alice, who continued talking as if unaware of the interloper. The half-dozen others already in the room also pulled out pens and folders and chatted; intent, it seemed, on conveying disinterest.

Crow, meanwhile, stared ahead at the blackboard, elbow on the back of his chair and slunk down low – it was possibly an attempt to hide, but it couldn't have been a more provocative pose – twiddling his pencil around in his fingers, tapping it on the vinyl desk. Perhaps his fidgeting wouldn't have been such a distraction outside the confines of a hot, airless classroom of women politically opposed to noticing this acute display of virility. He looked like he should have been hosting on MTV, not sitting in a Women's Studies class discussing the anti-pornography movement.

As soon as Horsfall entered the room and put her leather briefcase down, she turned her attention to Crow. 'So, Mr ...'

'Crowley. Damien Crowley. You can call me Crow.'

'Mr Crowley. You're the first male student to ever enter this class.'

Crow was rocking back in his seat; then, remembering his manners, he stopped and sat upright. He shrugged, gave her that lopsided smile I now know so well, and said, 'I guess I'm just not like the other guys.' A few titters could be heard around the room.

'Unlikely.' She pursed her lips. 'So what does bring you here?'

'I was thinking of enrolling in this class next year. Friend said I should try it out.'

Horsfall's gaze didn't waver.

'Well, I've learned a lot of male history at school, so now I want to learn about female history.'

The girl sitting on the other side of Alice – half-head shaved, nose-ring – looked to the ceiling, visibly unimpressed. But others, like the redhead next to him, who communicated her ardour to her neighbour with wide, dreamy eyes, seemed to be almost swooning.

Horsfall was unmoved and pressed on, questioning his motives further, waiting for him to falter. He looked about at no one in particular and squirmed in his seat, trying not to grin as he made attempts to legitimise his presence. It was impossible to tell if he was performing or truly uncomfortable, just as it was difficult to infer if Horsfall's interrogation was actual disapproval, or whether she was merely curious (as we all were) about what would motivate a young man like Crow to learn about the plight of the subjugated other half.

When Horsfall let us out, Crow made straight for the door. The redhead, who'd been sitting closest to him, hurried to be by his side.

'Jeez. She's a bit of a ball-breaker,' Crow whispered to her as they passed me.

'Tell me about it,' said the redhead, laughing.

Alice, waiting as I hitched my bag on my shoulder and watching them also, mumbled, 'Looks like he got what he came for.'

At the top of the stairwell, looking down, I could see Crow and the girl, still chatting. He pushed open one of the glass doors and she walked through, looking back at him over her shoulder as she thanked him or laughed, with an expression best described as euphoric. He stepped through behind her, his head dipped, and they took off towards the wide expanse of the lawns.

Our next Women's Studies tutorial came around and no tall, dark-haired rockstar blessed our class. We were back to being just a room of serious young *wimmin* sitting around discussing Gender and the Media; all perhaps feeling a bit peeved at Horsfall, who drily delivered the tutorial, making no mention of the abscess that had been so neatly removed.

Over the following month, leading up to end-of-year exams, I saw Crow a few times around campus, loping along with his long bounding stride, central among his coterie of friends – boys with eyeliner, girls with piercings and tattoos – and had tried to catch his eye. But he was always preoccupied, his large bony hands waving about as he spoke, his friends turned inward, nodding, laughing theatrically, or bantering back. Other times, he'd have his arm draped over whoever he was speaking with, male or female, pulling them in close.

I once walked behind his group to listen to what they were chatting about. 'Johnny Farnham?' he said, laughing. 'Me? No way! I'm not wearing a colostomy bag!' He lifted his shirt to reveal his scrawny abdomen and bellowed with laughter, as did his friends. Then they all stepped inside the union building's second-hand record shop, so I continued on my way. That night, I mentioned my sighting to Alice, who replied that she'd seen him just the other day as well: snogging a girl on the south lawn, with his hand up her dress. I detoured past the south lawn several times over the following week. I couldn't get the image out of my head.

Then one day, late autumn the following year, Alice met me at the glass doors to the union building, where I was going to get my lunchtime coffee; she was rugged up in one of her bulky knitted scarves, puffing into her hands. 'Glad I found you,' she said, taking my arm and leading me inside. 'Come check out who's on stage,' she said as she leaped up the stairs ahead of me, two at a time.

When I reached the top of the stairs I could just make out, over the lunchtime throng, a rich, jangly guitar sound, a heavy, slow drumbeat and a low, caressing voice, distorted by proximity to the mike. Alice surveyed the room with a frown: her look of concentration.

There were maybe fifty people watching the band; a dozen or so were around the perimeter, some leaning against the painted brick walls and some sitting cross-legged on the floor, eating pies or drinking from polystyrene cups. The rest were milling about, chatting or glancing at the stage as they walked along the vinyl walkway.

At the far end of the atrium on a black makeshift stage was Crow, hands tightly gripping the mike and lips against it as he whispered out his melody. He was wearing a shiny lurex cut-off top, black jeans and a bandana, and was crouched over slightly, singing towards the two hippy girls who danced in front of the stage, weaving their bangled hands through the air. Next to them was a sandwich board, which announced in green chalk, 'Earth Monster, Union House stage, 1pm.'

The music paused; the three other band members – Jas, on guitar, wearing a black suit and skinny tie; Simmo, virtually hidden behind the drums; and Mark, on bass, with his spidery arms and fingers – all looked around as if bored. Crow, now upright, eyes closed and mouth stretched into a pained smile, let out a note, soft at first, that reached higher and louder – falsetto, almost operatic – until the band joined him in a frenetic cacophony that drew cheering and whistles from around the room. The drum rolled and crashed, and Crow flopped down, head to knees, then whipped his long, sweaty black hair back up, fixing his bandana with his spare hand. The two dancing girls stood as close as they could to the stage, clapping above their heads; the rest of the small crowd cheered and whistled. Crow looked around, nodding.

When it had quietened down, he spoke: 'You'll have to pardon me, good people: *I'b god a bid ob a cod.*' He paused for a laugh that didn't quite arrive, then stepped back, still holding the mike stand, and surveyed the room. 'When Sydneysiders head out, they take ecstasy. Melburnians: we take a Sudafed and a beer.' This time he got laughter and a few cheers. 'But don't worry, I'll be chatting to my dear friends at the pharmacy downstairs before our gig at the Empress of India tomorrow night, see if they can get me something a little stronger.'

More laughs, and whistles, then a girl called out, 'I can get you something stronger, just call me.'

Crow laughed, then called back to the girl, who was leaning against one of the concrete pillars, wearing a plaid lumber jacket and eating a focaccia, 'Thanks, gorgeous, I will. See you at the Empress.' He pointed his finger, like a gun, at her, then picked up his guitar – an electric twelve-string – from behind the amp, plugged it in, pulled a plectrum out from his tight black jeans, then played a major chord. In a husky, Texan falsetto, he sang the opening plea of *Mercedes Benz*. When the whoops and whistles stopped, he turned to the band, braced with his hand above the strings, then hopped and nodded at once, bringing in a loud thrashing sound.

'So Women's Studies wasn't his forte after all. Who'd have thunk it?' I said to Alice as we walked down the stairs at the end of the show.

'Yeah,' she said thoughtfully. 'Not normally into the prisoner-of-war look myself, but he's got something going, hasn't he.'

The following night, Alice and I went to the Empress of India Hotel, and then, a month later, to Earth Monster's next gig at the Gershwin Room in St Kilda. Before the year was out we started seeing Earth Monster regularly listed on blackboards outside pubs around Carlton and Fitzroy, and we became regulars at their gigs.

Then one evening, at the start of third year, Alice came home while I was reading on the couch and plumped herself down at my feet, head lolling back to the ceiling. She sighed and said she'd just interviewed Crow for her radio program at uni. I told her to wait, then dashed to the kitchen and poured us both a glass of shiraz from the Stanley Leasingham cask that lived on top of the fridge, then sat across from her on the couch as she pulled out her knitting and started click-clacking away. She tried to describe her interview but kept resorting to breathy exclamations and platitudes about how intelligent he was, how funny, how kind, how worldly.

'We were talking about Earth Monster's *Gethsemane* album launch and the benefit gig he's doing for the Friends of the Earth. I asked him about the role of music in raising social awareness, and – you're not going to believe it – he quoted Lao Tzu. Something about the softest things in the world being capable of overcoming the hardest things in the world.' Alice was reading *The Way of Lao Tzu* at the time.

'Afterwards we went for a drink and a game of pool at the Clyde. I beat him two games to one. Don't think he expected that! And, this is crazy, last year he travelled to America and lived in a tepee in Colorado next to Hunter S Thompson!'

I prompted her to continue – not that she needed encouragement – relishing this proximity I now had to Crow. But I was also unsure what to make of her sudden ardour, when she'd shown no previous interest in him. I remember thinking, quite clearly: *this all should be happening to me.*

'He said he wanted to see me again tomorrow night. I suggested the weekend – because, you know, we'd talked about going salsa dancing tomorrow night – but he's going fly fishing in the Snowy Mountains. So I hope you don't mind ... I said yes. We can do salsa on Thursday.'

I tried to think of a reason why I couldn't go on Thursday, but couldn't. Alice finished casting off the maroon sleeve she'd been knitting, rolled it up, placed it carefully in her knitting bag, then lay back and gazed at the ceiling with her arm draped off the side of the sofa, smiling giddily. 'Oh my God, Lara. I think I'm in love,' she said, amused by her own theatrics. I leaned back in my chair, also, unable to really comprehend all of this, unable to think of anything to say, unable to even look at her. Finally I glanced over: she was still staring at the ceiling, and I noticed that the intricate lacy rash she'd occasionally get after drinking red wine had started spidering its way across her neck and chest.

And that was it, just like that: their relationship had begun.

Two weeks after Alice met Crow, she took me along to meet him in the city square. She told me he had 'a thing' about being on time and so she was anxious not to be late. As we approached, I think we saw him at the same instant: I could sense Alice breathe in and her pace quicken. He seemed to have been watching us, or Alice, for a while. He was sitting on one of the large concrete ledges at the top of the steps, cross-legged, straight-backed, hands on thighs. He was almost Buddha-like, except for the slightly tilted head and dazed smile. I felt I should look away, but I couldn't – what I was seeing was too extraordinary. He was seated, entirely relaxed, but hovering several inches off the ground. I could see beneath his crossed legs to the green of the bushes behind him, and there was a thick book in front of, and below, his left knee. He was just floating there, among the crowd, none of whom seemed to notice. I stared, unable to say a word, as Alice walked towards him.

Then he sprang up to his feet and toed the end of the skateboard he'd been sitting on so that it flicked up to where he could grab it. He jumped down from the ledge, put his book under his arm (*Zen and the Art of Motorcycle Maintenance*, I later saw) and walked slowly towards Alice. When he drew near, she took a few quick steps into his arms. I stood back, embarrassed, and looked over towards some pigeons, squabbling over bits of rubbish on the pavement, and waited for the embrace to end.

He was wearing black jeans, a black knitted vest and a small red scarf knotted loosely around his neck. Up close, he wasn't as handsome as he appeared on stage, or even at uni. But those eyes – porcelain blue – looked into mine with so much curious intent. I smiled in return, trying to hold his gaze, and waiting for that moment of recognition from him.

'Enchanté,' he said as he leaned in to kiss my cheek, his other arm pulling Alice in beside him. I inhaled his woody aftershave, and couldn't help but think of Alice inhaling it also, skin against skin.

He stepped back and laughed. 'Apologies for my pretentious greeting – your gorgeous friend has turned me into a blithering idiot.' They looked at each other – she, tucked under his arm. 'That's a lie, actually. I'm always a blithering idiot. Aren't I, babe?'

I was a tad affronted by his frank adoration of Alice; perhaps I'd expected him to be a little more aloof. But as I came to learn over the years, that was his nature: he'd flaunt his love for her in his lyrics, describing the way she sipped her raspberry tea and chatted to her pot plants, calling her his Górecki Number Five.

'We're off to see *Impromptu* – would you like to join us?' he asked.

'Thanks, but it'll have to be another time. I've got an essay on memory due tomorrow, which I'd completely forgotten about.' I laughed, wishing I could have added something other than feeble, rehearsed jokes and polite cordiality to the meeting. I said my goodbyes then left, afraid that both my awkward aloneness and poorly-hidden veneration of him had been quite plain.

I watched the two of them walk away, arms around one another. Their step was slow, as if they were walking through a meadow, not a city street. I noticed other people turn and stare straight at their faces as they passed, knowing that they were invisible to Alice and Crow. I remember thinking that this is what it looks like when two people are deeply in love, and that maybe this was just the first time I'd ever really seen it up close.

I stepped onto the tram to head home, the loneliest I'd felt in a long time. When I arrived, the house was quiet and cold, and our breakfast dishes were still piled in the sink. I turned on the heater and sat on the couch, looking around our ugly living room at Alice's belongings – a charcoal drawing of a mother and child on the wall, funny little wire puppets made by street kids in Lilongwe, and her teapot painted with scenes from *Pinocchio* – and felt a choking sadness, as if this moment were already far in the past.

I was reading in bed when Alice came home, around midnight. She knocked on my door then came and sat on my bed.

'I like what you've done to your room,' she said, looking about. Above my desk, I'd hung the framed photo of Einstein poking out his tongue that had been over the living-room mantelpiece; I'd also brought in my silver Art Deco candelabra and lit the candles, as well as the oil burner. The room smelled like mandarins.

I shrugged, now embarrassed by the evidence of my domestic evening.

I hardly said a word before she launched into a detailed description of her night: the French restaurant Crow had taken her to after the movie, then going back to his place, where they'd kissed on the couch for an hour and he'd tried to convince her to stay.

'I think I've met the man I'm going to marry,' she said.

I couldn't believe it: my denim-wearing, guitar-strumming, Greer-loving friend. 'Marry?' My horror must have been evident.

'It's just a turn of phrase!' Her turn, now, to be embarrassed. 'I mean I just can't imagine ever being with anyone else.'

5

Our honeymoon was over. It was no longer Alice and me; it was now Alice and Crow. However, I soon came to realise this new addition to my life might not be all bad. Crow spent more time at our house than Alice did at his noisy above-shop apartment, and he never turned up with anything less than a packet of Tim Tams, but usually a whole lot more: vodka and rollmops, or mouth-searing vindaloo and a six-pack of Grolsch. He came up with numerous nicknames for me – Lars Bars, Grand Larceny, Lala land, Queenie (extrapolated from my surname, King) – but more often just called me 'sister', a term he reserved for a very select number of women in his life. He seemed genuinely happy – at least for that first year – to have me around.

And the feeling was mutual: even the most mundane task would be entertaining with Crow. Like, one time, early on in their relationship, when the three of us went into the Woolworths on Smith Street: we were all hungover from one of Crow's shows the previous night and he wanted to cook up a big brunch. Alice also needed to buy herself some laxatives – she always had gut issues, and they worsened if she drank too much. Crow took off swinging a shopping basket, singing 'It's Not Unusual' as he almost skipped down the aisle, while I accompanied Alice to the pharmacy section. By the time Crow joined us, whistling, with his basket overflowing, we still hadn't found the laxatives.

He stood tall – taller than his usual six foot – looking up and down the aisle for a moment, then called out loudly in a broad Scottish accent: 'Kin we get some hulp aroond here, then? Ah cannae fin' th' laxatives.' A mother, pushing a trolley and with two kids at her feet, glanced over, as did another couple further along; Alice glared at him. 'Ah said ah neeeed some hulp tae fin' th' laxatives,' he continued. 'I've git me a lassie 'ere wha has nae shat in three days, a' that porridge 'n' scones. 'N' unless she gets some laxatives quick smart she'll be heading ower tae th' gardening section fur a trowel 'n' scrrraping it oot herself.'

Alice had one arm around his neck, pulling him towards her, and was trying to muffle him with her other hand. I just stood back, laughing. Crow was trying to fend her off and just continued, booming even louder. 'Ah tell ye, th' brassic lassie is ferr deranged, ah think she's jibbed some o' her stitches, that's th' kind o' pain she's in. Noo if someone cuid please hulp us fin' her some laxatives, we'd be gey muckle appreciative 'n' be richt oan oor wey—'

'If you'll just come with me, sir?' A tall pimply boy in supermarket uniform arrived at Crow's side.

Crow picked up his basket and turned to us both, one hand on his hip. 'Ah, th' service in this land is boozer none. Juist lik' hame.'

Alice put her arm around me and burrowed her head on my shoulder, I could feel her shaking with laughter. I wiped my tears on the back of my wrist. Crow put his arm around the staffer's shoulder as they walked ahead of us, then turned back to us, flicked up one eyebrow – James Bond style – and grinned.

That's what it was like, hanging out with Crow.

Over the following year, Earth Monster went from playing pubs around Melbourne, and occasionally Sydney or Brisbane, to touring as support for international bands and performing at The Big Day Out. When *Rolling Stone* magazine crowned Crow the sexiest new kid in rock n' roll, he grew that big 'bushranger' beard, ginger around the edges, and sported a pair of non-prescription glasses, just to have the final say. That was his greatest time, I thought, when he still wore his talent with such majestic innocence; when he was simply doing what he enjoyed doing: strumming on his guitar and singing spiked love songs and murder ballads. We were part of his entourage, accompanying him night after night as he played in front of swelling crowds. Despite his growing fame, he'd still buy Alice an enormous bunch of lilies or tulips every Friday, without fail, and sometimes even a vase to put them in, finding her Hungarian pickle jars a tad quaint for his exotic bouquets. He hosted dinner parties, usually at our place, with a dozen or more guests, pouring us all vodka martinis and bloody marys upon arrival. Then he'd circle us with a tray of oysters kilpatrick ('off the boat from Tassie this morning'), pulling paper napkins out of his back pocket. He carried us through his string of new obsessions – sushi, flaming cocktails or Jägermeister – inducting us like an evangelist, getting high off our happiness. There was the 'Lick, sip, suck', which he sat at the dinner table to demonstrate, pouring salt onto the hollow between his thumb and forefinger, and lining up a shot of tequila and a wedge of lemon in front of him. He must have spent a small fortune on entertaining us all (well, what seemed a fortune for the rest of us, mostly poor students): caviar, sushi, dope cookies and cognac in heated balloons.

The nights on the town were my favourite, though. If there was a pool, he would end up in it; if there was a bar, he would dance on it. Alice never complained about Crow's ways, as whether he performed Shakespeare soliloquies to a gathering of cheering drag queens, or body painted himself and others with a fan's cherry-red lipstick, he remained his effusive, loyal and generous self. Alice and I walked into the living room at one St Kilda cocktail party to find Crow naked except for a tie, sitting astride Maria – a tall Polynesian woman who worked the door at a few clubs, down on all fours and wearing a tutu – whipping her playfully with his belt and singing 'Raw Hide', to the cheers of the rest of the room. As soon as he saw Alice, he stood, held his wine glass high in the air and proclaimed to his audience: 'Here comes my muse, my angel. She's like an apparition, isn't she?'

On nights like these his mood was infectious. We followed him from the St Kilda party to Razor nightclub to 4am skinny-dipping at the beach. Then at the end of it all, when he collapsed naked on the sand, stared up at the stars and exclaimed, 'Oh God! We're *sooo* insignificant!' I looked up and felt it too, some seismic shift in my being. I'd enjoyed a night of nonstop partying and Crow's blistering affection, and just when I thought I couldn't feel a more exhilarating sense of freedom and love, I'd been reminded of something even greater: an entire galaxy, millions of light-years away, shining down upon us.

There was another side to Crow though, a vulnerability that was most evident in his music but of which I saw glimpses on other occasions.

One time, in a psychology class, we'd been asked to each draw our family, then afterwards, in pairs, we analysed and discussed one another's family relationships, based on their depiction in the drawing. I remember in mine, my older sister, Miriam, and her then-boyfriend were standing centre-left, in front of the dining-room table, and my dad was centre right, sitting on a dining-room chair, leaning over his golf clubs. Mum and I were both smaller and squeezed in at the sides: my mum was sliced in half by the kitchen bench, and I was reading a book, my back to everyone else. I was stunned when the teacher revealed to us what the exercise was about, and how well the drawing summed up the roles and fractures in my family.

When I got home and found Crow at our kitchen table making a pot of tea, I asked if he'd draw his family for me. He grabbed a pen and pad of paper, and, without pause, started scribbling away.

I didn't know much about Crow's family at the time, but it was clear they weren't terribly close. I'd only seen his parents once, at a gig – an elderly couple, dressed as if on their way to church, in cardigans, pale blues and browns. They'd been huddled against the bar amid that drunk and animated crowd, like frightened sheep herded into a corner. I also knew that Crow had a much older brother (whose name I can't even remember), who was estranged from the family and had lived for over a decade in a mining town in Western Australia. Alice told me that Mr Crowley, a Vietnam vet, spent most of his days drinking whisky on the brick porch of their house somewhere north of Geelong, while his wife fussed about dusting their china display shelves or preserving fruit for church fetes. I recall that Alice would often take the kids to see their grandparents on her own.

'Here,' Crow said with a smile, handing me his drawing.

In the bottom-centre of the page was a child dressed in a Batman outfit, gleefully happy as he leaped off the branch of a tree, his cape flowing behind. To the right of this figure was an enormous slingshot aimed at the boy, being held by a giant pair of hands. A face, maliciously grinning, hovered above the slingshot – this must have been Crow's older brother. In the top right-hand corner was a small, decrepit man seated in a chair, tumbler in one hand, bottle in the other. A dark stain ran down his pants to a pool of liquid at his feet. In the other top corner was a blindfolded woman trembling on her knees, crossing herself underneath a crucifix.

I stared at the drawing a moment, unsure what to say, embarrassed by my naiveté and earnestness – at the thought that I could have quietly snuck into his interior, poked around, unnoticed, and been able to unravel everything.

'Well, doc?' he enquired. 'Read anything into it?'

'How boring. You happy middle-class families are going to put us psychologists out of work.' I smiled and returned his picture. He shrugged and continued with his sketch.

And then there was Crow's car accident – it was the night after he found out that his old school buddy Josh had hanged himself. I'd never met Josh, who'd been living mainly in London since school, but Alice said he and Crow had been close, both having ridden into their elite private school on scholarships (Crow as a runner, Josh as a footy player), though Crow only lasted a few years before losing his scholarship and ending up at the local state school. Alice had spent most of that day with Crow, and she told me he was in a pretty bad state. He'd been ranting about one of their old PE teachers, who'd taken Josh and him to gigs when they were fourteen, plied them with drugs and alcohol, and, in her words, done his best to screw them both up.

That evening Crow went out drinking with old school friends while Alice, Freya, Nadia and I sat on the sofa eating spaghetti marinara that Alice had cooked up. We spent a lot of time with Nadia and Freya back then. Nadia was studying media, but spent most of her time waitressing, acting in student films and staying out all weekend at country doofs. I loved hanging out with Nadia – she oozed positivity and laughed flirtatiously at everything you said. Freya on the other hand – with her short, scruffy self-cut hair and dowdy fifties dresses – I wasn't so keen on. One of the first times I met her, she stayed overnight on our couch and left behind an apple core, a glass of water and a pile of blankets where she'd slept. I felt like my mother, mumbling to myself about manners as I cleaned up her mess the next day.

Alice told us all a lot about Crow's background that night, things I'm not sure she would have mentioned if our emotions weren't already running so high. She sat there with her red wine, her voice shrill as she described how Crow and Josh would hang out at their teacher's flat, just near their school, drinking and smoking dope, then would head off to strip clubs.

I shrugged. It seemed typical that Crow should claim such a scandalous past.

'There was a teacher at my school a bit like that ...' Freya's dreamy, childlike voice trailed off.

'Was the guy a – you know?' Nadia asked, leaning in, her fingers positioned delicately against her chin. Nadia had such poise that, despite her streaked red-and-brown dreadlocks and eyebrow piercing, she was still able to make such an enquiry sound like she was discussing Descartes.

'Well, if you count giving them both blow jobs ...'

Nadia gasped and leaned back. Freya just blinked her eyes even wider. Possibly, like me, unsure what to make of this.

'Did Crow have, like, a choice?' I asked.

'He was fourteen!' Alice replied.

Nadia had her eyebrows raised and was shaking her head, Freya still said nothing, and I – remembering how unequivocally boring my own teenage years had been, and how I would have done anything for a bit of intrigue – failed to provide the reaction Alice was clearly after.

It wasn't just my own teenage ennui that I recalled, but also the belief I had, at the age of fourteen, that I was old enough to be in charge of my own fate. It was in Year Ten that I heard Tamara Lebedev, a girl in my class, was having an affair with Mr Lawson, our hirsute and nuggety maths teacher. Tamara looked like a supermodel and studied opera singing out of school, and Mr Lawson loved cricket and American soapies (while we were doing our maths work, he'd walk around the class practising his hook shots and blocks, while chatting about the goings-on of David and Maddie on *Moonlighting*) so the alleged affair was of great amusement to all of us. He'd often be seen walking her to tennis practice after the bell rang, and even giving her lifts to school in his mint-green Commodore. Then when Tamara suddenly left school mid-term, and Mr Lawson soon after, word went around that Tamara had ended up in a psychiatric hospital following an abortion, and that Lawson had negotiated a payout with her family then moved to a different school. After a while, the rumours about Tamara died down, and we all just assumed she'd been a bit loopy to begin with – allowing herself to be seduced by a Neanderthal like Mr Lawson seemed testament to this.

I see things differently now – very differently. I haven't given Tamara a thought in all these years, and now – my God, I can't believe I thought what happened to her was okay. But Alice – even with Crow telling her it was fine, that the affair with the PE teacher hadn't affected him at all – even back then she was furious: furious that it had happened, and furious that when Mrs Crowley found out about her son and the teacher, she either ignored it, didn't believe it, or hoped it might simply go away.

At some point Alice clammed up and didn't want to discuss Crow and the PE teacher any further – I suspect she felt guilty, suddenly, for gossiping about him in the first place. So Freya went on to tell us all about a grant for some sound recordings she was doing in the Mallee, and Nadia gave us an update on Ben, the guy she'd been seeing, whose housemate's pet python had escaped. (The update was that they thought the escaped python was probably living behind the oven, but until the snake was returned to captivity Nadia refused to visit.)

It was past midnight by the time we got the phone call about Crow's accident; we'd polished off four bottles of red and our pasta bowls were still sitting on the coffee table in front of us. Alice answered the phone, as we had all assumed it was Crow, drunk and morose. Then she just stood there, staring blankly down at the carpet, holding the phone receiver in one hand and the cradle in the other, saying, 'Oh God … oh God …'

'Crow's had an accident,' she said after she'd hung up, looking past us all and heading for the kitchen. I followed her, asking what had happened, but she just looked around, picking up piles of letters then going through her handbag. She found her car keys then headed to the door. Nadia stood in front of her, took her by the shoulders and guided her back to the sofa, telling her to sit down while we called a cab. Alice sat down obediently, slumped over then shook her head. 'He crashed into his school gates. He's at St Kilda lock-up,' she said. I put my arm around her while she sobbed, Nadia called a cab and Freya made her a peppermint tea. It was decided I'd accompany her in the cab.

At the police station, the officer in charge refused to let Alice see Crow, so we sat in the moulded-plastic chairs against the wall in the foyer and soon fell asleep, Alice's head on my lap and me slumped back in my seat. I remember waking into a groggy state several times as people spoke with the officer at the counter, or when swearing drunks were dragged in by the cops. At dawn I woke properly, to sobbing and what sounded like the voice of a child. I looked up and saw Alice and Crow holding each other tightly; he was the one crying. 'I'm so sorry, babe, I'm so sorry. I promise I'll do better,' he was saying.

Earth Monster's album *Phantasmagoria* had recently debuted in the Australian top ten, so photos of Crow's car crash ended up all over the papers: his crumpled Holden underneath those twelve-foot-high wrought-iron gates, uprooted from the school entrance like weeds. So were the reports of marijuana and speed being found in his glovebox. The court case, the suspended sentence he received, the drug and alcohol education program, and the media scrutiny of his 'substance abuse' made the next few months a difficult time for Alice and Crow. In fact I barely recall seeing him: he cancelled all gigs and appearances during that period, and Alice more or less lived at his place.

But that night in the police-station foyer, as Crow sobbed in Alice's arms, I closed my eyes and pretended to sleep. Alice's voice was a caressing murmur; she seemed to be telling him it was going to be all right. It seems crazy now, when I think back on it: she was comforting her drunk, bloody, damaged boyfriend, who'd just spent the night in the lock-up and would now have to front up to court. And yet all I could think about as I listened to the two of them was how lucky she was to be holding him right then, kissing away his tears.

I remember, around that time, learning about Maslow's hierarchy of human needs in my psychology class: that after our basic physiological needs and the need for safety had been met, the next most important need was for love and belonging. I walked from that lecture brimming with my new knowledge; it was the day something profound in my life had been named for the very first time. I realised at that moment that I was part of a *tribe*. These friends – Crow, Alice, Nadia, Freya, and others like the guys in the band – were more than just people with whom I shared interests: they were *my* people. And what connected me to them was some sort of psychic glue that had bound communities together for hundreds of thousands of years.

I've heard that penguins sleep in groups lying on the ocean's surface, and should any single penguin start to drift an alarm will resound throughout the raft. There are examples among herding mammals, schools of fish, bee colonies – so many groups of animals – of behaviour that makes them seem to operate, in many ways, like a single organism: a kind of telepathic community consciousness that still baffles neuroscientists. And so it seemed with us that what drew us together was the very thing that had bound ancient Homo sapiens together, ensuring their survival as they'd trekked and hunted across the savannah. Yes, we were a tribe, and it felt like Alice and Crow were *our* glue. The three of us, in particular, would have done anything – *anything* – for each other. And that's one of the things that makes Alice's death so difficult to accept. Because the last time I spoke to her, she'd asked for help, and I'd refused. Then when I went to visit her a week later, she'd set her house on fire.

6

I'm remembering that flinty look Crow gave me tonight when I tried to speak about Alice. It takes me back to the early days and the friction that began to arise between the two of us. Not straight away – maybe about a year into Alice and Crow's relationship – and not all the time; he mostly remained his usual charming self around me. It started with the occasional quip: there was one about Alice and Crow being in their dotage with me in a granny flat out the back, and others about me never paying for anything, even though Crow feigned insult if I ever pulled out money. I ignored these remarks, and Alice did too, putting them down to a churlishness that would exhibit itself when Crow was hungover, had played a bad gig, or had suffered some other minor upset. But then his prickly behaviour started to become more frequent, coming to a head at the beginning of 1994.

I met Rob at a nightclub at the top of Swanston Street. I noticed him as soon as Alice and I arrived. He wore a vintage western shirt and cowboy boots, and was leaning his elbow against one of the chest-high drinks tables, holding a bottle of Corona and gazing out over the dance floor below – though I'd noticed him stare in my direction several times. Alice and I were chatting at the bar, but as soon as she ran off to find Crow Rob appeared, standing in front of me. He leaned on the bar and, with his green eyes six inches from mine, said, 'Come home with me.' Just like that. I'd had a couple of half-hearted relationships over the previous years, but I'd never had a man look at me or speak to me in this way, let alone someone as handsome as Rob. I'd also never gone home with a stranger before, but I'd had a few drinks and was feeling fearless. Over Rob's shoulder, I could see Crow wrapping his arms around Alice, lifting her off the ground in his embrace. 'Sure,' I said, with a shrug intended to match Rob's nonchalance, then took a swig of my beer to hide my grin.

He took me back to a tiny room above a pub in Richmond owned by his parents. I remember remarkably little about it all: not much more than sitting next to him on his single bunk bed, smoking a joint and barely listening as he chatted away – about his friend's ski lodge and the Renault his parents had bought him for his twenty-first – staring at the clothes and surfing magazines strewn across the floor. Growing tired and swallowing yawns, I was no longer so thrilled by my temerity. I began to wish I was tucked up in my own bed, but resigned myself to the idea that everything that was about to happen was inevitable.

I noticed a copy of *The Fatal Shore* among the mess on the carpet. I hadn't spoken for some time, so asked, 'You reading that?'

'Oh, yeah, kind of. My aunt gave it to me. I've read a bit – enough to get the gist,' he took a drag on the joint. 'You know, I reckon colonialism gets a bad rap. Humans have fought against each other throughout time.'

'There's waging territorial battles and then there's rocking up on someone else's land and systematically dismantling and obliterating their culture and language, and enslaving them to your own ...'

'Yeah, I just reckon these things have always happened ...'

You intimidate guys: I remembered the words of my old school friends, trying to find a reason for my singledom, and said nothing more. Besides, he was clearly no Alice, and I was too tired to argue. I handed him back the joint, now almost burning my fingertips.

He took a final puff, butted the joint out on a saucer on the table then started kissing me, grappling with my buttons and bra.

The only other clear memory I have is from the morning, scrambling around for my clothes on the floor while Rob lay in bed, smoking a rollie and watching me. 'You've got a top body,' he said. I hurried to put my shirt on, shoving my bra into my bag.

Once dressed, I kissed him goodbye, wondering if I'd see him again; if I *wanted* to see him again. Then he leaned across to his bedside drawers, grabbed a pen and a Tally-Ho paper, and asked for my number with the same breezy indifference with which he'd spoken to me all night. 'Lara, isn't it?' he said; no irony, I'm sure.

Rob never called. Alice convinced me that a number scribbled on a cigarette paper in a messy bedroom was bound to get lost, so the following week we turned up to the club. Rob wasn't there.

Another week or more passed and my period was late. I whispered the news to Alice in the corridor outside class, a part of me revelling in the drama of it all. She dragged me to the union building pharmacy to buy a pregnancy test, then ushered me into the toilets and waited outside my door.

'Christ. Two lines,' I said from inside the cubicle. 'That's not good, is it?' I was trying to be humorous.

'Shit,' I heard her respond.

So that's how I found out I was pregnant. And all I remember feeling was a kind of heady confusion. Was this the excitement of adulthood for which I'd longed? Had I finally superseded the spectacle that was Crow with my own thrilling drama? We skipped our lectures, went to the pub and got drunk. 'I'll support you whatever you decide to do,' Alice said, inebriated, her arm around my shoulder. 'No, seriously. Whatever you wanna do, I'm there for you.' But for me, there was never any decision to be made.

Outside the clinic, a dozen people stood about, mainly older men, some of them with pamphlets or clipboards in their hands. Several had sandwich boards displaying photos of foetuses; one board was cut in the shape of a tombstone with 'Massacre of the innocents' written on it, decorated with posies of flowers at the base. One of the younger men wore a board adorned with plastic models of a pregnant woman's womb at six, eight, twelve and twenty weeks. At six weeks – my stage – a small baby, the size of my thumb, slept curled up in a cosy red cocoon. Alice had her arm hooked around mine; I stared at the footpath as she towed me along. I became aware of someone walking alongside me, then a pale, wrinkled hand held a pamphlet in front of my eyes. 'Would you like some information, madam?' It was an elderly male voice with a lilting cockney accent. 'Just talk to us, please. We'd like to help you. Life won't be the same ever again if you go in there.'

His hand touched my elbow. He had a long, pale face, with a ginger beard, and wore a beige bomber jacket and a tweed peaked cap. His eyes looked at me pleadingly, 'Please think about the baby; it's your own son or daughter you're killing.'

'Get away from her,' Alice said, leaning across me and pushing him back. I kept my head lowered and pushed on towards the front steps.

I didn't know where I was when I woke from the abortion. I was lying on my side on a bed, covered with a blanket. A nurse put her hand on my arm and asked how I was feeling, then propped the bed up so I could sit. I was in a room with five other beds; three women were asleep, and two, both of whom I recognised from the waiting room, were sitting up, staring straight ahead into the centre of the room and drinking cups of tea. No one spoke. My breasts were still sore and my abdomen ached. I thought about Rob's laconic, enigmatic smile as he lay there smoking his morning cigarette in bed, and wondered what he was doing now – if perhaps he somehow knew. The nurse brought me a cup of tea and two Scotch Finger biscuits on a plate. She put her hand on my shoulder and smiled in an apologetic way. I was shivering and asked her for another blanket. 'Of course, dear,' she said. As she walked away, I took a bite of the biscuit and started crying for the first time since this had all begun.

Out in the waiting room, Alice gave me some large black sunglasses to wear and tucked me under her arm as we stepped back outside. They were all still there; I could see the ginger-haired man approaching a woman further up the street. Alice guided me in the opposite direction, towards a pale blue Holden Special pulled over at the curb in a No Standing zone, with both the front and back passenger doors wide open. There were Venetian blinds hanging in the back and side windows, and a 3RRR sticker on the bumper bar. It was Crow. She hadn't told me he'd be coming.

Alice ushered me into the back, onto the tasselled bedspread that covered the ripped red vinyl seat, and closed the door. Then she slid onto the front bench seat, beside Crow.

There was a blanket folded on the seat, and on top of it a bunch of chrysanthemums, wrapped in purple tissue paper and tied with a piece of string.

After kissing Alice, Crow leaned back towards me, puckering for a kiss. His face was covered with stubble and he smelled of Grey Flannel, the cologne he was always splashing himself with. 'Hey, it's Michael Jackson.'

I remembered the big black sunglasses I was wearing and attempted a weak smile.

Then more tenderly, 'So how you feeling, sister?' He reached back and put his hand on my shoulder.

I shrugged as I settled onto my seat and gave another close-lipped smile, afraid that if I spoke I might cry.

'Flowers are for you,' he said. He looked ahead, indicated and turned out into the traffic.

I wrapped the blanket around me, then put the flowers in the footwell, lay down on the seat and closed my eyes. The grassy waft of the flowers cut through the mouldy sponge-and-vinyl smell of the seats.

'Well. No more late nights and cheap alcohol for you, hey, girl?'

'Crow!' Alice snapped.

Crow turned the radio up and started singing along to Donovan. He stopped to respond to something Alice asked, but I couldn't make out what they were saying over the music, a tram bell and other traffic noise. It sounded like they were arguing.

The music went down. 'So we're heading back to your place,' he turned to the side to speak to me over the click of the indicators. 'I'm going to pick up some takeaway for you, and get you set up with some videos. Then Alice and I are heading out to see Ween. Going to be hanging with the band afterwards, I reckon. Nadia is home tonight and said any problems, just give her a call.'

'Thanks,' was all I managed to get out before closing my eyes once more.

Once home, I went into the kitchen and put the kettle on, out of habit, then decided against sitting up with Alice and Crow. I went to my room instead, embarrassed by how poorly I was dealing with this. I took off my clothes, leaving them in a puddle on the floor, looked at my belly, which seemed quite the same as before, then climbed into bed. That's when I felt the absence of what had been whirring within me. Pregnancy makes women feel powerful: we're creating a *human being*. It's impossible, in this state, not to acknowledge the tug of the future, the reach of a hand, belonging to a tiny unformed being. This person. *My child*. I lay there and let it happen, that indulgent fantasy I'd denied myself: Rob and me, living in some shabby inner-city weatherboard cottage, cradling our baby. I lifted my knees up to my torso and hugged them tight, then tried to picture myself marching alongside de Beauvoir and the other French women – the Manifesto of 343 Sluts that I'd written about in first year – who claimed to have had an abortion, and who forced their will on the French parliament in the early seventies. Legal abortion was nothing to be sad about, I reminded myself: it was a gift.

I hadn't been in bed long when Alice came in and sat on my bed. I had my back to her and the doona pulled up around my face. My nose was running, so I sniffed, then wiped the tears from my cheeks with a fist of doona.

'Fuck this,' Alice muttered, then got up and left the room.

Within the quieter moments of the Ween CD playing on the living-room stereo, I could hear Crow's raised voice and, occasionally, Alice's quieter but more insistent one. Sometime during the third song I heard Crow's firm march down the hallway, the floorboards creaking and my bedroom door trembling as he passed. The front door opened and slammed shut. Shortly afterwards, Alice returned to my room and again sat on my bed. 'I'm going to stay in,' she said, sounding much brighter.

'Sorry I caused a fight.' But I wasn't sorry at all. Thoughts of Rob and the abortion now felt quite remote. I was even ashamed of my previous melodramatic distress, and relieved I hadn't voiced any of it. I was now just looking forward to sitting on the couch with takeaway food, wrapped in doonas, watching videos, with Alice.

I didn't see Crow that weekend, or all the following week, but Alice seemed to have been forgiven and stayed at his place often. I next saw him ten days later at the Esplanade Hotel. He gave me a peck on the cheek, asked how I was, then ordered me a black Russian from the bar. All seemed harmonious again, so I accepted Alice's invitation to accompany them to a party in the city. At eleven o'clock, we stumbled out the glass double doors onto the marble-tiled verandah of the hotel. Crow threw his arm around Alice's shoulders, and they both trotted down the concrete steps towards the road; I was a few metres behind. Halfway down, Crow turned to Alice and – loudly enough for me to hear – said: 'Why does *she* always have to come with us?' I stopped in the middle of the stairs, held on to the metal railing and waited. Alice replied, 'Because if she doesn't come, I don't go either.' I continued down behind them, head low, wondering whether I should go home instead. When Crow didn't respond, Alice added, 'It can get a bit tedious, you know: watching you get hammered every night and entertaining your admirers.' He still didn't reply, just shook his black mane and looked around as he hit the pavement, letting go of Alice and lifting his arm to hail a cab. Alice turned to me and reached out her hand.

Later that night, as Alice and I drank champagne and leaned against the marble benchtop in the kitchen of the party, Alice thanked me for coming along, telling me how boring she found these parties. 'There's only so long I can fawn over someone's Clergerie boots.'

'Any time,' I said, reaching for a salmon vol-au-vent as a tray the size of a small coffee table slid past.

'Christ, would you look at that?' Alice's eye followed the tray. 'You could feed an entire third-world nation on those canapés alone.'

I reached for another as a Hot Chocolate song came on and a cheer went up from the living room.

Alice grabbed my hand and pulled me away from the kitchen bench, past the white leather couches and onto the zebra-hide rug of the dance floor. 'Stick with me. If a guy dances near me, Crow'll hit the roof.'

We shimmied around, holding hands, bumping hips, for hours; no one dared interrupt us. I did, however, notice Crow – who spent much of the night smoking joints outside on the balcony – glancing through the large glass window at us. I told myself he should have been grateful I was there.

The following night was my twenty-second birthday. Six of us went out for a Thai meal on Swan Street and were heading over the road for an Earth Monster gig at the Corner Hotel. I was walking up front beside Crow as he complained to me about his rider at the Corner. At least Max, one of the barmen, always gave Alice and him free drinks, he said.

I laughed. 'Reckon he'd love to give Alice more than free drinks.'

Crow looked at me, said nothing, then quickened his pace to step up to the heavy green door of the front bar.

It was already crowded inside, the carpet sticky, and the air thick with cigarette smoke and the tinny smell of draught beer. Alice, Nadia, Jason and I headed to the only free spot at the far side of the pool table, and Crow went to the bar to get the first round. Max lined the drinks up on a tray and was about to walk away when Crow leaned over the bar and grabbed his wrist, then slapped a note into it. He put one hand on Max's shoulder, and with the other he gently held onto the yoke of Max's shirt as he spoke, inches from his face. Max turned his head as he listened, looking straight down the end of the bar, nodding. When Crow finished, Max looked at him and nodded again. Crow let go of his shirt and patted him on the back.

Later, during the band's second set, Alice and I were leaning against the bar, and Crow, sweat dripping down the sides of his face, panted into the mike that he wanted to dedicate this next song to a very special lady. He lifted his T-shirt to wipe his face; a few whistles went out. He laughed and looked in our direction, and I turned to Alice, who still blushed every time Crow singled her out at a gig. 'That foxy lady at the bar in the silvery black top is Lara, and it's her twenty-second birthday today, so how about we give her a birthday song to remember.'

As the two-hundred-strong crowd belted out 'Happy Birthday', Alice's face beamed next to me. Crow stood centre-stage, mock conducting the crowd. After the applause, Crow yelled out, 'Now I want everyone here to buy Lara a drink. Tequila, lime and soda is her favourite. Max! You listening? The first one's on me, unless you'd like to pay?'

Alice, up on her elbows, leaned in to the bar to get one of the bartenders' attention. I stepped away from the bar to let others in, and watched Crow, up on stage, as he hung his twelve-string around his neck, plectrum between his lips, and plugged its cord into the amp. He returned to the mike, and as he adjusted its height and strummed a few chords, he looked in our direction, squinting to see us.

The three of us – Crow, Alice and I – stepped out from the hot chalky air of the pub into a summer's night, the streets glistening black after a rain, the asphalt steaming its stony perfume, the sky a murky violet. Crow's 'unwinder' joint had made him particularly frenetic and he was running ahead of us, leaping about in his black jeans and faded Metallica T-shirt, waving his arms and hollering about everything he came across. 'Look at the weight of it all!' he said, springing up onto the tray of a Holden ute, 'Five tonnes, you reckon?' Then up on top of the cabin, which didn't even quiver under him. 'I mean, look at that, would you?' He flung his arms out, presenting the city buildings that glimmered beyond the rail overpass. 'The sheer mass of it all'.

His tone was part awe, part condemnation. He jumped off the ute then ran under the bridge, disappearing down the street, singing and ranting, lucky not to be arrested. Watching him flitting about in the dark like a moth, this chimeric figure garbling about the tonnage of modern civilisation, made me feel quietly exhilarated, like a bit part in some dystopic arthouse flick.

Crow ran back to us and started smothering Alice in kisses, combing her hair with his fingers and whispering in her ear; I marched ahead and around the corner into a narrow street crowded with single-storey terraces, towards where my car was parked.

I must have been twenty metres ahead of the lovebirds when an orange Cortina slowed down alongside me, and a young guy leaned out of the passenger window, his hairy arm hugging the outside of the door to his chest. I could see another man peering across from the driver's side. The Guns N' Roses playing inside quietened, and he called out, 'You want a lift, gorgeous?'

'No, thanks,' I replied without lifting my head.

'Wouldn't let my dog fuck ya anyway!' he yelled back, breaking into laughter. His window went up, the music got suddenly louder and the brake lights went off.

I only realised that Crow had been sprinting up the street when he was almost at the car's bumper. As the car screeched away, Crow launched himself onto the boot, spread flat. The car lurched forward; Crow slipped backwards and grabbed the aerial, which snapped in his hand as he slid onto the road. As soon as he'd landed, down on all fours, the car's brake lights flashed on like a baring of teeth and the car came to a stop, humming loudly. The muted sound of the music through the closed windows went quiet as the driver revved the accelerator several times. Crow picked himself up off the bitumen, only metres behind the car's rear, taking his time. God knows what he was planning.

'Crow!' Alice screamed out, running from behind. I memorised the number plate – all I could think to do. Crow stood in the middle of the road, dusting his side, glaring at the Cortina – as if this car posed no threat at all. Then he ran towards the driver's side, still clenching the aerial in his hand like a weapon. The car accelerated and sped off before Crow could reach the window, the guy in the front passenger side yelling out, 'Fucking lunatic!' and Crow yelling back, 'Motherfucker!'

'You didn't need to do that,' I said as Crow returned, hands on hips, to the footpath where Alice and I stood with arms around each other.

'That's gratitude!' He shook his upper limbs, bristling. His face was shiny and red, with dirt from the road on one cheek. He handed me the aerial. 'Souvenir.'

I took it and let my arm dangle behind me, then dropped it to the footpath.

Alice and I exchanged an uneasy smile, a smile like a handshake closing a deal. Then we walked on; Crow was a few steps ahead of us, singing.

I didn't really know what to think. I felt like that often back then: my deference, my appreciation, my horror, all bound up together, impossible to untangle. Alice possibly felt the same; she didn't sidle up to Crow, or to me, but dallied behind to pick some jasmine off a gate, returning moments later to poke a stem behind my ear. No, I didn't know what to think, so I went with feeling. I felt rattled, but safe.

Alice was smelling a sprig of jasmine as she walked alongside me, twirling the stem between her fingers. I clutched her hand in mine, pulled it towards me and took a big sniff.

I'd been singled out, but in a good way. Perhaps that was it: I felt loved.

Alice read a lot of Foucault back then. She was quite obsessed with his notions around power and madness, and this is something I've thought about a lot since her death, not as a way of reframing what happened to her as some sort of foreseeable or inevitable destiny, but more because I recognise that from very early on she seemed aware of the struggles that may lie ahead for her. There was one quote in particular that I remember her pulling out: something about how if you are not like everyone else then you are abnormal, and if you are abnormal then you are sick. And that these three things are in fact very different, but society has reduced them to the same thing. She liked this quote because she enjoyed being different and outspoken, and aligned herself with outsiders. The crazies, for Alice – people like Crow – were the unrecognised geniuses, the oracles, of society (and following that, their indiscretions could be more easily forgiven). Everyone else – the 'mindless masses' – existed in ignorant servitude to a corrupt, unjust system. She talked a lot about the difference between the hypnotic evil of people like Hitler, Himmler and Hoess, and the *banality of evil* of 'office boys' like Eichmann.

'Germany, 1939: imagine you were alive then. A non-Jew. What would you have done?' she once asked me.

I shrugged, confessing I'd never given it any thought.

'Johann Elser, that's who I'd want to be,' she said. Elser was, of course, the German worker who infamously carried out an elaborate – and almost successful – assassination attempt on Hitler, and later died in Dachau. His psychological report at the time concluded that he was a 'fanatic' with a pathological desire for recognition.

That's how it was with Alice: 'crazy' and 'mad' were never criticisms, but labels to be worn with great pride.

There's one other event from that time that's important, an afternoon I forgot about for almost ten years. A memory that, once recovered, seemed to underpin everything that came later. It was spring 1995 – I remember it was spring because of the clematis coming into flower on our gate; the great waft of it as I walked up to the house. I was doing a masters in media studies by then, and co-managing a restaurant near the stock exchange three days a week. On this day, I arrived home from work around five. When I walked inside, the house was quiet except for the soft click of Alice's bedroom door closing. I went through to the kitchen, dropped my bag on the table and put the kettle on. I took my handbag back to my room, pausing outside Alice's – there wasn't a sound, so Crow couldn't have been there – and hung my jacket in my closet. On my way back to the kitchen, I knocked on Alice's door.

'Alice? You in?'

There was a long pause before she replied. 'Um, yeah.'

Inside, Alice was standing, dripping wet and naked, and with a towel just held over her front, a couple of metres in front of her open wardrobe doors. The phone was in the centre of her room, on the floor; the receiver was off the cradle, quietly beeping.

'Everything okay?' I said, placing the phone back in its cradle.

She seemed to attempt a smile. 'What should I wear?'

'Wear whatever you want.'

She didn't move; her eyes were wild, panicked. 'I mean, what would I normally wear?'

I looked at her closely, to scrutinise what she was up to, whether she was drunk, stoned, mucking around, hungover. 'Are you okay?'

Her mouth twitched.

'You're not, are you?' I walked towards her, grabbed her towel and wrapped it around her, then put my arm over her shoulder and started leading her out. 'I've put the kettle on; come into my room, we'll have a cup of tea.' I grabbed her red towelling dressing-gown from the hook on her door and put it over her shoulders, then removed the towel from around her – she stood like a child, letting me do this – and began to dry her hair with the towel. 'No. You're not okay, are you?' I said again.

She shook her head and blinked. Tears ran down her face.

By the time we were sitting on my bed, cups of tea in hand, she looked more relaxed; those animal eyes had gone. She said that she wasn't sure what had started it. She'd been in her room, cleaning up, and had been thinking about all the things she had to get done over the next week – she was volunteering at a soup kitchen in St Kilda as well as DJ'ing three nights, working in a bookstore and playing a role in a short film of Nadia's. She just wanted to stay home tonight but knew that Crow would be upset if she didn't join him at his gig.

'I kept calling the Tote to leave a message, but this weird panic was coming over me. I began to feel like I wasn't me anymore, but someone else; I didn't know who Alice was at all. George, the barman, kept answering the phone, and I knew it would have been the simplest thing in the world to pass on a message for Crow, but I just didn't know how to say it. I thought he'd know it wasn't me, but someone pretending to be me. Each time, before I called, I'd rehearse the kinds of things that I thought Alice would say, but I was scared he'd say something off-script and I wouldn't know what to do. I just gave up and decided to have a shower. 'Cos I knew that's what Alice would do.' Her body was hunched and curled around the tea in her hands.

'So I went to the shower. I turned on the taps and took my clothes off, and I put my hands under the water, but I couldn't feel if it was hot or cold. I could only feel the pressure of the water, no temperature. I was so scared. I knew that wasn't normal. I worried I might burn myself so I turned the hot off and just washed in cold. And all the time, my brain was whirring at this terrifying pace, this extraordinary worry – not of anything, but of what was happening to me. This incredible dread. It was like the walls were coming in on me. I thought I was going mad. I got to my room, and it just started to get worse, this feeling like my mind had become dislodged. It was like I was an alien in my body. I looked out onto the street, watching the cars drive past, and I decided if I still felt like this tomorrow that I would kill myself; I'd just run out onto the road in front of a car, because I couldn't bear to live like this, to lose my mind.' Her words were gushing out, urgently. 'But I was also trying to pull myself together, because I didn't want to have to kill myself. That's what I was trying to do when you got home, I was trying to get dressed, but I didn't recognise any of my clothes. I didn't know what Alice would wear ...' She put her teacup down on the windowsill, lifted her hand to her face and started crying.

I put my arm around her and rubbed her back, then said. 'I'll ring the Tote. I'll tell them to tell Crow you've had a migraine and gone to bed.'

She closed her eyes and rested her head in the nook of my neck. 'Thank you.' Then a moment later, 'Don't tell Crow. Please don't tell him.'

'Of course not.'

She looked up at me. 'What happened to me?'

'I don't know. I think it was just a panic attack. But it's all over now and I won't say a word.' I hugged her again, then took the phone into the next room to call the Tote, happy that she'd turned to me, happy to share her secret.

7

Though Alice and I never discussed her panic attack, I felt that the belt around our friendship had been tightened: I had been there when she'd been in need; Crow hadn't. But I'd also seen a more vulnerable side to her that made me, for the first time, question her bravado.

One night over dinner, she asked me if I thought she and Crow were a 'good match'. She was tiring of his partying lifestyle, it seemed. 'He keeps saying he's going to stop. But then other times he gets angry and says it's got nothing to do with me.' There was also the issue of his regular touring; they'd already had several fights about his upcoming US tour, and whether or not Alice would join him. Alice wanted to stay behind. 'I mean, if we were ever to have kids together ...'

This was the first time she'd ever mentioned kids, so I gave it little attention. And I'm not sure I bothered to try to quell her fears either. As much as I loved Crow, as much as I wished I had more of his flamboyant spirit, I was also glad to be the stable force in her life.

Instead, I reminded her of our plans, hatched near the beginning of our friendship, to travel together overseas after we'd finished our degrees. Alice had finished her honours the previous year, and since then had been working odd jobs – mostly DJ'ing and bar work. I'd be finishing my masters at the end of the year, and I'd been at a bit of a loss about what to do next. I assumed Alice wouldn't want to travel, because of Crow, but as soon as I uttered the words even I was impressed with how flawless my proposal sounded: timing the stopovers to be in Vancouver for her cousin's wedding, as well as in the States to meet up with Earth Monster on tour and appease Crow. She got to her feet, grabbed my upper arm, and shouted, 'Yes!'

I ran for the atlas at the bottom of my bookshelf while she poured us both a wine, yelling out to me that I had to promise not to say anything yet to Crow.

'Of course, of course, of course,' I said, opening the large canvas-covered atlas on the table, closing my eyes and jabbing a finger on the page. *The Greek Islands! Perfect!* We raised our glasses and clinked.

I was used to Alice's paranoia regarding Crow. She'd already asked me to stash her old photos and diaries in my room, worried that Crow would find them, and had instructed me on which subjects I wasn't to mention in his presence – in general, any topic that involved another male, especially one from her past. I'd never seen Crow once get irritated by anything that she did; to the contrary, I'd only ever witnessed his utter adoration of her, his showering her with gifts: Valentino silk lingerie, an antique Cartier pearl ring – the list seemed endless. But I was only too glad to have parts of her to keep to myself, so I played along with the request.

So naturally I was floored, four weeks later, when Alice announced she was pregnant. She'd mentioned only recently wanting to have children with Crow, but I hadn't taken this to mean she wanted them anytime soon; especially *then*, just a matter of weeks after promising to travel overseas with me. Whenever she'd mentioned children I'd assumed she was referring to that 'one day' in the future when we were all grown up, working grown-up jobs, living grown-up lives. We were still in our twenties, going to parties every second night, discussing itineraries for overseas adventures. We were feminists, for crying out loud. I'd never considered that I, or anyone I knew, would have children yet. Well, that's not entirely true: I did know of one or two other women in our crowd who'd become pregnant, and had either moved up north or to the outskirts of Melbourne. We'd never really heard from them again. I recall one guy returned to the fold after a few years, with little to say about his absence. We simply heard that 'Linda and the kid' had stayed up north or moved in with her mum – something along those lines – and that was the end of the conversation. Though I don't recall it being explicitly discussed, parenthood was generally deemed something that no man wanted anything to do with; it was something inflicted upon them. Likewise, we'd always been taught that having children was not something educated young women – women with choices – did. At school they used to show us documentaries on teenage mums who ended up on welfare, living in council housing, with the fathers nowhere to be seen. We were told alarming figures about the gender wage gap, but that every extra year of schooling raised a woman's eventual wages by up to twenty-five per cent. Motherhood for young women was synonymous with domestic violence, poverty and substance abuse. Back in those days, the subject of babies would never have hit the pages of women's magazines – nothing was considered more banal. (Okay, so Demi Moore's pregnancy was an exception, thanks to *that* photo, but she was also naked and dripping with diamonds at the time.) Young, sophisticated, successful women simply didn't have children, and if they did, they kept them hidden. Teetering on the brink of womanhood, we didn't admire *mothers*; the women we looked up to were sassy, ballsy and answerable to nobody: Kim Basinger in *9 1/2 Weeks*, Sharon Stone's bisexual killer who flashes her vag during a police interview. And, oh, to feel as alive as Thelma and Louise as they drove their car off the cliff into oblivion! These were the women we wanted to be! Even off screen these actresses had spunk: they didn't gush in interviews about their Prada-wearing babies like celebrities do nowadays; they didn't panic when childless at the age of thirty and rush off to an African orphanage. In fact, the only one of those actresses to have a child before the age of forty was Susan Sarandon, and that was at the age of thirty-nine! Geena Davis only started pushing kids out at forty-six! When Madonna gave birth to Lourdes, it wasn't plastered all over the tabloids like a Grammy celebration: it was quietly slipped into the paper on page five, like an apology, a brief note that the 38-year-old pop star welcomed a daughter at the Good Samaritan Hospital in Los Angeles. If she'd sprained her ankle in rehearsals it would have received more coverage.

Christ, to be honest, when Alice told me she was pregnant, I was horrified. The two of us were going to travel the world, drink cocktails on Mykonos, hike through the Black Forest, ski Val d'Isere; we were going to do these things *together!* Now I had images of her pushing a pram through the suburbs, trackie daks on, bum sticking out, nappy bag over her shoulder and baby vomit down her front. I couldn't understand what she was doing.

'Are you really sure you want to do this?'

We were over at Crow's new apartment – white walls, polished floorboards and Deco ceiling roses and light fittings – where she'd been increasingly spending more time. I was sitting back in the armchair, drinking one of Crow's Peroni beers while she sat across from me, perched on the edge of the black club lounge, sipping peppermint tea.

She didn't say anything at first, then her body collapsed a little, and she started crying.

I leaned over towards her and held her hand in mine. 'I mean, that's not to say you won't have children together in the future. But do you really want them now?'

She kept hold of my hand as she put her teacup down and wiped her eyes with the back of her other hand.

'It's not now or never. You're young, you can have kids later, after travelling, when you've done everything you want to do, and when Crow's settled down.'

She nodded.

'I've had an abortion. It's *no big deal.*'

I'd have said I was just presenting her with options, reminding her she had choices. But the line I took wasn't just about not wanting to lose her. It was also to do with my image of motherhood, which was one of drudgery. My mother told me, when I was a kid, that if she'd had a severely disabled baby she would have drowned it at birth. I didn't think much of it at the time – it was just a part of the prevailing sentiment in our house that raising kids was nothing to get giddy about; it was something one endured, a part of one's civic duty. Life, as it was meant to be lived, was happening out there, in the world, far away from domesticity.

But there was something else at play. I'd already gone through this: an unplanned pregnancy. I'd got rid of mine. So somehow I figured that she must do the same.

'What does Crow think?'

She dabbed her eyes with the edge of her sleeve, then smiled. 'He's been talking about babies since the moment we met.'

'Right. So where's the problem?' I sat back.

'He doesn't want me to return to Canada, which is what I'd do; at least in the short-term, him being away so much.'

'Fair enough; it's his kid too.'

She looked into her teacup and nodded.

'Anyway, whatever you decide, you know you've got my support,' I said as I stood to go, mimicking the words she'd once said to me, looking around for my handbag.

'I know,' she said, as she stood and stepped forward, giving me a hug. 'Sorry about our trip.'

I shrugged. 'Well, it's not going to stop me seeing the world.' But I wasn't thinking about her pregnancy or even about our trip;

I was thinking about her comment that Crow wanted children. It was meant to be women who wanted children – needy, ambitionless women – not men. Even after I left, I couldn't stop thinking about it. I didn't know *what* to think about it; it just kept needling me, and I couldn't work out why.

Crow's career had been on a steady trajectory for several years, and I'd grown accustomed to how it had consumed not just his and Alice's lives, but the lives of us all. The glamorous parties, the backstage passes: they'd all been bestowed upon us by Crow. So when Alice later told me that Crow was taking a break from the industry on the eve of his first overseas tour – to the US of all places – and the two of them were moving down the coast to have the baby, I felt more than shocked and disappointed: I felt betrayed. But there was nothing to discuss; he'd already informed the band, and his tour was in the process of being cancelled. He'd also bought his parents' holiday house, on a large bush block in the Otways, half-an-hour from the coast where he'd spent his weekends and holidays as a kid. 'His fondest childhood memories are from down there: building tree houses, farming glow-worms and tadpoles, fishing for eels and yabbies, spotting owls and platypus at night,' she told me over the phone. 'It's how he wants his children to grow up. And he's a bit over carrying the band – reckons he's better off without them. Seriously, Lara, since making the decision, I've never seen him so happy.'

The rest of the band, especially Mark and Jason, were furious. Even though Jas and Crow were constantly fighting, and all of them complained about Crow being a control freak, they still all wanted that US tour. As we all stood around drinking black-and-tans at the Punters Club, dissecting this recent turn of events, word began to circulate that Alice had tricked Crow into fatherhood.

'She was supposedly on the pill,' Sandy said, 'but you don't get pregnant on the pill.'

And Louise: 'Jas reckons Crow's freaking out. He's just doing the honourable thing. But it's really not fair on him.' She glanced over at me.

'Alice said the pregnancy was an accident,' I said, but I was also beginning to wonder whether having children now had been secretly a part of her plan.

I didn't realise it at the time but there was a parting of ways between Alice and me at that point, and for me it was Alice who was breaking the oath – the oath of feminism, of our friendship – not me.

Sandy stood there shaking her head, 'My dad's a psychiatrist, and he reckons there's no such thing as an accidental pregnancy.'

I found myself nodding in agreement with the others.

8

Within six weeks of her announcement, Alice had rented a removal truck, emptied our house of sofas, pictures and crockery, and left town. Before I knew it, Caleb was born: the 25th of June, 1996.

I went down to visit a few days after Alice came home from hospital, driving the inland route and getting lost along the way, even though I'd already been down half a dozen times. There had been heavy rain the night before, and the sodden bush glowed teal, silver and icy green. In the valley near their house, the air was damp and misty. Neighbouring farmyard properties cut lonely figures, like subjects of McCubbin paintings, their chimneys puffing exhaustively out into the lead-grey sky. Cows and sheep congregated in the mist under the few trees in their paddocks, but otherwise not a soul was about.

Their house sat at the end of a short gravel drive and a bluestone path, tucked in among a small cottage garden. That old wooden bench that Alice loved sat halfway along the front walkway, hemmed by pansies and several pots of orchids. Beyond it was the thin stand of acacias, bottlebrush and eucalypts that separated their house from the dirt road and the state forest on the other side. The driveway ran around to the right of the house, to a large corrugated iron shed. Between the shed and the far end of the house was one of several large cypress trees, a large chopping block, and a small tin shelter filled with chopped wood. The house was weatherboard with peeling white paint and thin powder-blue aluminium window frames; a wooden verandah ran the width of it. At the front entrance – a flywire door, and behind that, another door covered in chipped black paint – two pairs of muddy work boots sat next to the doormat.

Alice greeted me wearing a thick, plush pink bathrobe, the belt knotted between the bulges of her belly and bosom. Her hair was loosely tied back in a bun with stringy wisps falling about her pale, blotchy face. Despite her maternal heft, she appeared small and frail. I wanted to say that she looked well, but couldn't quite manage it, so I gave her a hug. 'Congratulations, angel.'

She took me down the hallway – it smelled of burned toast and lavender – which ran to the right and into the living room. They'd done it up since I'd last seen it: the old floral carpets had been pulled up, exposing floorboards, which were now covered with an Afghani rug; the cement sheet walls with thin wooden beading, which had been a musty pink, were now a sunflower yellow; they'd pulled down the lace curtains, letting more light in through the bank of windows; and with Crow's black club lounge, Danish armchair, and pictures – a framed charcoal nude, and a linocut of a boat – the room looked less bleak than I remembered. However, the low ceilings, large eaves and the grey skies – visible through the window above the wooden deck – still made the room feel dark and damp.

Crow stood in front of the hearth, where a fire crackled and hissed, his feet firm and widely spaced on the floor. In his arms he nursed the tiniest black-haired figure, curled up and wriggling like a pupa, making tiny squeaky grunts. Crow's hair was wet and scruffy and, although he was unshaven, he looked dewy and fresh from the shower.

'Congratulations,' I said and gave him a kiss, then peered at the peculiar little face, with its black eyes and 'o' mouth, that peered out from his arms, hands scraping in the air.

'All congratulations should go to this amazing woman,' he said, smiling at Alice.

Alice reached her arms out towards Caleb. 'He's awake?'

'Can't believe you didn't hear him. I've changed him, so now he just needs a feed,' he shifted the baby into her arms. 'Hey, watch his head,' he said. 'You have to support it, remember?' Crow turned to me, rubbing his hands together. 'Drink?'

Crow popped the bottle of champagne I'd brought and poured us both a glass – Alice wasn't drinking – while Alice breastfed Caleb. Then Alice went to change Caleb's nappy and returned with him tightly swaddled in a flannel so that his body looked like a large blue cigar. She placed him down in his white wicker bassinet and tucked some blankets in around him.

'Jesus, babe, look how many blankets you've got on him! Haven't you heard of cot death?' Crow put his champagne glass down on the black bakelite side table, walked to the bassinet and took off the top blanket, tossing it on the couch. Alice walked over to the blanket, folded it then carried it off to their room.

Crow and I drank and chatted for a while, then I suggested I start cooking dinner. He thanked me, mentioning that they hadn't had any lunch, and adding, as he walked into the kitchen, that Alice couldn't eat garlic or onions. 'We think that's what's making Caleb cry so much,' he called out from the fridge.

Alice returned as Crow walked in with another bottle of champagne, twisting the wire cap around the cork. '*You* think that's what's making him cry so much,' she said.

I looked up at Crow and he returned a po face so ridiculous I had to stifle my laughter. He popped the champagne, letting the cork shoot out across the room and land on the floor behind the sofa. He skipped towards me with the bottle, which was beginning to foam over, and filled my glass. Alice was looking down at her lap, so I raised my eyebrows and smiled to him in reply.

I only stayed one night, making an excuse to leave immediately after breakfast in the morning. Alice had returned to the bedroom after eating half a piece of toast, so when I'd packed my car, I poked my head around her door to say goodbye. She was asleep in bed with Caleb in the crook of her arm. There was no curtain or blind, and the full-length window opposite her bed looked out through clumps of agapanthus toward a cypress tree and vegetable garden. A cot was set up against her bed, with one side removed abutting her mattress. Above the cot was a picture that I hadn't seen before, pinned to the freshly painted coral-orange wall. A watercolour, painted in her distinct childlike style, on thick parchment paper with pearlescent silk threads throughout, sparkling in the low winter sunlight. The picture was of a large, reddish weepy love heart, with two tiny figures standing on one of the bulging ventricles, like ants atop an apple, holding hands with an even tinier figure in between. Underneath, scrawled in her unmistakable naive font, were the words: 'How can there be so much love?'

Crow was in the kitchen eating toast. He looked up as I walked in. 'Don't worry too much about Alice. The maternal health nurse says it's normal.'

'What's that?'

'The tears, the crankiness. You would have heard her yelling at me this morning? They call it the baby blues. Hormones apparently go berserk a few days after giving birth.'

'Oh, okay.'

'Friend of mine who's a Chinese doctor is going to send some stuff to help. I'm going to cook up a big chicken stock this afternoon. We'll have her right as rain in no time.'

'Good to hear. Keep me posted on how she's going, won't you? And if there's anything I can do.'

He finished his last mouthful, sucked his honey-covered fingers, then put his arms around me and gave me a kiss on the forehead. 'Thanks, Lars. Think I've got it covered. She'll be good.' I wiped away the imprint of honey and crumbs on my forehead as I turned and said goodbye.

I was in a strange mood as I walked outside to the car. I felt both edgy and exhilarated. I wanted to get home as quickly as I could, ring a friend to come out with me, and get drunk.

It started raining – lightly at first – almost as soon as I drove out onto the dirt road. The car fogged up so much I had to pull over several times before I'd even reached Geelong and clean the inside of the windscreen with the sleeve of my jumper. The de-mister wasn't working, so I drove with the windows open two inches, letting in flecks of rain that hit the side of my face.

I was thinking about my parents. I remembered going into their bedroom one morning when I was around eight. Even though it was the weekend, I expected my mother to be there alone. I didn't like being around my father and tried to avoid him, which was fairly easy: on the weekends he was usually at the races or out playing golf or fishing. I probably wouldn't have entered their bedroom, wearing only my underpants, if I'd known he'd be there, sitting up in bed and smoking a cigarette with the newspaper spread across his lap. His chest was covered in thick black curls, matching his wavy hair and handlebar moustache. My parents were chatting about the dinner party they'd been to the previous night, and as I waited for a chance to speak to Mum, I found myself gazing at my full-length reflection in the mirror inside their open wardrobe door. I held onto the vertical wooden post inside the wardrobe and started rising up and mincing about on my toes. I spun around, catching glimpses in the mirror of my long hair as it fluttered out like a veil around my pirouetting body. Then I hung my head back, admiring the length of my hair, which tickled the knuckles of vertebrae that protruded in the curve of my back. I curtsied, and wove my arms through the air, mesmerised by this elegant ballerina I saw in front of me.

'You're like your mother, Lara. You've got a big El Conder Pass,' my father called out from the bed.

I looked over at his amused grin. Then at my mum, standing behind me in a bra and slip, who I thought was the most beautiful woman in the world.

'Arse. You've got a big arse,' he said, then started laughing.

'Shut up, Graham,' Mum said, in the weary voice she mainly reserved for Miriam and me. She was gazing at her half-naked reflection as she spoke, stepping her lean legs into a skirt, her mouth in a frown. Still on tiptoes, I signalled for my mum to lean down. I could smell her gardenia perfume, and her chain and pendant dangled against my cheek. I whispered in her ear, 'Mummy's the best.' She stroked the back of my head, then stood upright again and told me to go get dressed. She pulled a blouse from her wardrobe and I turned and skipped to my room. My father's words didn't upset me much back then – or, maybe I just don't recall being particularly bothered. I was used to the way he spoke to the three of us. My best friend back then, Charlotte, had an Alsatian dog that used to sit in the bend in her hallway and snap its jaws around my ankle each time I walked past. It would hold me there, lightly in its teeth, gazing up at me as I stood paralysed. I'd wait there until one of Charlotte's family found me, laughed, then growled at the dog to release me. I hated this horrible dog, but he was a part of Charlotte's household, so I had to put up with him. That's how it was at home with my dad. We all just learned to put up with him.

My father spent as little time as possible with us, which seemed to suit everyone. But when we were forced to share each other's company, he'd suddenly take the role of disciplining and cultivating our minds very seriously, teaching us skills such as how to correctly hold and swing a golf club, or decipher the label on a bottle of wine. He also handed out life advice whenever he saw the opportunity. 'Men and women have different brains,' he told Miriam and me after we'd been watching a female politician on the TV – 'a stupid cow', according to him. 'Women get very emotional, can't make decisions. They make terrible politicians, doctors and judges. Good carers, though. They make much better carers than men.'

Miriam and I always rolled our eyes when he spoke like this, especially as we got older, making it abundantly clear to him that we were dismissing everything he had to say. But we must have been listening. Miriam announced, as a teenager – so I'd have been around nine – that she never wanted children, and later went on to make Dad proud by becoming a successful estate agent in New York, married into a well-connected Republican family. I never went quite so far as Miriam, but I was still not about to admit any maternal feelings to anyone, least of all myself. To show a caring side would satisfy him too much: prove him right about a woman's worth. Too emotional, my foot.

Yes, Alice was very lucky to have found Crow, I thought on that drive home. Her life looked serene, and even though I convinced myself this was most definitely not what I wanted, I still found it hard to be entirely happy for her. She'd found a beautiful home and partner, and she'd slipped into her new life with absolute ease. Too much ease. And for some reason, for me, this was wrong.

9

I wake to the bell-like chime of children's laughter. For a moment I'm without bearings: I could be in my childhood home, waking on a summer's day; I could be middle-aged, listening to the sound of my own children. As my eyes adjust to the daylight I see a large sheet of black plastic nailed to a round wooden frame set in a rendered wall. Sharp bright light shoots in around the edges like a solar eclipse. I can hear the screech of cockatoos flying outside, and then, like an afterthought, the lazy caw of a raven. I smell dry grass and eucalyptus. Then a man's voice – loud, playful and suggestive. It's Crow. I'm at Crow's.

I drag my legs out from under a doona covered with moon, planets and stars, and heave my body up, landing my feet on the stone floor. As well as a book shelf, an old wardrobe and desk, and two Motorhead posters, there's a large round mirror on the wall – is this what eleven-year-old boys have in their rooms these days? I stand and strip off in front of it, and admire my ripe-fruit body from the front and then the side, running my hand along the rounded lines.

I've never liked my body very much – like most women, I'm sure. I've constantly looked at it and found fault. But not anymore. The perfect arcs of my torso; my pendulous breasts, ready to ooze; I love everything about it. I stand on my tiptoes and spin around, then lift one leg up into an arabesque, which throws me off balance. But even my stumble has its own beauty, like a rocking nesting doll.

I sit back down on the bed. My baby, a soft-boiled egg resting in my lap. Not long now, I think, giving her a stroke. The thought of meeting her soon fills me with a warmth that almost makes me light-headed, and then I remember, with some shame, a conversation I had with Alice when she was at a similar stage of pregnancy with Caleb. We were walking through the Botanic Gardens in the low winter sun, kicking through the autumnal leaves like children. We'd been talking about Bowlby's attachment theory, which she'd been reading up on, and which I'd learned about when I studied psychology. Alice was telling me – well, gushing, really – about how she was going to co-sleep with her baby because she wanted her child to feel loved, even when asleep.

'Attachment isn't about *love* at all,' I responded. 'All children are born with the drive to stay close to their caregivers. It's to do with protection from predators and other dangers. A child who's too independent will die. Attachment is just a trait evolved over millions of years to increase an infant's chances of survival.'

I don't know why I thought my heartless response might in any way diminish the intensity of feeling she already had for her child. It was more that I didn't want to hear about it. In fact, despite my enjoyment of theoretical discussion, I didn't want to discuss Bowlby's theories on the mother–baby bond either; I found them problematic for the brand of feminism I'd subscribed to, one whose main goals included the need for women to be able to exercise complete autonomy over their bodies, as well as having access to affordable childcare; these were paramount for enabling women to strive for equality in the workplace. For me, one of the greatest struggles for women was in finding ways to share the burden of child-rearing, not in surrendering to it. My only interest in attachment theory, back then, was limited to how early childhood relationships set the blueprint for later adult relationships. For example, there's the work of Heinz Kohut – a contemporary of Freud's – who traced adult narcissism back to childhood needs not being met. So according to Kohut, when my baby is born, she won't understand that I'm separate from her – she'll see me as an extension of herself – and so, she'll need to look into my eyes and see and feel love from me: that's how she'll develop self-love. If my child is showing off, and I ignore or humiliate her, I'll be actually teaching her that there is something shameful about wanting to be special, and that my love for her is conditional on her behaviour. Narcissists spend their lives compulsively searching for that unwavering parental gaze that they never received, the adoration they feel is owed to them, raging violently – like a toddler tantrum – when their supply is threatened. I found Kohut's theories on narcissism fascinating (I got my only high distinction in psychology for a third-year essay on Kohut) and especially helpful in trying to understand my father.

I can still hear the kids laughing, so I peer through a gap at the edge of the black plastic. The sky is blue and there's not a breath of wind. I can see Crow and the kids, about thirty metres away, near the chook shed: Crow is holding a big white meringue of a chook, clutching her to his body, leaning over, holding her with her beak just above the ground, at the end of a white rope that runs along the grass. 'Okay, get back, get back,' he calls. He holds her there for a minute, then places her carefully back on the ground while his three children laugh and point. Crow commands, 'When I count to three I want you to bark like a dog ... one ... two ... three ...' The kids are now shrieking with laughter. The chicken looks around then quickly dashes away.

'I'm having a go, Dad,' says Caleb, running after a red chook.

'Meow like a cat, Caleb, meow like a cat,' yells Tom, jogging on the spot.

'What on earth are you guys doing?' I call out to them.

Maeve is the only one to turn. 'We're hypnotising chickens!' She yells back.

I laugh. 'Of course you are.'

Crow's a great dad. Those kids are going to be fine.

After Caleb was born, Alice was ensconced in her little family bubble; meanwhile, I had finished my masters in media studies and was now managing the restaurant where I worked in the city, three days and five nights a week. For a time I was going out with a nerdy sound engineer called Daniel, who wore socks with Birkenstocks and large white calamari earrings. I didn't like going to stay at Alice and Crow's on my nights off, only to be woken early by a crying baby when I had a shift to work that evening. It was a long way to drive and I rarely felt I had Alice's attention when I got there. She and Crow would be at each other the entire time, bickering about everything from the amount of time Crow spent surfing to Alice's apparently incompetent installation of the baby capsule, and Caleb seemed to spend most of his waking hours crying. Sometimes their fights would get so bad that Crow would storm out, not returning until after I'd left. Other times I'd be trying to tell her of a new job I was thinking of going for, or about a relationship drama, and she'd be barely listening to me as she stomped around in circles, rocking Caleb and humming Brahms's Lullaby, or darting from room to room as she washed and hung out nappies. The best time to talk with her was when she was breastfeeding. Pinned to the sofa for half an hour, she seemed relaxed, her face open and receiving, and Caleb would, at last, be quiet. But chatting to her about the goings on in Melbourne as she sat serenely with her baby made me feel like my life was somehow trivial. Instead of chatting with my best friend, I felt like I was confessing to somebody's mother – which of course was exactly what I was doing. As I briefed her on our circle of friends in Melbourne, she'd respond with a benevolent smile, absently stroking Caleb's head. Conversations were stilted as we searched for topics to which we could both relate, without having to resort to gossip.

I never would have told her this, but I was always quite indifferent to babies, and failed to understand the veneration that others displayed as they crouched down beside them and cooed. I also couldn't work out why looking after something that couldn't move around and seemed to sleep most of the time could be so tiring. Her contentedness annoyed me, and I'll admit it now: I felt she'd taken the easy path, sitting there each day drinking cups of tea, knitting bunny rugs and singing nursery rhymes. I once asked Alice what she was going to do with herself down here now, expecting to hear of ambitious work, study or activist plans, but she just shot me a stunned glance and said 'Mother', as if no more potent word had ever been spoken. I never broached the subject with her again.

I don't think I ever really tried, until now, to imagine what Alice's life might have really been like: it was the life she'd chosen, away from her friends, and that was all that seemed relevant at the time. It's hard for me to think about it now because, to be honest, I remember feeling a little sorry for Crow at the time. When that photo of him appeared in *Who* magazine, walking down the main street of Apollo Bay with Caleb on his hip – he was wearing black jeans, cowboy boots and a velvet blazer, and the caption ran, 'Does fatherhood get any sexier than this?' – he said he was going to sue the magazine for publishing a photo of his son. We all knew how much Crow loved being in the media, but I think seeing that photo there on page fifteen – wedged in underneath two *Home and Away* stars frolicking on the beach – really threw him. I'm sure it must have made him question, as we all did, whether he'd made the right decision. He could have quite easily kept the band going. He seemed to spend much of his time in Melbourne, anyway: at the Punters, the Espy or the Corner, being his old larrikin self, shouting rounds of shooters at the bar. Whereas I never saw Alice unless I drove down to see her, hushed my voice and sat patiently on the sofa, or made pots of tea and washed the dishes while she took an hour and a half to get Caleb to sleep in her room.

I started seeing Alice less and less. She became a discontented voice on the end of a phone line, Crow's keeper, ringing up to find out where he was, or to let me know what he'd just put her through. I couldn't tell her I didn't half blame him. Alice's world had shrunk; Caleb, swaddled up in his basket or strapped, African-style, around her body, was the sun at the centre of her orbit. We – the rest of the universe – were now just deep space, hardly relevant to her anymore. Crow, however, was still Crow – run-around-the-pool-table-with-his-pants-down Crow. He hadn't changed, and he was still loyal to his Melbourne crew. So we were still loyal to him.

Over the following months, Alice gave herself a few projects to work on at home. With Crow's help she built a giant hen house and was slowly building up a flock of laying hens; she'd put in several above-ground vegetable gardens, placed inside a wired enclosure to protect them from kangaroos and birds; and she'd also planted more fruit trees and bought herself a Vacola preserving set at auction. She mainly stayed holed up at home, away from her friends, so when Caleb was about ten months old I convinced her to come along to a birthday that Crow's friend Sam was having at his folk's property outside Daylesford. Crow would be going, and if it wasn't for me insisting on it, Alice would have stayed behind.

When I arrived at Sam's with a carload of others from Melbourne, Alice was set up with her esky of Tupperwares, plastic bowls, bottles and spoons, and was feeding Caleb in the kitchen. Crow had pitched their tent already and was sitting with Sam and half a dozen other early guests, drinking beers on a lounge settee that had been carried outside around a large fire, dug into a grassy clearing not far from the house.

'Well, we made it!' Alice said as I greeted her, as if she'd just hiked to the top of a mountain. I poured her a weak gin and tonic, helped her clean up, then we went outside and sat on a log near her tent where she breastfed and we chatted, watching the new arrivals pitching tents, unpacking eskies and settling in for the evening.

Caleb sat up and looked around on the embroidered blue rug that Alice had laid on the grass in front of us, and while she stroked his fluffy head, she told me how last week she'd left him to cry in his cot for three hours. She'd just got so sick of his crying and his refusal to sleep, she said. So she'd sat on the front deck and read the weekend paper from front to back, something she hadn't done since before his birth. 'I never expected him to cry for so long. I kept thinking he must be just about to fall asleep,' she said. It was an experiment to see how long he'd cry for, but it was also an experiment, she said, to see how cruel she could be. 'It sounds strange, and I don't know if you'll get what I mean, but having a baby – I've got so used to being so bloody nice all the time. I just wanted to feel that other side of myself, the selfish side. You know, sometimes I can be really cold in the way I think. This other side of me – kind of ruthless – takes over, and it makes sense to me to do things that … I don't know, probably aren't normal. Like leave your baby crying for hours. But it was easy. It was as if it wasn't even my baby.' She was almost laughing as she told me this; I wasn't sure if it was pride or embarrassment. But she was right: I didn't really understand, though I was a little impressed – I had always been impressed with how her mind worked – and I presume that was why she was telling me. She was confessing, wanting some kind of pardon or absolution, and she knew she wouldn't get it from Crow or her mums' group. 'Jesus, they'd freak if I told them. They'd think I was some kind of monster,' she said.

I looked down at Caleb as he sat contentedly chewing on his thumb. 'He seems fine to me. Don't think you've done too much damage,' I said, making her smile.

About thirty metres away, the crowd steadily grew around the fire. At one point Crow yelled out, 'Alice, Alice, watch this!' But she had Caleb laid down on the change mat and was scraping away wads of poo with baby wipes. As putrid as it was, she was cooing down at him, and he seemed equally mesmerised as he gazed back. 'Hey, little fella,' she said, and he gurgled a reply. I don't know if she didn't hear Crow, but she didn't turn to look. I was watching him, though, and could see him with his jeans rolled up, stepping briskly across the ground, while others stood about him, cheering.

He had stopped and was calling out to her again, then turned to the others. 'I walk across burning coals for that woman, and she's not even looking!' Everyone laughed, and I remember wishing I was sitting around the fire with them all.

But ten minutes later, Alice *was* watching. She had Caleb all cleaned up and wearing a velvet leopard-print grosuit, and she was breastfeeding again as the two of us sat facing the fire. Crow filled an empty beer bottle with petrol, nailed a hole in the lid, hammered the lid back on then placed it back in the coals. 'Okay, stand back everyone. Just wait ...' He shepherded everyone away from the fire.

A plume of blue flames spurted up from the bottle, and the fireside mob applauded. As the fountain of flames died down he reached for another stubby and started filling it from the jerry can that had been parked next to the arm of his sofa, then placed the second bottle in the fire.

Alice shook her head. 'God he can be a dickhead.'

Flames shot up in the air, eliciting hoots and cheers from Crow's mates. A log in the fire collapsed and the bottle tipped over, spewing fire out towards Sam and a few others. They jumped and leaped away from the flames, laughing, clutching their beers to their chests, then started stomping on the ground where the fire had ignited the grass.

Alice clipped up her bra and called out to Crow. Crow looked over, as did a dozen or so of his audience. She stood up from the log, frowning, with Caleb on her hip. They were like a bunch of grinning school kids, heckling ('You're in trouble now, Crowsy'), as Crow walked towards her. The two of them stepped away, out of earshot, and talked. Afterwards, Crow shrugged, took Caleb and the baby backpack from Alice, then walked back to the fire. 'Caleb wants a bit of fireside action, don't you, mate?' he announced to his audience as he returned.

With Alice free of her mothering duties for a while, we went inside and played some old records, danced and drank. Then I helped Nadia and some others carry food to the outside tables, while Alice went off to check on Caleb. Sam said that Crow was down near the octagon hut, so she headed down the grassy slope to find him. I could see the area next to the wooden hut, lit up by the headlights of a parked car. The Funkadelic track being played on the house stereo ended, and I could hear faint guitar music coming from the car stereo at the hut, beneath the intermittent revs of a motorbike. There were six of them down there, standing around, leaning against the car. It looked like they were smoking a joint, and in front of them was Crow, riding the motorbike, doing donuts, with Caleb on his back in his baby backpack. Alice must have already seen them, as by the time I noticed her she was halfway down the hill, screaming out to Crow. I turned and walked back inside, not wanting to witness the scene.

I didn't see Alice again that night; I assumed she'd put Caleb to sleep in the tent and fallen asleep herself. Sam pulled some amps out near the fire, running them off extension leads from the house, and was blasting everyone with Radiohead until Nadia jumped back on the turntables to play Motown and other dance tracks that got a few of us girls up dancing. Sam brought out a bottle of his homemade absinthe, and Kate produced a bag of magic mushrooms that she and Pete had picked from the pine forests near Macedon on their way there. I had to work the following evening so just stuck to vodka but, after dancing for much of the night, I ended up sitting around the fire until near dawn.

At one point, Pete's staffy-cross, Jaffa, walked over to the edge of the couch, squatted and laid a steaming, stinking turd.

'Hey, why are women like dog shit?' Sam called out as Pete got up and started scraping the dog turd onto a paper plate with a stick.

'They get easier to pick up the older they get,' Sam said.

'Well, there's hope ahead for you then,' I said. 'Wait a couple of decades and you might get lucky.'

Sam sat there grinning drunkenly among the laughter of his friends.

Crow kept disappearing from the group and returning dragging massive limbs of ironbark that he'd lay across the fire, releasing a hiss of steam among the smoke, and golden flecks that shot up towards the starry cloudless sky. The fire burned so fiercely that we had to keep shifting our camp chairs and couches backwards until our huddled group had become a large ring encircling the fiery spectacle metres away at the centre. I knew I should go to bed, but I felt such a drowsy contentment, sitting among my friends, listening to their fireside banter, that it was only the faint tinge of pale blue in the sky over the pine forest to the east, and the first perky tweets from the honeyeaters, that sent me off to my tent.

When the heat of the day forced me from my sleeping bag in the late morning, Crow and Alice's tent and car were already gone.

I spoke with Alice the following week and she sounded amused by the memory of the party. I wondered if her breezy attitude was partly to compensate for the dark admission she'd made to me that night. In any case, I took it at face value.

'I don't know why I didn't realise people would be running around screaming all night on mushrooms,' she said, laughing.

I couldn't recall us being particularly noisy, but perhaps we had been. It was a party though, after all.

When I was young I remember spending the occasional Saturday following my father to the racetrack under the pretext of a family outing. However, we'd barely see my dad on these days: back then, only men were allowed to be full members at Randwick Racecourse, so he'd spend his day betting, inside the member's lounge in comfort, while Mum, Miriam and I remained in the women's and children's zone, outside. We'd meet with him briefly in the late morning at a prearranged spot on the yellow line which delineated the two zones, so he could lean across (I specifically remember him doing this, as if unwilling to set foot in our world) and give my mother lunch money: a handful of notes or coins from his pocket, this gambling play-money of his. It was only in the early eighties that women were finally elevated off the children's ticket and allowed full membership at the track, and the yellow line was abolished. But I suspect that for a long time many women still felt like guests in the member's area. I was old enough to avoid these outings by then but I can imagine my parents in there together: my father's rotund body and wide stance, like the buttress roots of a tree, gesticulating three feet in each direction, his voice booming around the room, each red wine adding more volume and theatre to his countenance; and my mother, whose body had seemed to shrink over the years in direct proportion to my father's ballooning torso, arms clutched to her side, anxious to take up as little space as possible.

Back in Women's Studies, I remember a lot of talk about how social life is divided up into public and private realms, and how this is replicated in geographic space: public space, dominated by ideas of production, emancipation, politics and power, is considered male; private space, concerned with issues around domesticity and reproduction, is female. We discussed how when a lone woman in a public place is attacked by a man, she's often questioned about her reasoning for being there; and men are just as often depicted as foreigners to domestic life, dropping in only to lend a hand and give their spouses a break. Back then the numerous yellow lines of public space and life were slowly being erased; cheers were going out as women filed in to each new zone, proclaiming they had as much right to be there as anyone, but then seating themselves along the edges, hands in laps, taking up as little room as they could.

I think back to that night in Daylesford, and try to reimagine that sense of comfort and community I had felt while jokes – about women, homosexuals, Jews – flew across the firepit, and Alice tried to settle her baby alone in her tent. In my defence, I can only suggest that my apparent complicity, my blindness to all that was happening, was the result of a kind of spiritual drunkenness: the enthralling fog of acceptance. Because isn't acceptance among one's people – the state of being approved of, applauded, of being deemed *acceptable* – the highest currency there is? The most intoxicating – but obscuring – feeling a human can ever know?

10

It wasn't long after the Daylesford party: Caleb was almost one; Alice was busy canning, curing and preserving everything in sight and was already talking about having more kids; Crow had started recording a solo album; Nadia – who'd moved in with me after Alice left – was starring in and directing plays and short films; and even Freya seemed to be getting numerous grants to create her bizarre sound installations. And me? Since Crow and Alice had moved down the coast, I'd felt a little lost. I was twenty-five and already feeling nostalgic, craving that life together that we'd all shared before Alice became pregnant. I fumbled through a string of month-long romances with men I had little interest in, and spent my free time going to parties, waking up with hangovers, then walking around St Kilda taking super 8 footage, pondering the idea of doing yet another course, this time in photography or film. Then on a whim, realising that a year and a half had passed since Alice and I had discussed our plans to travel overseas – she'd gone and had a baby, and I'd done virtually nothing – I booked myself a one-way ticket to London, leaving in three weeks' time.

Then the week before leaving for the UK I bumped into Christian, a close friend of Crow's from the private school he briefly attended, who'd been in California for the last three years doing his PhD on environmental economics. Although he'd only arrived back in town a few weeks earlier, he'd decided to head to the Otways rainforest and camp for the night in an old-growth coupe earmarked for clearfell logging, having already entrenched himself in the local activist scene. I'd finished up at work and had nothing planned over my final week in town, so I offered to join him and get some footage of the forest, the loggers and the demonstrators – something he could use for media and events.

I didn't know Christian well but had seen him often over the years: at uni, before he left for the States, and then since, during his university holidays when he'd fly back to Melbourne and step straight into Crow's partying entourage as if he'd never spent a day away. The first time I saw him, though, was years earlier, at the twenty-first birthday party of a guy he and Crow had known at school. It was at an ivy-covered white neo-Georgian house; outside, the lawn was freshly mown and edged with withering blue hydrangea and camellia, and fruit trees strung with fairy lights. On the slate patio, among concrete pots of azaleas, there was a large outdoor table and bench seat setting, made from old grey sleepers. I noticed Christian immediately: he was perched on the end of the table with another guy; several others – mostly girls – stood on the patio, encircling them. Christian sat tall with his legs dangling over, a beer in his hand, wearing a broad, tipsy grin as he spoke; his female audience, it seemed, were enthralled. I was a little beguiled, also, by his beauty, but told myself we were definitely not each other's type. He appeared too assured, too *rich*, too impervious to others. I assumed someone like that would find me complicated, needy. Given all that's happened in the past few years, I wish in many ways I'd heeded that first impression.

The girls merged together in my mind, except for one: her hair and skin appeared to be the same honey-brown colour, buffed with the same sheen – a complexion not dissimilar to his. Around her neck she wore a locket of rose gold, which hung just beneath her protruding collarbone. If she hadn't been so immaculately groomed, she might have seemed quite plain, but her skin was so flawless, her hair so thick, clean and straight, her fingernails so pink, that she gave the impression of great beauty. Her smile was mild and knowing, and her gaze – at Christian – rarely wavered. Only occasionally she looked about the garden, her chin high, before returning to him with a modicum of impatience.

I didn't meet Christian that night and didn't see him again for another six months. But he'd made an impression on me, although I wasn't quite able to work out why. He was not someone I'd normally be interested in – all cheekbone and jawline. Yet the following week, whenever I thought about the party I'd see his face, and furthermore see her face too. I wondered if he'd gone home with her, whether she really was his type.

The next time I saw him, though, my image of him shifted. It was at uni, and he was up the front, speaking, at an Environment Society meeting, organising a day for volunteers to prepare for an upcoming march.

When someone called out that the day he'd nominated was Father's Day, Christian responded with the mildest of smiles, then said, 'Well, that will test my theory that all environmentalists have father issues, won't it?'

Although I hadn't seen Christian since the party, I'd already formulated a character and life for him – this captain of a grammar school first eleven, probably already betrothed to a leggy heiress. But this unexpected humour – the hint at introspection and failings – changed all that. He'd been reduced to my level and, consequently, had risen immeasurably in my esteem.

We camped a short walk off the track we'd ridden in on, in a small clearing that had been used by demonstrators, and loggers before them. When we'd packed the panniers on his motorbike, he'd questioned me about all the plastic containers I was bringing along, but was thrilled, once we'd set up at camp, when I brought out Moroccan marinated chicken, a tub of yogurt, and a box of couscous for us to cook over the fire. He'd only brought two-minute noodles, dark chocolate and red wine. We pitched a tent, but it was a clear night so we lay our sleeping mats and sleeping bags outside next to the fire, then sat on logs, drank and chatted. He told me about the post-doctorate project that he'd applied for, how he would team up with a group of ecologists from Southern Cross University who were studying coral health and matching it with satellite photographs, enabling them to create computer models to track marine health. It would be used worldwide to help countries monitor and calculate the economic costs of coral reef bleaching. He explained the project in great detail, and with such passion, that I felt like I was listening to the most important advance in environmental science in decades. I wondered what it must be like to be so absorbed by such a clear vision. How much I envied that passion and dedication, while I fluffed about, going to parties, trying to exude that focus and independence that came so effortlessly to him.

We went for a walk after dinner and sat on a lichen-carpeted log next to a running stream, surrounded by pulsing glowworms. In the dark bush on either side of us, two powerful owls duetted back and forth. Then when the moon came up, a silvery light was cast over the forest, turning the mountain ash into glowing monoliths, whose silhouetted heads towered above us, nearer to the stars, it seemed, than the earth. The downy moss and the delicate filigree of the unfurling tree fern fronds seemed to sparkle under this ethereal light. The forest had that magical quality that it had seemed to possess when I was a small child, when the real world would slip away, and another, more fantastical world full of fairies and spirits and unknown possibilities, opened up. We returned to the fire, and already I felt that I was caught in a spell. We sat on the log, we kissed, then we spread out our sleeping bags and pillows and spent the night in each other's arms. For years I'd been an acquaintance, simply 'Lars'. Now, suddenly, he was gazing into my eyes and calling me 'babe'. When I lay back staring at the sky, almost powdered white with stars, I was filled with a contentment that I felt I'd never known. I started to wonder if getting on a plane the following week would even be possible when another force had taken hold of my life. I couldn't help but smile, my glee invisible in the darkness, as I wondered if he might be having the same thoughts.

Then Christian, with his arm under my neck and his hand stroking my forearm, spoke in that low, calm voice of his, almost a whisper: 'I think it's amazing what you're doing. Getting on a plane with no idea where you're going. I don't know many people brave enough to do that.' I waited a moment for him to continue, to change tack. When nothing came, I said thanks, suddenly questioning whether any of this would have happened between us if I wasn't going away.

I lay awake staring at the stars long after he had fallen asleep, thinking about his words – how admiring he'd been of my trip – and realised that, as much as I wanted to stay with him in Melbourne, I had no other option but to leave.

It took four hours to ride back to Melbourne on his motorbike. I had my arms around his waist, my head on his jacket against the caramel-blond hair that curled out from under his helmet. As the wind whipped past us and the sunlight flickered down through the overhanging eucalypts, I started to suspect this moment, riding along on this quiet bush road, was precious, and might haunt me throughout my travels. I tried to convince myself, though, that other adventures and romances overseas would supersede it. And kept trying to convince myself, for the entire five years I spent away.

It's strange: I hadn't thought too much about my time overseas until recently, but now I'm beginning to wonder if that's when it really began – the deepening of the schism between Alice and me; and I don't mean by the distance my travel created between us.

We'd always debated issues, but that was back when nothing was at stake. We were no longer sitting next to each other in the study hall, eating our salad rolls, sipping our coffees and writing our essays – Alice on Emily Davison; me on Sigmund Freud. We didn't realise (well, *I* didn't) that those differences – the subjects we enrolled in, those essays that we wrote while picking the alfalfa from one another's teeth – might be indicative of something meaningful one day. I'd adored Alice and treasured our sameness, and believed this sameness would remain. I mistook ideas for things that you talked about, not lived.

We had our first real fight over a phone call I made from Biarritz, three weeks after I'd left. I'd just met a Californian girl called Sharni in the Biarritz youth hostel; she was holidaying after finishing her degree majoring in community studies in Berkeley and worked on the weekends as a lap dancer and escort in San Francisco. She was thrilled to meet someone from Mel*born* and gushed about the semester she'd spent there while writing her thesis on the sex industry. She told me all about the St Kilda sharehouse she'd lived in, the North Melbourne brothel she'd worked in, and Alex, the gigolo she'd dated, with whom she'd starred in several porn flicks, filmed in Canberra. I was enthralled by the ease with which she chatted about her profession, which she maintained, somewhat adamantly, was just temporary. It afforded her a fabulous lifestyle, gorgeous clothes and jewellery, and she got to dance all night and wiggle her cute little toosh around on men's laps while they ogled and pampered her.

'You're a hot chick, Lara,' she told me. 'You can talk about all sorts of intelligent shit and you've got an Aussie accent, which makes you real exotic.' She beamed from behind her dark glasses, flashing her blindingly white teeth. 'Six months as an escort and you could make a packet. *Seriously.*'

I had left Australia in order to reinvent myself, to empower myself, and to show myself and others that I would do something interesting and unexpected with my life, so the more time I spent sipping coffees in beachside cafes with Sharni, the more I considered her suggestion to return with her to work in San Francisco.

When I told her I wasn't sure if I could do it, she replied, 'Do what? Sit at fancy restaurants and look pretty? Chat with rich guys who adore you and buy you beautiful things? Have the occasional bad sex? I mean big deal. What woman doesn't spend half her life putting up with bad sex? At least you get paid.

'Besides,' she told me, leaning in with a hand on my arm, 'I always make sure I get off. The whole experience is actually very empowering.

I'm the one in control; he's just the client. I mean I sometimes see my job as being like a healer. Prostitution is the oldest profession in the world, you know.'

Sharni seemed so incredibly normal in every other regard: she was considering studying acting or psychology, then hoped to one day marry a wealthy guy, have kids and raise them in the Bay Area. The more I watched her splash around her money – buying accessories, bikinis, overpriced cocktails in ritzy bars ('I only ever pay for the first drink – if no one's around to buy me another, I leave'), the more I considered the logic in everything she said.

I called Alice in the middle of the night from a broken phone booth (I had to wait in line behind two other Australians and one Japanese tourist), that allowed you to call anywhere in the world as long as you could reload the phone with coins as quickly as it spat them out the bottom.

'So I'm thinking of becoming an escort,' I said offhand, then waited, looking around at the quiet cobblestone street – in the moonlight, the *boulangerie*, the shoe shop and the empty corner cafe with its collapsed maroon awning were infused in a ghostly blue-grey. Then, as several coins tumbled out, I hurriedly slotted them in the top. 'Yeah, there's a girl I've met from San Francisco who's going to take me back there and show me the ropes. Says it's great money, the guys are usually really nice, they mainly just want someone to talk to. The sex is a tiny part of it and you can just switch off if you're not into it. So yeah ...'

There was another pause, but I could hear Caleb's soft babble not far from the phone. 'Are you serious?'

'Sure, why not?' I was aware my voice sounded less than convincing. I'd been prepared for her disapproval but felt armoured for any debate that might ensue.

'You think you're going to enjoy this new career? More than managing a bar or working in TV or radio? You know, stuff you're actually qualified to do?'

'I can leave if I don't like it.'

There was a pause before she spoke in a more considered tone. 'Lara. Why do you want to do this?'

I realised I had no ready answer to this question. I'd prepared answers for why I *could* do this – how I could justify it within my feminist paradigm; how it might add to my resume of being an interesting, provocative, progressive woman. But *want* – whether I actually *wanted* to do it was something I'd somehow overlooked. 'Have you got a problem with women making decisions about how they use their bodies? I always thought you took a hard line on people policing women's behaviour.' A response I'd rehearsed.

'Of course.' She paused for a moment. 'I don't judge sex workers, of course not. But I judge the industry. It's an industry that exploits women.'

'Not if a woman chooses to do it.'

'Jesus, Lara.' She laughed, mockingly. 'Most women who work in the sex industry don't actually have much of a choice. Many of them have had a very different life from you; they don't have the opportunities you've had.' Again she paused. 'They don't have a family to bail them out if they're in trouble.'

I was thrown by her mentioning my family. I'd only been able to even contemplate doing this work after flying to the other side of the world.

'Still—' The coins jangled noisily out of the phone box. I scraped them up, then, for a moment, considered not reinserting them. 'I can still do it!'

'Lara! The entire industry is fucked. And you waltzing in with some Hollywood idea of what you'll be doing, with this come-or-go, see how I like it attitude. I mean ...' she let out a groan. 'Look, I'm sorry. You're right, it's not my position to tell you what to do. Do whatever you want to do. Just be careful, okay?'

I was riled as I left the phone booth and walked the quiet street back to the youth hostel. I should have let the phone hang up on her. How dare she take such a high-and-mighty position? She – a *mother*, and supported financially, no less, by a man! It was unimaginative, I thought, for her not to see that both a mother with a husband and an escort with a client were engaged in contracts, with terms that both parties could negotiate. I played out this hypothetical argument the entire walk home, furious with her, furious with me, furious with us. The wife and the whore. Was this really the best we could do?

I can't remember the exact reason I gave both Sharni and myself, but I never did follow her back to San Francisco, which clearly annoyed her. ('Well, you enjoy your youth hostels and backpacker boyfriends,' she said, smiling.) But for a time, I enjoyed thinking that I almost did join her: that I had it in me to challenge my moral codes, my upbringing, *even Alice*, in such a radical way – to be released from such conservative ideas about what a woman's life could and should be.

After a month of travelling around France and Spain, I settled in London and found work in a pub. Then, soon after, I met a couple of young fast-talking guys in skivvies, vests and flat caps, who were setting up a small production house, and who let me work for them as a volunteer. They had no money, at this early stage in the business, to pay me a wage, but I was happy to gain experience. It started with making real estate promos and in-house training videos, but soon moved on to other, lengthier pieces, which required more research and creative input, such as a series of secondary-school art history videos, focusing on the lives of famous European artists. I worked for George and Elias for two years, and when I left, for an extended holiday through Egypt and Morocco, they gave me an exquisite smooth leather The Bridge satchel worth two-hundred quid (they let the price slip over drinks at the bar), which I absolutely adored – until I found out a week later from a mutual friend that the two other lackeys they'd had working as runners and office boys for the past six months, lads they'd gone to school with who had no experience or training in media, had been getting paid from day one.

Over the following few years, I found sporadic work on film shoots. I lived in mice-infested sharehouses with no heating, and survived on beer and baguettes. I had a few unremarkable relationships with mostly kind but unremarkable men. Whatever money I did make I spent on travel, telling myself repeatedly how lucky I was. No one was making me do any of this; I called all the shots. The reality was, however, that I was miserable. I missed Alice and I missed Christian.

I never told Alice any of this and instead wrote her elaborate tales about my adventures. It was important for me to be proud of my choices; I was intent that my life should appear better – more interesting, more fulfilling – than hers. I was also aware of the weight of letters arriving from abroad – that so much is read into every word, and that any minor sorrow would be received quite gravely. I knew which story to sell.

Alice's letters were far shorter than mine (she used to joke about my novel-length correspondence, with handwriting so small that she suggested I save myself the paper and write on the back of a stamp), but I knew she was busy, especially after Maeve was born. However, her words were as dense as Haiku as she told me about harvesting and preserving fruit, when she had to drench her parasite-infested chickens, and when she'd just eaten a sandwich using home-baked sourdough bread and her first ever cured prosciutto. Then she'd tell me that she and Crow had got married on Marengo beach, just in front of their kids and neighbours, and how much she wished I could have been there. In another letter she asked me to be Maeve's godmother. Reading these words, my Mediterranean sunset (I was spending three weeks at a friend's aunt's home in Chania at the time) withered into a kitsch watercolour, and I desperately wanted to return home.

Christian didn't write me many letters – probably only one or two a year. But each time one arrived, I was taken aback. Just the touch of the envelope in my hand would send my heart into a gallop. I'm not sure what I was expecting to read as I ripped each one open – a proclamation of his eternal love? A demand I return? I knew he'd never write these things. The letters were usually not much longer than one page, with very little news. Usually, they were just a snapshot of whatever had been on his mind: a rumination about green tea or primate communities, or a description of a surf he'd had on the weekend with Crow, painted for me like Hokusai's 'Great Wave'. But he'd always finish with words like, 'I miss you, Lars. God, I missed you before you'd left,' or 'I can remember every line in your hand.' Words that could mean everything or nothing. And I chose everything.

I finally landed a well-paid job, as an assistant producer in an ad agency in London, and soon after was sent to their Hong Kong office. But it was almost too late by then; I seemed to have forgotten why I wanted this job in the first place. And that's where I was when I received Christian's final letter, scribbled, he claimed, at seven o'clock in the morning, after an all-nighter with Crow that finished up with a joint on the end of Port Melbourne pier, staring out to sea, contemplating the path of currents and deep ocean trenches between him and me. I read his letter four times as I lay on a bunk, below deck (at the time I was working on a series of Kent cigarette ads, filming just off Kowloon), listening to the gentle slap of the waves against the hull. I thought about Christian and Crow, sitting on that old weather-worn pier under a butter-coloured dawn sky, staring out towards all the container ships on the horizon, in a sea that looked like rumpled mauve satin. The Melbourne early morning traffic would be waking up behind them, and plastic bottles and bags would be skiffing about the pylons beneath them, on this same great watery lung I lolled about on now, inhaling and exhaling around the globe. After five years of travel – working in London bars and production houses; weekends in Amsterdam; backpacking around France, Spain, Morocco and Egypt; now finally ending up in Hong Kong – I could finally admit what I'd denied to myself for years: I was lonely. My peripatetic existence had been symbolic, for me, of living in a society where women like myself, for the first time in history, could make their own choices and live as they pleased. But other times I just felt like another middle-class kid, recolonising the world, playing Monopoly with other people's money. *Why do you want to do this?* Alice had asked me that time over the phone in Biarritz. Her words still stung, because they reminded me of how little I understood – and hence how little I could strive for – what I actually wanted.

I must have read Christian's letter more than a dozen times that night and couldn't think of anything else for days. By the end of the week, I'd worked out what it was I wanted: I wanted to return home.

11

My increased optimism – about Crow, the kids, my stay – has put me in a good mood and piqued my hunger, so I slip on a dress and head out into the kitchen, where it looks, from the mess on the bench, like Crow made bacon and eggs. I'm not sure I can be bothered, so I opt for coffee and toast, carrying them out into the dazzling sunlight on the back deck.

I spend most of the morning reading on the daybed as Crow – in old jeans, boots and a Stetson hat with a red-and-white feather in it – digs a trench for the water tank. Maeve is nearby, connecting pieces of black pipe together with the joiners that Tom hands her. She hollers down the pipe, and Tom puts it to his ear and laughs. The air is still, and the sun already has a bite: it's going to be a scorcher. There are the quiet caws and mutterings of the chickens poking about in the shade of a nearby cypress. The scene is ridiculously bucolic: Crow and his kids on the grass in dappled morning sunlight, against a backdrop of mountain ash and manna gums.

It was the right thing to do, coming down. I'll cook a frittata for lunch, and hopefully, if Crow takes a break in the afternoon, we'll go for a walk and have a chat. I can tell he's more relaxed today. It dawns on me that it may have been confronting for him, me arriving last night; we've seen little of each other since the funeral. I've been so worried that Crow might blame me for the state Alice was in before the fire, but it seems I've been working myself up for no reason. I keep replaying that scene, of her last visit to me in Melbourne before she died. But I have to trust Crow – trust Lisa – when they tell me I couldn't have changed a thing.

'I gotta say, Lara,' he looks up while digging. 'You're looking great. I mean you've always been a very beautiful woman, but I seriously don't reckon you've ever looked any better. Seriously.'

I take a bite of toast, chewing and suppressing a smile. 'That's very kind of you – shameless lying, but very kind. So I'll let it go.'

'I never lie.' He's smiling now too. 'I embellish, but I never lie. You're looking great.'

I pop the last piece of toast in my mouth and follow it with a sip of coffee, then lift my feet up onto the daybed and into the patch of sun at the end, propping a few cushions behind my head and shoulders. I stroke the smooth flesh of my torso and the hard bump I'm told is a knee, trying for a response. Nothing immediately, but then a slow shifting within. I hope she can feel she's safe in my hands.

'So I've got an idea for a doco,' I call out to Crow. 'On oxytocin.'

'Yeah, what's that?' He keeps digging.

'It's the *lurve* drug. The hormone in our bodies that makes us crave belonging and closeness. It gets released into our bloodstream in a steady drip, and it spikes when we're flirting, hugging, having sex, giving birth, hanging with friends—'

'Oh yeah, yeah, Alice talked about that. Used to make her breastmilk squirt across the room when the baby cried, yeah?'

'Yes, that's the one. So the ultimate purpose for oxytocin is to keep us all entrenched in the tribe, looking after one another, safe from predators.'

'Right.'

'The oxytocin system is built during a baby's first year of life, based on the love and comfort it gets from its parents. It's basically the biochemical explanation of attachment theory.'

'Yeah Alice was into that, I think.'

'Right into it. All those African wraps she used to wear? Attachment theory. Anyway, so parent and child have this need to be close to each other – it's the oxytocin doing that, keeping them close. When the child wanders too far away from their parent and gets scared, their fight or flight response gets triggered, cortisol floods their system, and they cry and shoot back for a hug – for their oxytocin fix.'

Crow keeps digging, head down. I think I'm boring him. But, Christ, how many songs of his have I sat through?

'So obviously if they don't get that hug, that's a problem. Depressed mothers and fathers have lower oxytocin levels than non-depressed ones and, because of the interactions they have with their children, those kids end up with lower oxytocin levels too. Later on, they have a significantly higher chance of developing psychological disorders.'

'Uh-huh.'

'So now they're doing these trials – which I'd love to get footage of – where they're treating depressed and anxious people with oxytocin. They're going to pump that feeling of love straight into their veins.'

'That sounds all right. Where do I sign up?'

'Be nice, wouldn't it? It's fascinating stuff, the way our brains are drugging us, *brainwashing* us, to be team players – making us believe we *need* to love and be loved by others. I mean, when you think about it, it's weird, isn't it? We're not living in the wilderness anymore, why do we need these things? I used to think that maybe I didn't need it. All those years I was overseas, I just wanted to be independent, doing my own thing. But we have no choice. We actually have this drug in our body making us feel that if we don't have connection, if we don't belong to a tribe, then we'll die.' Crow squats and tries to dislodge a rock from the ground with his hands. I can tell he's not listening but I'm on a roll: I could talk about this stuff all day. 'You know, loneliness has twice as much influence on predicting an early death as obesity? It affects people on a cellular level; you can detect loneliness in your blood.'

Crow stands, squinting towards me. Then, leaning against his shovel, he says, 'So I don't hear much from Christian these days.'

I try to not show I'm taken aback. 'He's pretty busy with work.'

'Bit too important for us these days, ol' Christian, hey?'

I ignore this. Why would he say that to me? Christian's the one he's annoyed with, clearly. 'I'm going to start the frittata.' I get up and hold onto the arm of the seat, then wait for the light-headedness to subside before I turn to go inside.

'Yeah, sure. I'll keep going here. Gotta get this done before the rain.' He looks over towards the west.

It's not like I need reminding to think about Christian, but something about Crow's provocation bothers me nonetheless. Christian texted me only yesterday, telling me I shouldn't come down here, that I needed to stay in Melbourne, close to the hospital. Such a simple, prosaic text. And yet, I was overcome by this feeling of love for him – or perhaps it was nostalgia. The thought that he was up in Sydney airport, about to board a plane for Dubai to deliver a keynote speech at some international conference, and he was worrying about me going into labour far from home. He really is a good man. Perhaps it's the incoming tide of hormones – the oxytocin – but I've been thinking a lot about Christian over the past few days; snapshots appearing, unbidden, in my mind. There's one in particular – I get a lightness in my limbs when I think about it – from the first time I saw him after returning from overseas.

The moment I walked into the velvety lamp-lit room of The Gin Palace, I could feel his presence before I could even see him. Then – seated at the mahogany bar, wearing a navy pinstripe suit and chatting to the barman – there he was. I walked up behind him in my black-and-white satin jumpsuit and Charles Jourdan heels. The barman, polishing glasses, acknowledged me with a nod, then returned to his conversation with Christian. I stood there for a moment, inches behind him, savouring the flux of heat moving between us, looking down at the whorl on his head, his messy caramel curls and the broad reach of his navy jacket. I was struck by that memory of sitting behind him on the motorbike, breathing in the mossy smell of his hair. I squatted down and put my arms around his waist, as I had that day on the bike, and as he turned his head I kissed his cheek. He got to his feet, holding me around the waist at arms' length, while his eyes caught mine then inched their way down my body; he didn't even try to hide what he was doing. 'You look incredible,' he whispered into my ear. People along the bar turned to look. I didn't usually enjoy the spotlight, but with Christian it felt different. We were like two exotic birds performing our courtship ritual in a rainforest. In that noisy bar on a Saturday night, sipping watermelon martinis and munching on lupini, we were both aware, from that first glance, where the evening – where *we* – were headed.

Sometimes, it seemed, I did really know what I wanted. But he was more than a want. Christian, my oxytocin fix. No better words for it.

I started seeing Christian about two weeks after returning from overseas, and then a fortnight later again, Nadia invited me to Friday-night drinks at a pub near her work in Richmond. There she introduced me to Michael, owner of RatTrap – a production house that made documentaries. Michael was tall, hairy, and had the strong, bloated body of an ex-sportsman who drank with the same ardour with which he once kicked a footy. He had shiny, tanned skin and looked like he was about to burst, Hulk-like, out of his expensive, but slightly ill-fitting, olive-green suit. He had large wet lips and watery blue eyes, and as Nadia and I both agreed, while getting drinks at the bar, he was a strange mixture of incredibly gross and sexy; we joked that there was probably a German word for such a thing. When I returned to the table with my glass of red wine, Michael called me over, throwing out my name like an old friend, and patted the seat next to him. He asked me about my travels, commenting on every country I mentioned, every nationality. He then found the opportunity to tell me a sexist and homophobic joke, to which I replied with another, even worse. The following day he emailed me and offered me a job as a production assistant.

So this was the new me: well-travelled, sexy, ambitious, back in town. Enough of the soul-searching and earnestness, I decided. In an unwitting tribute to my dad, I became that oft-joked-about rare breed: the feminist with a sense of humour. Or so I thought. I was being shrewd, a chameleon. Michael was old-school, and I was merely buttering him up, having fun, being one of the boys. I would cringe when I thought about my younger self, arguing the usage of every pronoun: the feminist slogans, the theory, the righteousness. A woman doesn't assert her will on the world through following manifestos, I decided, but by getting among the men and getting things done.

Yes, I was back from overseas and found myself with an enviable job and an enviable relationship (I say this because that's how I'd have expressed it at the time, only realising now what a strange measure of success envy is). Life appeared good. I'd found my people and hit my stride. And for a time it seemed to be true: I could indeed have it all.

Was I really *in love* with Christian back then? I thought I was, but it's hard to know. Enough people said we made a great couple for me to believe it. We loved each other's minds and were proud of each other's achievements, and in the beginning – even after we first moved into that mission-brown Californian bungalow in Brunswick – we rarely fought. Perhaps I could have fallen in love with Christian, if not for the nagging thought that he hadn't really 'chosen' to be with me. No, I had chosen him. He had simply flirted with me, as he flirts with every woman he meets. I just happened to be back in town and calling him up – the closest attractive woman available – when he'd most recently found himself single.

After the first few months of living together, small domestic issues – that I told myself were too trivial to worry about – began to arise. He couldn't stand the way I left kitchen knives in the sink, vinyl records out of their sleeves. He found me chaotic; I found him fastidious and sometimes cold. Then when he came along to my work Christmas party, he disappeared after half an hour; I eventually found him outside, sitting in his car, working on his laptop and listening to Frank Zappa. 'It's your night,' he said, as we sat in the car arguing. 'Go and enjoy yourself, don't worry about me! If you left a party I'd dragged you along to, I couldn't care less!' And that became our signature problem, the essence that every major or minor issue boiled down to: I cared too much, and he couldn't have cared less.

Once I start stripping back the veneer – the giddiness I felt that first year at having such an impressive human being shine his light on me, followed by the *habit* of sharing a life that seemed more-or-less compatible with mine – it's hard to know what was really there. But maybe that's the entirety of what love is? Honeymoon then habit with someone you've part-consciously, part-randomly, chosen to care for.

There's also the undeniable reality that there's just something about Christian; anyone who knows him would say the same. He has this *power* over others – he certainly did over me – but in a way that people, on the whole, don't seem to mind. In fact, it's something they *enjoy*. Though it's an invisible force, it's as plain to me now as those chooks dusting themselves in the dirt under that cypress; as plain as the fact that Maeve – she's got her hands on her swinging hips, doing the 'Nutbush' – looks like her mum.

And it's the same for both men and women. I mean, it's understandable that women fall for Christian. Crow once claimed that the difference between men and women was that men want to love, and women want to be loved. Whether or not there's any truth in this assertion, Christian makes women feel loved. He just adores them, all of them, whichever woman is in the room with him at the time. He enjoys the gaze, the dance, the play – his ability to hypnotise and magnetise. He loves the thought of being in love, and exploring this possibility with anyone sitting in front of him. He loves the idea that his best friends are women, thinking this demonstrates a certain softness in him. But when it comes down to it, those he'd far prefer to hang out with, and talk to, are men. And men, on the whole, seem to be equally as besotted with him as women are.

Crow, for example, always seemed to adore Christian. And this was despite the fact that Christian was everything Crow derided: Christian was wealthy, academic and relatively conservative. Christian told me that they'd bonded in Year Eight over a mutual love of German avant-garde rock band NEU!. Even after Crow had moved schools, they would go on bike rides and camping trips through the High Country and along the Great Ocean Road. But I still wasn't sure what really drew Crow to Christian. Maybe it was Christian's self-effacing humour, his nonjudgmental nature, his sense of justice and passion for the environment. Or perhaps it's simply that even Crow wasn't immune to that undeniable charisma of his.

I remember one day, a few of us were down here at Crow and Alice's place – their old house – drinking beers and watching a news item on the upcoming federal election campaign.

'If Labor wants to differentiate themselves, they need to take a stronger stance on the environment,' I said from the couch. I have no recollection whether I truly thought this or whether I was just trying to appeal to the others.

Christian was sitting back in his chair, drinking a beer. 'The problem with the Labor Party is that they're too apologetic,' he said. 'The Liberals – they behave like they're meant to be in charge, even in opposition. They've got a born-to-rule mentality, and it rubs off on the public. Even Labor seem to believe it. You watch: if Labor wins this election, which they won't, they'll freak out and do something stupid.'

Christian hadn't disagreed with my comment – he was too polite for that. Instead it was as if his words had magically erased mine; my assertion may as well have never been spoken. But I was as bad as everyone else – I accepted Christian's words without question. (I even remember, in later weeks, trumpeting out his opinion about Labor, which was now *my* opinion also, and enjoying the feeling of being able to speak with such authority.) I nodded admiringly, while he, having finished his spiel, leaned back and took another sip of his beer.

'They're as bad as each other,' Nadia added. 'Look at them, kissing babies. Do people really fall for this shit? Can't they just behave like normal humans?'

'Yeah,' Crow agreed from down on the beanbag. 'They need to show us Howard lying on his sofa with his hands down his trackies, smoking a fag, drinking beer and watching porn.'

Christian lurched forward in his chair, a hand covering his mouth and nose, trying to contain his laughter. He turned to me, sheepishly grinning as he wiped the snot from under his nose.

Another time we were in Christian's beaten-up Volvo station wagon, his mum's old car, after a few drinks at the Apollo Bay pub. Within one hundred metres of the pub, Christian was pulled over by the police, then breathalysed. One of the policemen said to Christian: 'You were driving with your seatbelt dragging on the road, you didn't indicate, and you've just blown 0.07. Give me one good reason why I shouldn't throw the book at you?'

Crow was in the passenger seat, looking out his window. I slouched down in the back seat next to Nadia and Alice, hiding my face in the darkness. I could only see the policemen's uniformed torsos through the back window.

'I'm sorry, officer, I can't give you a good reason,' Christian said, then paused. 'But I can tell you a good joke?'

I couldn't believe what I was hearing. Nadia, Alice and I glared at each other in the streaks of grey light thrown across the back seat by the policemen's torches.

The policemen didn't reply straight away. 'Okay, then. Let's hear it,' the other voice said.

'Well,' Christian cleared his throat and gave an endearing giggle, then launched into an irreverent joke about Kerry Packer.

When he'd finished, there was silence, and then the first policeman said, 'Put your seatbelt on and get out of here.' They walked back to their car. I could hear them talking, even laughing, on their way.

'Fuck, man!' Nadia exclaimed as soon as the police were a safe distance away. 'You are unbelievable!'

Christian started the ignition, eyes on his rear-view mirror, waiting for the police to drive away.

Then Alice added, 'Yeah, you pretty private-school boys. You could get away with murder.'

12

Six months into my job at RatTrap, Jane, my production manager, who'd just returned from maternity leave, called up to say she couldn't come to work. Her child had had an asthma attack and she was in an ambulance on her way to hospital. She was calling me, she said, because she needed me to help her out and cover her job. I assured her I would, then knocked on Michael's open door, poked my head inside and walked in. He was staring at his screen, eating a salad roll, flecks of grated carrot and lettuce on his lap. As I told him about Jane's situation, I was aware of the disapproval in my words: 'Her baby's unwell.' I may have even snuck in the word *apparently*. I realise now that even though I knew Jane's son's name – it was Toby – I only ever referred to him as 'the baby', as if he were not even human, but rather some toy she was going home to play with each day.

'Jesus!' Michael thumped his roll down on the desk.

I sighed in agreement, as if acknowledging that Jane had carelessly left us in the gravest of situations. I offered to cover Jane's work as well as my own, and left Michael's office charged by the thought of all I had taken on, of feeling indispensable, loyal, reliable.

I was still in the office at nine o'clock that night. Michael had ordered a delivery of spring rolls and pad thai for the three of us who were still there. As I was typing up the last of my emails to the talent for the next day's shoot, Jane called to thank me. I told her to think nothing of it, and that I would run the shoot tomorrow if Toby was still sick. Then Michael appeared at my desk and put a large glass of shiraz, three-quarters full, in front of me. When I looked up, he said, 'You're good. Keep it up.' Spoken like a threat. He pulled out some Lindt chocolate balls from his jacket pocket and put them next to the red wine. 'I'm not meant to be eating them. But you could do with a few more pounds.' He gave me a look that wasn't quite a smile, then walked away. I continued typing, enjoying working late, sipping Michael's wine and eating his chocolates.

Last week I spent an entire day in my pyjamas at my computer, reading up on oxytocin and social theory (the closer my due date looms, the more urgency I feel about firming up this documentary proposal, as if motherhood is some hot air balloon that's going to carry me far away and I'm frantically trying to anchor myself to familiar ground), and I came across an interesting study on male and female friendships. The findings were that men's socialising tended towards larger, more loose-knit groups – like clubs – where men bonded over shared activities.

Women generally preferred socialising in smaller, tight-knit – even dyadic – relationships with other women; they bonded less through shared activities, it said, and more through shared feelings. I started thinking about how true that was of Alice and me: how our friendship, in the early days, did seem to be founded on points of similarity, and a mutual understanding of each other's lives. I'd always assumed that this was how all friendships worked. I also remember coming home from overseas and feeling uncomfortable about the differences that had sprouted between Alice and me. At the time I blamed these changes on her. I was the one, so I thought, who was the natural extension of those young women we'd once been. I'd been faithful to *us*; she hadn't. And yet now – after she has so recently self-destructed – *now* I feel a sameness with her that's even stronger than the bond we once shared at university. And it has both everything and nothing to do with me having a baby. It's to do with growing up – the scales falling from my eyes. And admitting, I suppose, that I became a person who I never really wanted to be. I imagine, if given a chance, that she'd have probably said the same thing.

This whole documentary idea has been sparked not just by my impending motherhood but by a desire to better understand – *Why did I do the things that I did?* I'd always treated individualism as the pathway to self-actualisation, but now I was beginning to wonder if individualism was actually just the most effective way of shoring up one's place in the pack.

It's common practice for people my age to reflect upon their younger years and cringe, but I wasn't so young when the events that

I'm thinking about – shortly after I returned from overseas – took place: I was thirty. This was only four years ago.

Looking back at my behaviour, I'm embarrassed to admit that the words 'inferiority complex' come to mind: a term coined by Alfred Adler – another contemporary of Freud's. Adler thought that feelings of inferiority originate in childhood, when children become aware of their relative incompetence among powerful adults. For many children, these feelings later motivate them to strive for achievement. Some children, though, never grow out of feeling inferior and, as adults, they try to cope by finding ways to delude themselves and others that they are, in fact, superior.

Adler's 'inferiority complex' ties in to Kohut's ideas on narcissism, Anna Freud's ideas about 'identification with the aggressor' – the bullied child becomes the schoolyard bully – and also, to a degree, with Stockholm syndrome – falling in love with one's captors. They're all related to the way that a person who feels weak may latch on to those in power, or even just the *ideas* of those in power.

But I'm still just trying to figure it all out, making excuses for my behaviour – this person I'd become – when I'd returned to Australia (Christian always did joke that I had an honorary doctorate in *post-factum* rationalisation). Why I fell over myself for people like Michael and turned my back on others. People like Jane. Like Alice. But I'd had a difficult time overseas, and now I'd returned and was being given opportunities – opportunities to find love, to build a good career. Things were, at last, beginning to happen for me. So yes, my allegiances *had* changed. I enjoyed working for Michael; I enjoyed – in a perverse sort of way – his crude, randy behaviour. He made me feel needed, valued, *sexy*, and he rewarded me for these things. I enjoyed being with Christian too – that attention we commanded when we entered a room. These things might not sound like much, but I'd never experienced them before, and they were far more enjoyable than anything I got hanging out with the likes of Jane. Or even Alice, for that matter.

I have two memories of Alice from the time shortly after I returned from overseas. Two memories, that is, that I think about, over and over, as if I might, by watching the show reel for the hundred and forty-third time, be able to glean something new. I treated them as outliers at the time – because our relationship was otherwise strong – and tried to paper over both without giving them too much thought, believing, as I often have, that it is possible to dilute the effect of an event by refusing to acknowledge it; that that will somehow dilute it for others also. Besides, we'd always engaged in a bit of sparring, albeit usually within a discussion on ideas. But looking back on these incidents, I realise now that they were early glimpses of the troubles that were stirring in our friendship, and were also predictive of where the fault lines would appear in our own lives.

The first occurred during a visit to her place, not long after I arrived back. We'd spent the afternoon walking arm in arm around her property: she'd shown off their new smokehouse – a wardrobe-sized construction of cinder blocks and cedar wood – and taken me inside their large corrugated-steel curing shed, where the chipboard walls were lined with bottled tomatoes and stewed fruit; and sausages, salamis, prosciuttos and fists of garlic hung from the ceiling. We then had dinner with the kids; Caleb was now seven and Maeve was three. Crow wasn't home, and Alice and I sat in the kitchen. Since I'd left, Alice had painted the fifties wooden cupboards white, the walls pea-green, and there was now a display of children's artwork – paintings on butcher's paper, Caleb's line drawings, various other artefacts. But the familiarity of the marbled vinyl benchtops and the old wooden table (where we'd drunk so many pots of tea back in the Greeves Street days) made me feel that very little had changed.

I'd been nervous about seeing my old friends, including Alice; I was determined to appear more worldly, dazzling them with my experiences. However, I hadn't anticipated how stark the comparison between Alice and me would be. She appeared much older: her hair looked dull and thinning at the front, she had eczema across her cheeks to her temples, and she carried extra weight around her hips. The edges of her mouth drooped in a permanent frown, giving her a look of half-fought resignation. She even appeared shortened by a slight slouch. I also noticed small details in Alice's face that I hadn't remembered: two deep-set vertical lines between her eyebrows and a crooked canine. I wondered if they had always been there.

I was sitting on the church pew, leaning back against the wall, and she was on one of the odd assortment of chairs, slouched forward on her elbows at the head the table. At some point she confessed that she and Crow had had a bad couple of years after Caleb was born. She spoke quietly, her eyes on the door to the living room, where Caleb and Maeve were watching TV. 'Even before you left it wasn't good. We got into debt – well, Crow did – and he was drinking and smoking a lot.'

She ran me through a list of Crow's ventures: two solo albums, both critical and commercial flops; an organic food delivery business that he had to close after losing his driver's license for drink driving; Iyengar yoga teaching, which he'd stopped after putting his back out surfing. Then there was also the stint at gambling: pokies at the pub, the horses, the greyhounds. It had happened early on, and luckily Alice had cottoned on before they'd 'lost everything'. She topped up our wine glasses. 'But we did counselling and things got better. And then, of course, Maeve was born.'

It was only now occurring to me how much of her life I had missed. I had been treating my time overseas like a kind of space travel – believing that I would return after years of adventures to find everyone exactly as they were when I had left.

'So I ended up in the mother–baby unit for a while.'

'Maeve was sick?'

'No. I had postnatal depression. I think I was just tired. I actually can't remember it very well; I can't even remember Maeve as a baby. I look at photos of her and have no recollection at all. Nothing. I just vaguely remember one day, here in the kitchen, Caleb was lying on the ground having a tantrum, and Maeve was screaming in the high chair. I was cooking dinner and I had a frypan with oil heating up on the burner.' She nodded towards the stove. 'There was all this screaming, but it seemed far away – I couldn't really hear it anymore; I couldn't hear or feel anything. It was all happening somewhere else. And I was looking at the oil in the frypan, at the tiny bubbles, starting as golden specks on the bottom of the pan, growing like little eggs and rising to the surface. And it was all so silky-smooth and delicious looking, like honey. I was so cold, so far away, and it looked so warm and soft. I just wanted to *feel* something – so I lifted my hand and I stretched it flat and laid it in the oil.'

'You fried your hand?'

She nodded. 'I felt this amazing warmth, and – like a thunderbolt going through me. Next thing I remember was being in hospital – I was there for three weeks – on tranquillisers. It was *greeaat*.' she said, laughing.

'You never told me.'

'I'm telling you now.' She shrugged. 'What could you do? You were on some boat, drifting around the Mediterranean.' She flashed me her palm. 'All good now.'

Her attitude was simple: this was all in the past; she and Crow had sorted it out; they'd moved on. Besides, Crow was happier now, since he'd started his work as a volunteer firefighter. So I believed her when she said that all was now well; I had to. I was offended that she hadn't told me any of this earlier – but then, I'd only conveyed the good bits about my life overseas as well. I'd told her I'd been making good money working in an ad agency in Hong Kong, but I didn't tell her about the bullying from the woman who managed my team and that her husband, who worked in another department, had propositioned me several times. I told her about weekends snorkelling in Malaysian resorts, full moon parties in Thailand, and the many short affairs I'd had; I didn't tell her about my desperate loneliness, and that I hadn't stopped thinking about Christian the entire time I'd been away.

No, none of this made it into the letters, and even now, after everything she'd confessed, I was still determined to maintain the illusion created by my correspondence, of exotic locations and exhilarating adventures. I wanted my life to seem better than hers. I wanted – I realise now – for her to think that having a child, and not travelling with me overseas, had been a mistake.

But at the same time, I was saddened by what I saw. Alice's vitality had faded, or been transformed into a jitteriness. She tapped continually on the table with her fingers or with a teaspoon, her leg jiggled up and down, she chewed at her fingernails like a child. Earlier, she'd even ducked out the kitchen door, asking me to stay and watch over the stove, then returned, smelling of cigarette smoke. She'd only ever been an occasional smoker but had made a big deal about giving up altogether when she had kids.

I'd already told her about my relationship with Christian, so to change the subject I started telling her about Christian's work: his office at the University of Melbourne, where he lectured and worked; all the boards and advisory committees he was on; his weekly spot on 3RRR talking about sustainable energy, the environment and the economy. 'He's just written a great article for the *Financial Times* – "The Economy of Narcissism". I'll show it to you; you'd enjoy it. He writes that the world's failure to respond to climate change is an act of aggression by rich countries against poor.'

'You're clearly in love, which is great.' Her mouth twitched into a smile. 'And he's super smart and successful. But he's not exactly the family type. I mean, if that's what you want.'

'He's great with kids.' My response was a little abrupt. It was the reasoning I used with myself.

'He doesn't want kids; he's told me that several times.' Then she shrugged. 'Maybe you don't either?'

'He hasn't ruled it out.' *How can anyone be sure how they'll feel about something in the future?* That's what he'd say whenever I pressed him on this.

'Look, even if he did, you wouldn't want kids with someone like that.'

'I disagree.' I looked away, towards the kitchen door, wanting to signal an end to the discussion.

'Well, I hope you're right. But it's something to think about. The man a woman chooses to have a child with is one of the most important decisions of her life; it doesn't affect men's lives in anywhere near the same way—'

I scoffed. 'Jesus, when did you go all Jane Austen?'

She grinned. 'I'm a realist, baby. Guys don't care if you're a feminist. No one cares if you're a feminist – except for other feminists. The world goes on. It's not going to change its tune because of what you've been reading.'

'A bit jaded are we?'

She shrugged and gulped her wine. 'It just shits me. Feminism used to be about collectivism, and it's ended up just emulating the worst behaviours of the system it used to fight against. Women like us are fighting to become the new privileged class so that we can outsource to the underprivileged – mostly women – the shitty stuff that men used to make *us* do. Brilliant. Capitalism thrives on inequality. It relies on there being an underclass of people working for next to nothing – caring for the children, the sick, the elderly – so that the productive ones can get ahead. So if Christian wants to write about the greedy extravagant lives of us people in the West, maybe he should think about the part he plays: I'd say he does pretty bloody well. And modern white feminists? They're just as bad. They've just become another cog in this whole bloody corrupt machine.' She paused then gave me a sarcastic grin. 'So yes, you could call me jaded.'

I didn't return her smile. 'I forgot you were such a Marxist.'

She drained her glass and topped it up, stood, then leaned against the sink. 'You know how I visited my aunt in Malawi before I started uni? I might have told you this already – one time, walking through the rainforest near Mount Mulanje, I saw the most extraordinary thing: a colony of ants had used their own bodies to build a bridge over a small trickle of water. There must have been thousands of them, stretched almost flat, with their front legs grabbing hold of other ants, and their back legs gripping onto more ants behind. The rope of ants was a few inches thick and high, and the bridge must have been almost a foot long. And then there were even more ants marching along the top of the bridge. It was the most incredible thing. I have no idea how they engineered it. But what really fascinated me was how their roles had been assigned – who became the bridge, and who got to walk over it? Perhaps they'd been predetermined? Maybe some had been born with the particular gene that compelled them to risk their lives to help the others, while others somehow knew it was their job to wait behind until the bridge was built before marching across. I was lying there on the ground, watching them for ages, and I found myself focusing on individual ants – not the ones marching over the top, but the bridge ones – watching for any signs of weakness. I wanted to see how long they could stay locked in position. I mean – *What could those bridge ants possibly be thinking?* But of course, it's ridiculous to anthropomorphise—'

'What's your point?' She was drunk and I wasn't interested in trying to curb my annoyance.

'They just somehow knew what to do and did it. I mean, imagine that?'

'They're ants.'

'Yeah, but imagine just *knowing*? Do you think that on some level they were aware how vital a part they played in the survival of the colony? Because *why else would they do that?*' She shook her head. 'But of course, you're right – they're *ants* – clearly they wouldn't be thinking these things ...'

She'd put her wine down on the sill and her palms were flat and open as she continued, looking up towards the ceiling. I ran my hand through my hair and leaned down onto my elbow, letting her know I was tiring of this topic, but she was clearly consumed.

'So I watched and waited. But the trail of ants crossing the bridge continued on for maybe an hour, with no signs of slowing, and I had to get back. But I wanted to see because— I mean some of them must have *died* when they were constructing the bridge, and surely more were going to die when it was time for the bridge to come down. Was this nature's plan?' She shook her head. 'It makes you wonder about natural selection, doesn't it? Because if natural selection is happening at the individual level, how do you explain altruism? How do you explain self-sacrifice? But then if natural selection operates at the group level – well, so many group traits can be reduced to individual traits – just look at the ants ...' Her voice trailed off. She looked so red and flustered that for a moment I thought she was about to cry, looking up above the doorway to the living room, her face drawn and sorrowful.

'So – sorry – I'm a little confused,' I said. 'I'm a capitalist dating an arsehole, and we're just going to trample over everyone. Is that what you're saying? Or is Christian just going to trample over me? You know, you're not making a lot of sense.'

She looked down at her palm briefly, as if involuntarily. Then put on some dishwashing gloves and squirted detergent into the sink. 'I just don't want you to make the same mistakes I did.'

'You're blaming Crow for your breakdown?'

'Of course not.' She turned off the taps and faced me. 'I just want you to be happy. If you tell me you're happy with your life, then I'm happy for you.'

'Sure. I'm happy with my life. Very happy,' I said, leaning back in my chair, swilling my wine around in its glass. I let it settle then took a sip: a Vouvray I'd brought down with me, spritzy and clean. I'd gone on a wine tour in this region, in France. Just the memory of that place – the castles built into the chalky limestone cliffs, shimmering rows of vines covering the hills – and then looking around at where I was now ... my eyes fell on the row of mismatched mugs hanging from hooks near the window. Next to them was a woven-stick star hanging from a pin, and, on the window ledge above the sink, a bird's nest, an urchin shell, a kookaburra tail feather and bits of driftwood, gathering dust. Yes, I had every right to feel pleased with myself. I'd worked hard – very hard – and could afford nice things. I could understand Alice's resentment. My new Motorola phone, on which I'd been showing her photos from some of the shoots I'd worked on in Hong Kong, was sitting on the table in front of me. As I thought about all this – how far I'd come, how much I had to be grateful for – I started playing with my phone, out of habit: spinning it around against the table. 'And you? Are you happy?'

She looked down at the floor with a frown, blinking heavily. 'I don't know. Maybe there's something wrong with me. Everyone seems to think there is. Maybe I just don't know how to appreciate what I've got.' She took a swig of her wine, finishing it, her big pale-green rubber-glove fingers splaying out ridiculously around the stem; I noticed the top button of her jeans was undone. She picked up the empty wine bottle from the table, looked at it up against the light, then refilled her glass from a cask in the pantry, which she'd explained to me earlier was 'just cooking wine', and she hadn't got around to buying anything else. She must have snuck a few glasses of it before dinner; she couldn't have got so drunk on half a bottle of Vouvray. 'But I know one thing.' She looked down at my fidgeting hand on the table, sniffed and turned back to the dishes. 'I don't need a four-hundred-dollar phone to make me happy.'

I rose, put my phone in my back pocket, picked up a tea towel and started drying the plates in the dish rack without speaking.

The fallout from our argument didn't linger. The next few times I saw Alice, she didn't say anything more about Christian and had dropped the political ranting. I decided she was probably remorseful, or perhaps she'd been so inebriated at the time that she'd forgotten what she'd said. In any case, we'd always respected each other's differences of opinions, so I didn't let the altercation bother me. But I see it now as the beginning of her slightly untethered behaviour, which she fuelled further with alcohol. It was also a glimpse into her unhappiness, which she increasingly began to blame on the injustices in society. And Crow.

The second incident must have been around six months later, and it was the first time I truly suspected that something more sinister was stoking Alice's moods. It was a few weeks before Crow was going to Fiskville, as a part of his professional firefighter training, and I'd been trying to convince Alice, with the kids, to join a few of us on a road trip up to the Territory. If Alice joined us, Crow would fly up to Darwin to meet us at the end.

Leading up to the departure date, Alice started to frustrate me with her lack of commitment, her evasiveness, her prevaricating around every apparent obstacle – 'Crow doesn't like me going away with other men' was one of her many excuses. Then three weeks before we left, Crow telephoned, saying he needed to talk with me about something.

'I don't know if you've noticed, Lara, but Alice isn't well.'

'What do you mean?'

'She probably hasn't told you, but she's seeing a shrink. And, well, there are a few mental-health issues.'

I asked him to explain.

'She's always had problems. I'm sure she's told you already, she's got a pretty screwed-up family. Her stepdad is dodgy as hell. I mean, she's kept it together pretty well – really well – but motherhood has just brought it all up for her. She had a breakdown after Maeve was born.'

'She said she was better now.'

'Well,' he grunted a laugh. 'It's not quite that simple. She's pretty unstable. They made us go to couple's counselling after the breakdown, and she'd just sit there crying the entire time, making these crazy accusations about me. I convinced them she needed another psychiatric evaluation – they agreed of course. This new shrink seems a bit better, still not great though. She's a smart woman and she's good at presenting well when she needs to. Personality types like hers usually are – I've had it all explained to me. I hate telling you all this, and you can't say anything to her, but I know you really care. She's probably been telling you that I won't let her go on the road trip. See, that's just bullocks. I'd love her to be able to go. She has these delusions about me. She just makes this shit up, 'cos it's easier for her to deal with if it's not her fault. The reality is, deep down, she knows she's not well, and without me there it could be really tough.'

'We can look after her if she gets upset or anything.'

'Lara, you were away. You don't understand how sick she gets. If she comes with you, we'll have to fill out a crisis management plan, in case she has an episode while she's away.'

'Really?'

'Look, it's doctor's orders. They'd probably say she shouldn't go but, hey, I get sick of being the bad guy all the time. Personally, I don't think she should go. I think it'll be too much for her. But I don't want to stop her. I just want what's best for her.'

Over the following week, there was further vacillation from Alice: claims that Crow was making things difficult for her, though she wouldn't explain any further when I asked. I didn't play into it, though a part of me was beginning to hope they'd stay behind. I was looking forward to a relaxing adventure with my friends, not this. But to my surprise, Alice eventually said they would come. Nothing came up about the crisis management plan, and of course I never mentioned the conversation I'd had with Crow.

So we took off – six adults and her two kids – on an overcast late-autumn morning, with all our camping gear strapped to the roof of Sam's Jeep. Thermoses of coffee and chai and bags of chips circulated around the car, the CD player blaring as we headed towards the Red Centre. We stayed the first night with friends in Adelaide, then, on the second evening, we camped near Cooper Pedy. Jas and Christian put up Alice's tent, and she laughed when all five of us each offered her a glass of wine before dinner. In the evenings we'd sing songs around the fire with her kids and rate the toasting of their marshmallows out of ten. Alice would sit back contentedly in her camp chair, drinking a wine, watching her kids be entertained.

One time when I was telling Caleb jokes – and helping him make up and sing nonsense limericks – she lifted my feet onto her lap, pulled off my boots and socks and started massaging my feet. Caleb was chewing gum, and I started trying to teach him how to blow bubbles, so asked if he could give me some. He bit the gum in his mouth in half, then handed me a gob, which I popped in my mouth and started chewing. Alice shook her head and laughed. 'You're going to make a *great* mum one day,' she said. Christian looked over to her, then returned to his conversation with Sam.

Each morning, Alice was offered a cup of tea by everyone as they emerged from their tents, but of course she'd always been up for hours, started the fire we were boiling our water on and had drunk several cups of tea before any of us had even stirred. I'd often wake momentarily at dawn to hear her shushing her kids, whispering as she dressed them, then taking them off for a walk as the sun was beginning to rise.

From what I could tell, all seemed to be going well – she was the same old Alice – until day twelve, when we camped for the night at Koolpin Gorge in Kakadu. Up until then, Alice hadn't asked anything of anyone except for occasionally watching over the tent where her kids were sleeping while she took a shower, or leaving them with us for brief spells while she ducked off to the bathroom or to have a sneaky cigarette. On this morning, while Alice had been off on her morning walk and swim with the kids, the rest of us had sat around the fire, among the pandanus and melaleuca, and decided we'd climb the gorge and walk up to the plunge pools at the top, leaving immediately after breakfast so we could get there and back before we had to leave for Darwin. Simon had been deep into the gorge years earlier, and had told us about the incredible waterfalls and rock art that you come across after a few hours' walk.

When Alice and her kids returned, she made them both sandwiches, then sat quietly gazing into the coals. Her kids had been crying and complaining a lot recently; they were finding the long days in the car, the heat, the flies and the unpredictable meal times difficult. Alice looked tired too. Sam was walking around with his stovetop espresso coffee maker, pouring coffee the colour and consistency of melted dark chocolate into our mugs. As he held out the coffee pot to Alice, she looked up and shook her head, her elbows draped over her knees, only occasionally shifting to swat away flies.

'No heart starter this morning?' he asked.

'I was actually wondering if someone could mind my kids for an hour or so while I have a lie-down?' she asked, looking into the dirt.

No one said anything. It was quite simple: no one wanted to do it.

'We were going to walk up the gorge to the top pools this morning,' I said, figuring it was best to be straight up with her.

'My kids can't climb up the gorge!'

The rest of us looked about, at anything but Alice. Sam continued topping up coffees.

'Jesus Christ!' she yelled. 'All I want is a bloody nap!' Her face reddened, her jaw clenched and tears filled her eyes. There was a moment where she just glared at us like this, as if she wanted to scream or hurl a log. I sat there bracing myself for what was to come. More seconds passed, then she stood, picked up Maeve, grabbed Caleb by the hand and dragged him to her tent. Was she crying? I believe she was. But maybe I've just embellished it in my mind because, from the entire road trip, it's the memory that I've held onto, wishing to somehow undo it. I still feel uneasy thinking about how we all sat there, dumbly, like children told off by their mother, knowing they were going to return to the same mischief once she'd gone. And we did: moments after her dramatic exit, we all got up and quietly moved about the fire, piling up our dirty cups and plates in the washing-up basin, and kicking the fire out with our boots.

Five minutes later, Christian walked over to her tent. There were beeping noises coming from within, maybe a toy gun or some other kid's game. 'Lara and I will look after the kids for a bit when we get back, okay?'

'Yep,' short and sharp, was all she said from inside the tent.

Christian waited for a moment, then walked towards me with a pleased smile to let me know it was all sorted. But when we returned in the mid-afternoon, Alice and her kids were nowhere about, having taken off on their own adventure somewhere. She'd already packed up her tent and only returned as we were packing the car, ready to leave for Darwin.

Looking back, I'm still at a loss as to why I didn't come to her aid, especially after being warned she was unwell, and knowing that her behaviour could have deteriorated even further. That was one of the moments I really could have stepped up and helped her. Why did climbing a gorge suddenly seem so important to me? I can only imagine it had little to do with the gorge, little to do with her wellbeing, and something to do with my own understanding of the meaning of choice and responsibility, and the claims we were all quietly making on our own life decisions. Alice had chosen to elope with the rockstar. She had chosen to settle down the coast, away from us all, and to have children. We had chosen differently, and we expected to enjoy the benefits of our decisions, just as we assumed she enjoyed the benefits of hers.

As the five of us marched off towards the gorge that morning, I did feel bad leaving Alice behind, but I couldn't see why I should miss out as a result of decisions she had made – especially after she'd recently been so unsupportive of me. Later that morning, lying in the crystalline waters of a rock pool, gazing up at the fruiting pandanus, listening to the rush of the water over rocks and the warbling butcher birds above, I thought of her back at the camp with her kids and found myself clutching onto the words that Crow had used during our telephone conversations – *highly strung, volatile, unreasonable* – as if already formulating my account of what had happened. In fact, I'm quite sure those very words were used during one of the police interviews after the fire, when Detective Sergeant Hafley raised the topic of Alice's mental health and first mentioned the possibility that she may have, in a fit of rage, started the fire, just as she had once fried her hand. Though, come to think of it, I'm not sure who used those words first: Detective Hafley or me.

13

If I had to point to the time when things fell apart for me – when my view from Mount Olympus suddenly soured – it was three years ago, soon after my thirty-first birthday. And perhaps I'm projecting my own problems onto Alice, but it seemed that's when things started rapidly traveling further south for her too.

Christian and I had been living together in our weatherboard bungalow for about eight months; my career was going well, and the threat of childlessness hadn't yet hit. I had, so I thought, years up my sleeve to consider motherhood. Despite my ambition, and my apparent lack of family orientation or real interest in Alice's children, I always knew that one day I'd have kids. It was an assumption made with as little planning or analysis as the assumption that I'd get older and one day die. It would be something my partner and I would decide on, then go ahead and do – as simple as buying a new couch. Yes, Christian had told me he didn't want kids in the near and possibly distant future, but I'd professed a dislike for kids years earlier too, hadn't I? I assumed people just said these things when they were young. I assumed that, under favourable conditions, this would change.

Then one Saturday morning, mid-March, my period didn't arrive. That's how I found myself sitting on the toilet, staring at a white pregnancy stick as the moisture crept up the screen. I was back at uni, all those years ago, Alice waiting outside my cubicle door. One blue line, and within seconds, another. The very faint, distant voice of my long-lost child. I stared back and forth at the stick and the instructions, unable to really comprehend – fathom – the result. I put the stick back in its foil sachet and buried it in the bottom drawer of the vanity, like a secret love letter. The packaging went into the paper chemist's bag and into the bathroom waste bin. No need to hide it: Christian was not the type to fossick about in his domestic world.

I made a cup of tea and sat on the sofa. Of course I'll abort, I said to myself, but then found myself imagining otherwise. My lower abdomen had ached for about a week. No, not ached, *hummed*; just made me aware of its presence, only occasionally deepening into a menstrual-like cramp. I started to think of this feeling as a small ember, glowing, radiating a gentle, orange warmth. How different the feeling was to my first pregnancy nine years earlier; I'd been a baby myself back then. I cupped my hand over my lower belly and, when I caught myself doing this, wondered whether I was simply reaching for the gestures I'd witnessed in others, or whether this behaviour was a natural expression – my actions already being dictated by hormones – of my body's need to hold, caress and protect.

I spent the day walking myself through various scenarios. Booking myself in for an abortion, and not even confessing to Christian. Why did it seem important he not know? There was something about the way he might view me: my messiness; my fallibility; or alternatively, the power I had the potential to wield over him. Was it even possible that he might want to keep it, and me not? What kind of woman would I seem to him then? And then there was me deciding I might want this child. I could sit, obstinate, and do nothing, just let it grow – it surely knew what to do. Yes, the easiest, and yet most difficult, option. One small decision, or indecision, but then a lifetime of decisions to follow.

Christian had driven down the coast for an early morning surf and didn't arrive home until mid-afternoon; when he came through the door I was at the sink peeling veggies. We had friends coming for dinner that night, and I was slow-cooking a shoulder of lamb in the oven. The bloody smell of the greying meat and the sweet, melting fat were making me feel queasy. He walked up and stood close behind me. I turned my head to kiss him, steeling myself against the nausea. 'Hi, sweetheart. How was your surf?' I asked, immediately worrying I'd given myself away: wearing an apron, peeling potatoes and carrots, the wife-like greeting.

'All right!' He inhaled through his nose. 'Roast. You good woman.' He cupped my hips in his hands and kissed the top of my head. His hands slid around over my belly and I squirmed from his touch to the fridge. I felt vulnerable. My entire body had become a team of sentries to protect this fragile being at its core.

I imagined telling him, wheeling out one of the lines I'd heard one hundred actresses saying – *We're going to have a baby!* Except this time, it would be me at the centre of the drama. He would cover me with kisses, whirl me around, dash out for champagne or pick up the phone to make a restaurant booking.

But I knew that wasn't how he would respond. So I didn't tell him that night, or the next. Then, unfairly, I began to judge him for not knowing, not caring.

One night after dinner, he put down his fork and asked if I was okay, said I seemed quiet. He didn't usually pick up on my moods, or inquire how I was feeling, presuming, I suppose, that I'd tell him if anything serious was wrong. I looked down into my bowl, twirled a noodle around my fork and told him I was a bit tired, which was true.

'Okay,' he said and stood, then took his bowl to the sink. I heard the clink and rattle of dishes. 'I'll do these later.' Then he disappeared to his study for the rest of the evening.

How was it possible, I wondered, that his baby – yes, that is how I was beginning to see it, not as a zygote but as a fully formed being, ten fingers, ten toes – could be growing in the bed beside him each night, swirling around in its little bubble to the sound of his heavy breathing, and he hadn't realised? I'd lie there staring at the darkness ahead of me, tears spilling down my face, surprised to find myself praying that he'd love this child.

When Christian had told me in the past he didn't want children, I'd ignored his ambitious nature; I'd assumed his lack of desire for fatherhood was a result of the distant relationship he had with his own father: a self-protective response. Of course, Christian would never admit that his relationship with his dad was difficult. Christian abhored ambivalence, and perhaps there was no way of having an uncomplicated relationship with Philip – as he called him – so he simply chose to have none, which was fairly easy to do, given Philip had lived in the US since Christian was six. Christian had never refused to see his father – he would hate to appear wounded – so he saw him, if convenient, on the one or two occasions each year when Philip came to Melbourne. When they did meet up, they treated each other like two directors within the same firm: bound by company loyalty, but little more. After not having spoken a word to any of his sons for six months or more, Philip would stride into their lives for the evening, take them out for Peking Duck at the Flower Drum, then launch into a litany of life advice, as if the job of simply siring the boys was enough to earn him the prime mentoring role. He'd then demonstrate his more thoughtful side by offering to organise a good psychiatrist for their mother.

After Philip left her, Christian's mother, Brigit, grew increasingly devoted to helping the poor and homeless in the world, and worked in an orphanage in Vietnam for several years after Christian's brothers finished school, then moved to a bush block just outside Healesville where, to this day, she helps rehabilitate injured wildlife. Philip, I'm sure, would view Christian's ideological leanings as oedipal: a pathological flaw.

Christian always told me he was determined not to be like his father and seemed to go out of his way to prove his difference. He was good to his mother, who'd become agoraphobic over the years, and increasingly incapable of looking after her beloved fruit bats and joeys – or even herself. So he'd spend a day or two a month at her house, chopping wood, mowing the lawn, paying her bills and getting her prescriptions filled. He was always quiet and serious when he returned. If I asked how his mum was going, he'd stretch his face into a theatrical grin and say, 'Ohhhh, no more fucked up than usual,' then disappear into his office to work.

So this – according to me, back then – was why Christian didn't want children: he was damaged. And I assumed I could cure him of this.

The first few days had been the hardest, when I was riddled with anxiety and excitement, but after that I started to feel protective of my secret. It was like a precious new friend I didn't want to share with anyone. Moreover, I had made my decision, and as much as I pretended and hoped otherwise, I knew that Christian wouldn't be happy with the news.

Christian was in shock when I first told him. He acted as if I'd blurted out some nonsense that he hadn't properly heard. I kept repeating it, trying not to smile, with an applied seriousness in my voice. He sat on the sofa with a hand on his forehead. 'Fuck!' He turned and stared at me, looking desperate and frightened. 'I've told you. I don't want a fucking child!' His voice was pleading, as if my pregnancy was optional, an imagined idea.

But declaring my news out loud had strengthened me. I was resolved: *I was having a baby.* I felt stronger than he, and even sympathetic for his crushed state. I became aware that I was behaving aloof, even smug, during our arguments, which continued for two weeks or more. He spent more time at work, going out drinking afterwards with Freya – as if, I thought, to threaten me with the kind of father he'd be. He'd come home aggrieved and spout out lines like 'How do I even know it's mine?' I'd never seen him so addled, so out of his depth. I told him he could leave if he wanted, and I meant it. I felt like Superwoman. My body was quietly, miraculously making a baby. I felt like I was capable of anything.

Even so, Christian had rankled me. 'And what about your work?' he asked during one of our arguments. 'How many female producers have babies?'

My brain was whizzing along too fast, too locked on its course for me to stop and grapple for an answer. 'Loads,' I shot back.

'Really? Name some.'

'Okay ...'

'Ones without husbands at home, ones without full-time nannies. Face it, Lara. You have a baby then someone else is going to be making that refugee documentary for you. You'll be at home breastfeeding on the sofa, watching it on TV.'

That argument ended about there. He went to his office to work and I went to bed and cried.

Christian was right, of course; but he usually is, isn't he.

I could now finally admit to myself that motherhood was something I'd always, secretly, craved, ever since I was a child. This was what I wanted; this was the belonging I'd been searching for.

I couldn't wait to share my news with Alice – she would be the godmother, of course. She was heavily pregnant with Tom at the time, and I imagined our babies growing up together, like cousins. Our lives would once more be forged together, intertwined. But I couldn't tell Alice or anyone else yet. Not until things had calmed down with Christian.

During this time, my tiredness was overwhelming, like an extra gravitational force trying to pin me to the ground. And the nausea: some mornings I wouldn't really wake until I was running to the bathroom to vomit. I took two days off work, as if it might pass, then realised I had no option but to push through it, keeping a packet of rice crackers in my desk drawer to munch on all day and keep the nausea at bay.

It was a horrendous few weeks. I'd come home each evening wrecked, then sit on the sofa and cry. One day at work, after we'd been shooting some footage at a playground in East Melbourne, I volunteered to grab some cakes from George & Simpson and meet everyone back in the office. On the way, I walked past the clinic on Wellington Street where I'd had my abortion nine years earlier. Christian had thrust the address and phone number into my hand the day after I'd told him the news – 'Just speak with them, find out what's involved,' he'd insisted. I didn't tell him I already knew. But I hadn't been back there in all those years, and felt a strange need to see the place again – to acknowledge the baby I'd never had. The building looked much the same, still with its band of protestors out the front, clutching their gruesome signs. I didn't feel any regret for what I'd done back then – I did what I'd had to do – despite the overwhelming sense of loss I felt gazing up at the peeling white façade, which looked to me now like a grand old mausoleum, a monument honouring the passing of so many little souls.

I walked along the footpath, past a group of three women, heads bowed, holding rosaries, and murmuring the Lord's Prayer, barely audible over the other voices, the traffic and the trams rattling by. I kept my head lowered and walked straight past, remembering the woman at the desk who'd given me a tender smile and apologised for the protesters, and the counsellor who'd asked me about my relationship, my family, what support I had, and if I had someone to take me home. I also remembered how hard I'd pushed myself through the entire ordeal, telling myself that this was what a responsible young woman must do.

When I arrived back at the office, I put the cake boxes down on my desk, and took off my coat and scarf, making a big show about the bitter southerly wind that had made my eyes water.

Christian didn't move out, and at some stage, he seemed to surrender. One night, he held me in bed, stroking my belly, and asked me if I thought it was a girl or a boy, then started suggesting outlandish names – Nebuchadnezzar, Scheherazade. He came home the next day from work with a bunch of tiger lilies and a jar of folic acid supplements, apologising for his 'ratbag' behaviour. The following week he appeared troubled again, staying out late drinking, or retreating to his study after dinner. This to-ing and fro-ing continued for another few weeks but seemed to be running out of steam.

I made an appointment for my twelve-week ultrasound and mentioned the booking to Christian. I was trying to be as gentle as I could, telling him that a baby needn't impinge too much on his life. I didn't want him to feel compelled to join me, but secretly hoped he would. Surely as soon as he saw his little child, wriggling about inside me, he'd feel differently. Christian did want to come along, but I felt it was more out of a clinical curiosity than any sense of paternal excitement or anticipation.

I can still see the image of the little sleeping body up on the black and white monitor at the medical imaging clinic: its large round skull, button nose and body curled up like a nestling cat. Smiling and with tears in my eyes, I looked up at Christian standing beside me. He smiled back at me but seemed otherwise unmoved.

How long did I get to enjoy this image? Perhaps only minutes, or seconds. The clinician was sitting facing the monitor on her desk, moving the mouse around on the screen, taking measurements and, with her other hand, rolling a rod over the cold gel on my abdomen, seemingly searching for different angles.

She put down the ultrasound rod and pressed a button on the monitor. The screen went dark and she turned her chair from the keyboard towards where I lay, belly still exposed. 'I'm very sorry. There's no heartbeat.'

At first I didn't understand. Christian's hand touched my shoulder. 'So what do we do?' But I meant, *What do we do to fix this?*

'You'll have to book in for a curette, but there's a good chance you'll miscarry before then.'

A *good* chance.

She wiped the gel off my abdomen with a tissue, and as I pulled up my skirt and fixed my clothes, Christian's arm went around my shoulder.

'I'm sorry,' he said once we'd left the room. And it did feel like an apology.

'You'd be pretty happy then?' I said as we walked against the wind to the car, the first time I'd spoken.

'Don't be like that.'

'You always get what you want, don't you?'

'Lara.'

It had started to rain. I cried the whole way home, curled away from him in my seat, hugging the dead child I carried inside. Christian stared straight ahead through the beating windscreen wipers, occasionally trying to put a hand on me, which I'd throw straight back in his lap.

The experience should have brought me closer to Alice. I was edging towards her world: motherhood had beckoned. But for some reason, I couldn't turn to her, or anyone, for support. Was I not wanting to admit that she'd been right about Christian? Was it because I hadn't supported her through motherhood? Was it, quite simply, envy? That she had children and a partner who adored her? And if so, was it really so wrong of me to feel this way? To want the things that she had too?

14

I take the frittata from the benchtop oven and am just about to carry it outside to Crow and the kids on the deck when I hear a man on the kitchen radio – an economist, of all people – talking about love. So I put the frittata down on a bread board and collect the cutlery, plates and cups, not clanging them about too much as I listen. The man is speaking about every human's first experience of love, the one that sets the template for later on: that of the newborn baby with its parents. One theory as to why newborns fall in love with their parents, he says, is because they are completely helpless, and the best survival strategy in such a situation is to latch onto and identify with those in power. Complete sublimation. He goes on, quite strangely, to proffer the argument that paying tax is like being in love. People pay tax not because of the very small chance of getting caught for not paying, nor because of the negligible fines that they'll pay, but because they want to do the right thing by those in power: they want to feel a part of their society. Membership is important to people, he says. We need to belong.

I poke my head out the back door, squinting into the light. 'Lunch is ready. Crow? Kids?'

I carry out the cutlery, plates and cups. I'm partly blinded by the glare of the sun but make out Crow loping around from the side of the house, wiping his forehead with the bottom of his T-shirt. Maeve and Tom are skipping behind him.

Attachment behaviour is understandable – well, integral to survival – in a baby. But what's more interesting, for me, is understanding how these behaviours continue on as we mature. Apparently oxytocin levels rise in adult humans and other mammals under stressful conditions, such as during social isolation and unhappy relationships. Some think that the rise in oxytocin encourages people, or animals, to search out and bond with others. Another theory is that the oxytocin, through its calming effects on the nervous system, might protect against shutdown during stressful circumstances, especially occasions that require keeping still rather than fighting or fleeing. Which helps explain Stockholm syndrome, I suppose. The hostage, flooded with oxytocin, adapts to the traumatic situation they're in by unconsciously regressing, returning to an infantile pattern of behaviour where they fall in love with their captor – their parent – and do everything they can to please them. People can be living in a state of fear, it seems, and be happily duped by their own survival mechanisms, into believing that everything is okay. Better than okay – they can believe that what they are experiencing is, in fact, love.

I think about Alice, about our old conversations, and wonder what she would have to say. *Hey, Alice – have you ever realised how similar attachment theory is to Stockholm syndrome?* I can almost hear her throaty laugh.

With tea towels in both hands, I pick up the frittata and carry it outside.

Crow and the kids are seated when I bring the dish to the table, presenting it like a cake. It's sweltering out here; I was hoping for some relief from the heat of the kitchen. I sit with an exaggerated huff. It feels good, though, to get off my feet.

'You be mum,' Crow says, pushing the plates towards me. 'Good practice.' He smiles. 'Not that I doubt you'll be a natural.'

I wonder about his choice of word – 'mum' – and check on the kids: Maeve and Tom are whispering to each other, and Caleb is looking about, bored. I don't feel like serving them all, having just cooked it, but I stand, pick up the knife and stab the frittata. A wasp starts hovering around the dish and I bat it away.

Crow doesn't wait for me to finish serving, but starts eating as soon as I place his food in front of him, puffing as he tries to cool down the molten food in his mouth. He finally manages to swallow. 'Fantastic. Does this have nutmeg in it? It's great.'

'Yeah, a bit,' I say, sitting down with my meal. I'm still thinking about oxytocin and good angles for the documentary. It can be challenging working with babies, and I've decided it will be more interesting to look at adults anyway. Battered women who can't leave their violent husbands, perhaps? But then there's my biggest obstacle: how to get a documentary up when I'm a single mother without a job.

'So my work's made me redundant, did I tell you?' I say. 'Michael told me last week, just as I went on maternity leave. Bastard. Called me in, handed me a cheque, and that was it. After five years of loyal service.'

'Good payout?'

'Okay. But I'm pretty upset. Single mum, unemployed and all that.'

'Christian's got money,' he says, not looking at me, and reaches for the salt.

We're quiet for a bit, and I start thinking about Jane – my old production manager – who would always race out the door at 5.30pm to pick up her son from childcare, as the rest of us exchanged disapproving glances. She left RatTrap when she was pregnant with her second. I have no idea where she is now. I often think about her – the rhythmic squeak of her breast pump through the toilet door at work, and the hilarity Michael caused when he used the breast milk Jane stored in the fridge for everyone's tea.

'So I'll probably end up in a single mothers' commune,' I say, remembering Alice's mention of such a place in Canada.

'Huh,' he grunts.

It was a rash comment, made primarily for effect, but then I start thinking about the possibility of it, of maybe even making a documentary about my experience there. While I'm thinking about this, wondering if such a commune might exist in Australia, and the logistics and ethics of such a documentary, I take in snippets of what Crow is talking about: how well Tom's doing on his new strict diet and boasts about Caleb's guitar-playing skills. He promises me a recital later on.

I nod enough to keep him talking, thinking further about my idea.

'So, kids, I've got to run into town this afternoon,' he announces, scraping the last few morsels of frittata from his plate, then smacking his lips together. 'Lara's going to look after you. She's in charge. Got it?'

Caleb groans, and Tom looks to Maeve, who's sitting next to me at the table. She starts stroking my arm. I give her the best smile I can manage. I'm incredibly tired – I've been getting like this each afternoon since the start of my final trimester. I'd love a lie-down.

'Seriously, best frittata ever. Hey, kids?' Crow stands. 'Maeve, you can clear the table.'

Maeve lets me go and starts stacking plates. She's eaten most of hers, but the other two have mashed their meals, and just picked out and eaten the potato. I notice Caleb shoving Maeve with his shoulder as he walks past. She sticks her foot out and tries to trip him over. He stumbles but continues on.

I sit on the daybed and pick up my phone. There's a text from Christian simply saying, 'All okay? Are you back in Melbourne?' He's written it from Dubai; it must be around six in the morning there now.

I smile at the phone for a moment, tempted to pretend that the baby's been born. I realise I'm enjoying the attention he's now giving me. Sometimes I think that was all I ever wanted from him.

Crow walks out with another two coffees – reckons I'll need it – and places mine on the crate next to the daybed, then stands holding his mug and car keys.

'Who's put you in such a good mood?' he says, trying to peer at my screen.

I place my phone face-down next to my coffee and smile expectantly up at Crow.

'Anyway,' he says. 'I shouldn't be too long. Like I said, *mi casa es tu casa*. And hey, I don't suppose you can loan me a fifty? Get my payment Tuesday. Just got a couple of exxy things to get from the hardware. Fifty should be fine.'

'Oh? Sure.' I'd been planning on buying dinner tonight anyway but have now promised I'll cook with Maeve instead, so I collect the money from my bedroom and hand it to him.

'Cheers.' He shoves the note in his back pocket and I realise I'll never see the money again. I don't have a job; I should have told him I didn't have any cash on me. I hope he's not long, I really need a lie-down.

'Ciao, then.' He picks up a small backpack at his feet, gives me a peck on the cheek, and walks with his coffee mug and keys to the blue Peugeot 504 station wagon, Alice's old car.

I think about how this would look to an outsider: me, heavily pregnant, surrounded by Alice's children, kissing and waving Crow goodbye as he heads out for DIY supplies. I think about Detective Hafley, interviewing me in the days after the fire: leaning forward, elbows on his knees, rubbing his jaw with his fingertips. And there was his deputy, Vella, I think her name was – a small, fiery Maltese-looking woman – sitting at what seemed a prescribed distance away from him, creating a triangle from which I couldn't escape. Eyes pinned on me – his, lazily hooded; hers, dark and penetrating – I'm sure neither of them blinked. Filming me with their stares. Then that deep, weary voice of his: 'Ms King. Were you having an affair with Mr Crowley?'

I watch the rear of the car, kicking up stones and dust as it heads out of the drive, then look down the hill, trying to draw myself back into the present. There are a wood duck and three ducklings circling around on the dam, aimlessly it seems. I need to avoid these thoughts about Hafley – I'm sure the cortisol is bad for the baby. I only ever tried to help Alice, but she couldn't, it seemed, be helped.

As I turn to go inside, I meet Maeve in the doorway, walking out with a dishcloth. 'Where's Dad?'

'He's already gone. Sorry, you're stuck with me.'

She pinches in one side of her mouth, sighs loudly – her chest rising and falling – then pivots on her feet and takes her dishcloth back inside.

Tom was born three weeks after my miscarriage, in May 2003. I went down to visit them the day after Alice came home from hospital. I'd been unable to enter any baby stores to buy Tom a gift, so bought Alice an in-house massage voucher instead, wondering, as I wrote the card, if she'd ever be doing the same for me.

I have an image of Alice and her children from that visit; it hangs in my mind like a large Botticelli. I'd just arrived at their house, and she was sitting on the wooden bench in her front garden: Tom was wrapped up in a flannel, asleep in the crook of her arm, Maeve was sitting next to her with her hand on her mum's thigh, and Caleb was behind the seat, balancing his body over the top rung, swinging his legs above the ground and draping an arm around Alice's neck for support. It was a cool but sunny late morning; dahlias were in flower along the front of the house, and painted pots of violets and hyacinth were clumped together near the bluestone path. The three of them were licking homemade icy poles, lounging over each other with the ease and intimacy of a family of cats. Bees circled lazily over the clover around Alice's bare feet, and a few small butterflies – the black ones with orange spots – skipped about, like small flares in the sunbeams. The three of them wore covert smiles, as if they'd just been sharing a joke. In the past I hadn't always appreciated the presence of Alice's children: I'd found them undisciplined and rowdy, too demanding of her attention. But seeing them all on the bench, licking the drips off their icy pole sticks, the auras around their hair aflame in the velvety sunshine, I realised for the first time that these three children were her people, her tribe, and that I'd never seen her look any happier. It was everything I'd ever wanted.

Acknowledging this, as I did, was hard. When I went up to greet them, I more or less dismissed the kids and gave Alice one of those quick pat-on-the-back hugs, keeping it moving. I then turned my back on them and returned to scrounge around in my car for my bags. It was the best I could do.

'You finish your icy poles,' I said as I emerged back out of the car, then put the card and massage voucher on Alice's lap. 'I'm dying for the toilet. I'll be back in a tick.' Then I ran inside, straight for the study, where my sofa bed had been made up. A nasturtium flower lay across the pillow, and a large pickle jar of marigolds sat on the desk at the head of my bed. I lay down, buried my head in the pillow and cried.

Sometime later – I'd stopped sobbing by this stage and was lying on my side, exhausted and wrung out – there was a knock on the door. As soon as Alice saw me, she came in, squatted by the bed and leaned over me, as if at the bedside of a sick child. 'What's the matter? You okay?' Then with her finger, she drew a line from my forehead to my ear, dragging the hair that had fallen across my eyes, and pinning it behind my ear. And there was something about the way she did that – her maternal touch – that broke me. I clenched my eyes shut and started crying.

She wrapped her arms around my head, drawing me in to her chest.

'I had a miscarriage,' I managed to get out.

'Oh, Lara ...' She squeezed me in again, then released, and I felt her climb over me. She lay down behind me, pulled the eiderdown over us both and put her arms around me, her head nestled in behind mine. And she didn't say anything else, just lay there, stroking my head, squeezing me against her body while I cried and shook, as if trying to absorb my pain.

Over the weekend, sipping chamomile teas and kneading pizza dough, details spilled out: of my pregnancy, of my longing for a child, and of Christian's response to it all. 'It's as if nothing ever happened,'

I told her. 'He's completely unmoved. His child is dead and he couldn't be less interested. The night I miscarried, he was chatting to me about electric cars!'

Alice, uncharacteristically, said nothing; just nodded and let me talk. I appreciated this, but also felt that she was holding something back; as if she knew something that I didn't.

Later that week, back in Melbourne, Alice called me. I felt embarrassed when I heard her voice. I'd returned from her house – my catharsis – and slipped back into my life in Melbourne with Christian, feeling more optimistic. I was able to put the miscarriage behind me and show Christian my resilient side – the intrepid traveller that he'd fallen in love with. It felt good to be able to be this woman he so admired. Strangely, lying to him about my feelings didn't seem deceptive at all: it felt clever. And strong.

'So how's it going? How are things with Christian? Have you spoken with him about everything?' The old cage-rattling Alice, who'd kept silent over the weekend, was back.

'No, not really,' I replied, putting my basket of washing down on the carpet and sitting on the bed.

'Have you thought about what you're going to do? You can't just do nothing.'

I lay back, staring out the window at the quince tree in our front garden and the still grey sky behind, trying to distance myself from the content of our conversation, trying not to cry.

'Things have been really good since the weekend. We're getting along better than we have in ages. I'm just going to wait and see how things go ...'

I was hoping she'd tell me that sounded good – or better still, change the topic. But I just heard a discontented silence down the phone.

And then she spoke: 'Lara. You have to leave him.'

This was what she'd been wanting to say the entire weekend. And really, I don't know what else she could have suggested. Yet the advice she gave me, the obvious one, seemed not only harsh – I'd lost my baby and now I must lose my partner as well – but also like a personal criticism. Because I didn't want to end my relationship; I just wanted it fixed. But now I'd admitted its dysfunction to Alice. I had let her see an ugly side of me, distraught and desperately clinging to this intractable man.

'Your relationship's hardly a picture of domestic bliss,' I said.

'That's different.'

I didn't press her further; I knew the answer: *We have kids.*

I got off the phone and sat, covering my face with my hands, regretting everything I'd divulged. Alice had told me, not long ago, that Crow wanted them to have six children. I tried to imagine what it must be like to be with a partner who valued family so highly.

The next time we spoke, I lied and told her Christian had agreed to try for a baby after returning from his conference in America the following year. I couldn't believe it had got to this; I was like a teenager in some dreadful sitcom, lying to my boyfriend, lying about my boyfriend. But at least I'd got her off my back.

Christian's and my relationship returned to normal – or what became the new normal for us: the perfect ratio of stability and drama to provide enough reason to stay, as well as enough belief that things might change. The stability was in the form of a kind of choking cordiality, which would have given anyone watching on no insight into the gradual disintegration that was occurring inside of me – in fact I, at the time, was barely aware of it myself. The drama that punctuated this sharehouse-style bonhomie only ever occurred after I'd had too much to drink – and consisted mostly of tearful pleas from me to Christian. The only drama instigated by him came in the form of reckless lovemaking (the withdrawal method had always been Christian's modus operandi – surely, I told myself, a subconscious desire for fatherhood), after which I would lie awake in bed, wishing and imagining that some magical alchemy might be taking place inside me. I believed that if I longed and loved hard enough, I could miraculously create a life form. Each month I'd count down the days until my period, then when it arrived, I'd cry and curse Christian for not loving this little being enough, for obstructing its entrance, and I'd have trouble even speaking to him for days.

During our fights, he'd call me selfish. I argued back that he was the selfish one, unwilling to share his life with others. But his comment upset me: my father, bosses and other boyfriends had called me selfish in the past, and I began to wonder if it was selfish – my need for a child, my desire to shoehorn him into fatherhood. I remembered the words of a schoolfriend's mother – a psychologist – who said that the biggest cause of depression in the youth back then was entitlement. I began to wonder if that was indeed my problem: I'd believed my own feminist propaganda. I'd believed I could have it all – that 'all' was in fact rightfully mine.

15

It was September, shortly after Alice, Crow and their kids had returned from a week's skiing holiday in Falls Creek. I was sitting at the kitchen table with Alice and the kids when Crow arrived home, entering through the kitchen door. Caleb was squashing the few remaining pieces of cold sausage into his mashed potato, marbled pink from tomato sauce, and Maeve was tipping water from her cup onto her plate, mixing it into the mash with a finger. There were potato peelings on the bench, pots and plates stacked at the sink, puddles of water, pieces of sausage and daubs of mash all about the floor. Alice had just sat down after plodding from foot to foot, making up ridiculous nursery rhymes in an effort to get Tom back to sleep in the papoose on her chest. Cold cups of tea sat on the table in front of us, as did the teacups we'd been using for wine.

'Hi kids, hi babe, hi Lars.' He ruffled each child's hair, barely offering a glance, then leaned down to give Alice a peck. She offered him her cheek but didn't look at him.

'How's Abby?' she asked, still focusing her attention on Tom.

Crow shot her a stern look then glanced about the table. 'So what have the girls been up to, then? Keeping afloat the Sri Lankan tea plantations, I see?'

'Well, you do your bit for the brewers,' Alice replied, looking pleased with herself as she took a sip.

'Great idea.' He pulled a beer out of the fridge, twisted the top off and took a gulp.

'How was the snow?' I asked.

'Incredible. Perfect conditions. I've already put our names down to become members at the lodge. Best holiday we've ever had.'

'Had his family and his girlfriend there. Who could want for more?'

'Abby is a friend of ours,' Crow turned to me, 'who Alice has taken a dislike to, for no particular reason. She's a member at the lodge. If it wasn't for her we wouldn't have got to bloody go.' He turned to Alice, his face red. 'She looked after your baby, if I recall, so you could rest. It's a shame you can't appreciate any of this, or refrain from being such a bitch about her.'

'*My* baby? What about *your* baby? Maybe my baby's father might have helped out a bit too, instead of leaving it to his girlfriend.' She turned to Maeve and started spooning mash into her mouth.

Crow muttered something, staring at the back of her head. Alice continued with her mechanical feeding, eyebrows raised as if poised to speak. Maeve was waving her hands in front of her, trying to stop Alice's spoon. Caleb had a rubber band in his hand and was flicking the leg of the table.

Crow sat down across the table from Alice, leaned back in his chair and sucked on his beer, watching her, clenching his jaw. His pupils were large and black, his skin ruddy. The room was quiet for a good minute, just the tick of the kitchen clock on the wall above the shelves, the hum of the fridge and the occasional rattle of the kitchen door from the wind outside.

'So I was just at Jezza's house,' Crow said, 'and I met the guy who owns the new cafe that's opened up in town. Turns out that he used to write a column for *Beat* magazine, used to go to every gig, every festival. He met everyone – Chili Peppers, Sonic Youth, Primus, Bowie, Dylan – and you know what he said to me? He said that performance we did at the Falls Festival was the best live show he's seen in his life. Wilkie said the same thing in his *Age* review at the time, remember? "Osborne meets Jagger".'

Alice had turned her back even further to Crow, facing Maeve, mouthing words as she fed her. Maeve took the food without resistance, so entertained, it seemed, by her mother's animated face.

'It was a conspiracy, what happened to me. He reckons he's seen it hundreds of times. The bloody yanks, Triple J, that fucking tosser *Bose*man. It was a bloody witch-hunt. We were the best in the country, could've been the best in the world, and we were just screwed. I was just too bloody naive to see what the bastards were up to. I was just waiting for things to blow over, just doing what I thought was best by everyone, best by *my wife*.'

Alice looked at me and explained. 'Earth Monster had to cancel their US tour because of Crow's drug convictions, then the record label pulled out. But Crow prefers a different version of events—'

'That's a fucking lie. You were pregnant and acting like a complete lunatic, threatening to piss off to Canada—'

'No, no, no, you don't—'

They continued in this vein for a while, apparently under the guise of explaining to me what happened, but I was quickly, thankfully, forgotten. I'd heard mutterings of both stories in the past anyway and had decided that probably neither of them could be entirely trusted. When Alice made an exasperated sigh and turned her back on him again, refusing to continue, Crow launched into an extended monologue about how the entire music industry had 'started going down the toilet' around the mid-nineties: 'No wonder Kurt Cobain shot himself, must have seen where it was headed.' He tipped his beer, pouring it down his throat, then stood, put the bottle next to the sink and walked to the fridge for another. He popped the top off his beer and put the lid down on the bench top, next to the other one, then leaned against the kitchen sink. His eyes were locked on a point on the wall opposite him.

Alice paused, spoonful of mash in her hand, resting on the edge of Maeve's plate, and stared at the bottle tops on the bench. 'Are you going to put those in the bin? Or shall I do it for you?' She turned and looked straight at him. 'I mean, if you're too busy right now, I could get up and walk the bottle tops over to the bin. Shall I do that for you?'

I didn't raise my eyes from the table.

Crow stayed frozen for a few moments, as if he hadn't heard, then snatched the bottle tops off the table, walked to the bin, pushed the lid flap with the base of his beer, and dropped the tops into the near-full rubbish bag.

'Come on, kids, eat up,' Alice said, cheerily, putting an arm on Maeve's back and rubbing it. Caleb slipped off his chair and left the room.

'Oi!' Crow yelled after him. 'Did I say you could leave the table?'

'Can I please leave the table?' Caleb's voice could be heard from the living room.

'*May* I leave the table, not *can* I leave the table. Yes, you *may*.' Crow leaned against the sink again, ankles crossed, arms crossed, holding his beer, staring ahead.

Alice and I sat there, saying nothing as Alice tried to shovel another mouthful into Maeve. Then Alice looked up at me and spoke.

'I might come to Melbourne next weekend.'

'What about Tom?' Crow asked.

'You can look after him.'

'What do you need to do in Melbourne?'

'Oh, I don't know. Same as you, I suppose. Drink, party, fuck strangers, stuff like that.'

'You're not going to Melbourne,' said Crow.

'Why not?'

'We haven't talked about it.'

'We can talk about it now.'

'We can talk about it later.'

'What's wrong with now?'

'I said we'll talk about it later. Lara doesn't need to hear about our domestic arrangements.'

'I'm sure she'd be really interested in our domestic arrangements, wouldn't you, Lara?'

Crow looked away and his chest, with his arms and beer crossed over the front, heaved slowly up and down. I looked away also, towards the living-room door, wishing I was in there watching TV with Caleb.

'It goes like this. Crow lies in bed until whatever the fuck time he likes; Alice gets up – after being up all night, mind you – and gets the kids' breakfast. Then, when his lordship comes down,' Alice stood up and started swanning around the kitchen, her nose in the air and her lids half-closed, 'his lordship will let me know what he'd like for breakfast. Sometimes it might be poached eggs and bacon, or porridge, or French toast—'

'That's enough, Alice.'

'And after breakfast, because his lordship has had such a hard week, he'll often sit in his room and play guitar for three hours while I—'

He stepped in close to her. 'I said that's enough!'

'No, Lara wants to hear. She wants to know what it's like to be a mum, don't you, Lara? So I take Caleb to Auskick, with all the other dads, and then Maeve—'

'You're making a bloody fool out of yourself.' He grabbed her wrist.

Alice shook hard, her ranting barely coherent, her eyes heavy-lidded. 'Why don't you just keep skolling beers while I take the rubbish out?' She said, pushing him off, then removed the lid from the bin and edged out the overloaded bag. Tom – his head wobbling about in the struggle – somehow, stayed asleep at her front.

'Alice, stop it!'

Crow grabbed her forearm again.

She shoved him away. 'No! I'll bloody do it; I always bloody do it.' She grabbed the empty beer bottle off the sink, along with another two from a cardboard box next to the fridge, and heaved the rubbish bag to the kitchen door. As she opened the door, frosty air charged inside. The door banged closed behind her then bounced ajar. Moments later, above the soft moan of the wind, there was a shattering sound from the blackness outside: the beer bottle, I imagined. Then seconds later, another, and then again, another. And then a long, guttural scream. In the quiet that followed, Maeve started crying and calling out 'Mumma'.

I put my arm around Maeve as Crow marched around the room. 'Is Tom all right out there?' I said, barely audible.

But Crow wasn't listening; he looked at me square, his eyes fierce. 'See what I have to deal with?' He kept staring at me, eyes bloodshot. 'See what I have to fucking deal with? I've spoken with her mother. Says she's always been like this. Wished me luck.' He grunted, picked up his beer then stormed into the living room, leaving me there with Maeve. As I wiped her face she screamed and tried to push me away with her cold, sticky, mashed-potato-covered hands, still yelling out for Mumma.

I picked her up and started singing 'Five Little Ducks' – I'd heard Alice sing it to her earlier – but she grew more distraught, so I opened the back door and stepped out, accidentally kicking over the ashtray on the concrete step.

I couldn't hear Alice, but I could hear Crow – he must have come around from the front door – his voice a low growl. 'So it's the Alice show again, is it? Always the fucking Alice show. You're a fucking embarrassment.' With the sound of the wind, and cries from Maeve, it was hard to hear much else, but I thought I could hear Alice crying.

You see, it was happening to both of us: our new normal; our lives falling apart. This is what happens – you grow up with dreams and ideals, and before long you realise it's all a fantasy: everything that you thought was going to happen. So you just keep going, day after day, watching romantic comedies, following the tabloid lives of Hollywood couples, hoping that yours might somehow change. That was it: I was busy with my own problems. So, no, I didn't give Alice much thought.

I closed the back door. 'Shall we run the bath?' I said cheerily to Maeve. Strange to remember me standing there on the doorstep, where Alice smoked her night-time cigarettes, next to the kitchen bench. The seat of the fire – well, most likely – that's what Detective Hafley said: a cigarette, the toaster, the electric jug; could have been any of those things.

16

Months – no, a year or more – went by. Christian and I were now regularly engaging in momentous fights about ridiculous things. One night we had dinner at my workmates' place, and Christian refused the food we were having for dinner, on ethical bloody grounds. We were sitting there on the balcony of Kate's Marine Parade apartment, overlooking the bay, sun going down – a beautiful evening – and Kate was standing at Christian's shoulder with the food that he'd refused, swordfish steak, dangling in her tongs.

'Sorry!' Kate said, 'Lara didn't tell me you were vego.'

To which Christian replied, ever so politely, 'No, I just don't eat endangered species.'

She raised her thinly manicured eyebrows and responded as best as anyone could: 'Well, it's dead now, innit? Want me to give it a funeral?'

As for me, Christian's comment just made me chow down my steak with more gusto, but I was still unable to resurrect the atmosphere that he'd so deftly destroyed, so we left the dinner early and fought the entire way home. If I wanted to hang out with airheads, that was my prerogative, he said in the car, but he didn't want to spend his time with people who had so little regard for the world around them.

'Why do you always have to be right about everything?' I yelled at him, following him up the hallway as we got home.

'Everyone always thinks that they're right,' he calmly replied, sitting down on the bed, taking off his shoes. 'That's the definition of an argument: two people claiming different points of view.'

I kept following him, right behind him, as he carried his shoes to the wardrobe and placed them side-by-side at the bottom, then pulled out his ugg boots. 'Why are you so hell-bent on saving the bloody environment anyway? For who? The children you don't even want?'

He looked at me and almost smiled. 'So that's what this is about.' Then he walked across the hallway into his office, closing the door behind him.

The following few nights, he stayed in his office until late. I started to wonder if he no longer found me attractive, and imagined him having an affair. I'd wake as he crept into bed but be too angry to contrive any affection. Five days later he reached across to hold me in the middle of the night, pulling me in, kissing the back of my shoulders, but I knew I was about to get my period so there seemed no point in having sex. His hands on me felt greedy, his hunger infantile. He turned me over onto my back. I lay there, unresponsive, with my head to the side, unable to even kiss him.

Alice once told me, years earlier, about a relationship counsellor she went to with Crow, and how helpful it had been. In the first session, the counsellor had asked them both to list the qualities in the other person that they'd first been attracted to, and then they had to discuss whether they still saw those qualities in one another today. Alice said how much these sessions had helped Crow and her to rekindle their relationship. I started to think about this during these months, when Christian would come home from work and I'd be lying on the sofa eating potato chips, drinking a glass of wine and watching *Deal or No Deal*. The kitchen counter would be crowded with bread, cheese, Tim Tams and salami, ants trailing across the bench.

Listening to Christian in the kitchen, the sound of the dishwasher being unstacked, saucepans and frypans knocking against the edge of the sink, as he muttered, 'Let's just get a bit of order in here,' I'd think about the things I'd once adored in him. His drive and passion to do good now seemed like a form of egotism; that staunch, unflappable nature of his now just seemed like righteousness.

And how must I have looked to him? The morning after our first night together in the Otways, over a cup of tea around the coals, Christian told me that when he looked into my eyes he saw a wild forest, and that he just wanted to step inside, wander around and explore. I know Christian well enough now to understand that these were simply words. Christian loves words: he loves their musicality and the ease with which he can turn a few mundane sounds into a powerful incantation. His mastery makes him like a hypnotist, yet in his mind he's doing no wrong. Just beading a few syllables together; stringing pearls. Nevertheless, Christian did admire my gumption, my carefree, happy spirit. And now here I was, his irrepressible gypsy girl, miserable and sniping, pleading with him for a baby.

The term biological clock had never seemed so apt. I no longer felt time in weeks and months but in menstrual cycles, always knowing precisely where I was within mine, like an astronomer following the waxing and waning of the moon. And with this came a more astute communication with my own body. The food I ate became paramount. And when my cycles swung out to thirty-five days, which my GP blamed on stress, I started meditating – or at least tried to give it a go. The tiniest abdominal twinge was never ignored, as I imagined a zygote anchoring into the uterine wall, a miniscule fishhook catching and clawing at the fleshy bed. Then each month when my period appeared, I'd mourn it like a death.

I wasn't great to be around, but I didn't know how else to be. It only took the mildest comment to set me off: 'Haven't you had enough to eat?' Christian once asked me after dinner, and I hurled my second bowl of pasta right at his feet. I felt like a wild cat that had been chased into a corner and was being prodded by a broom. I was hissing, clawing, growling, not wanting to be there but with no idea how to escape. I think I just wanted to *engage* with him; I just wanted to have him look into my eyes: to talk, be heard, feel safe, feel loved.

We started fighting more often, over anything. 'Paranoid', 'overly sensitive', 'hysterical', 'hard work': these were the kinds of things Christian called me, and I'll admit it, I assumed he was right. (Christian's always right, *right*?) I believed I was all these things also because it *felt* like hard work, and I *felt* sensitive, hysterical and paranoid. But these were apparently the wrong things to feel; apparently I should have been more like him: calm, rational and in control. But I've only realised recently how clever these accusations are, how incredibly hard they are to disprove – but worse, how *silencing* they are. They're loaded with the implicit message: I have authority in these matters, and you, my poor girl, are not qualified to speak.

Personal power is essentially the ability to change something if you want to change it. It's the ability to make things happen. But it's also related to the ability to make choices, to have options. I've read a study which showed that people will trade power for choices, and vice versa, because both stem from the same basic human need: control. When a person is deprived of choices, they show a thirst for power; and when people are stripped of power, they can be satiated with more choices. Power is control over another person's life; choice is control over your own. Both of them feel good. Both of them, for me, seemed to be lacking.

Our favourite time to make love used to be the afternoon. We'd be chatting over Sunday lunch, or reading the paper. He'd be listening to me rant about the state of modern journalism, then I'd notice those languid eyes staring at me. 'Let's have sex,' he'd say. He never called it making love or fucking, always having 'sex'. I came to like the word too. He'd start kissing me, then undressing me, at the kitchen table.

We still occasionally had sex, but now we only did it in the dead of night, without speaking. As if it were a shameful, clandestine act, even to ourselves. Afterwards, we'd both lie there on our backs in the awkward silence of the room. Once we would have lain in each other's arms and talked, but these days we rolled away from one another, as if we'd had a misunderstanding and were politely offering time alone.

I started looking at couples differently, almost covertly. They needn't have been real couples – even couples in ads or movies; I'd watch them with a mixture of intrigue and grief. I'd find myself staring at the actress, trying to imagine what it must be like to be that character, wondering if I'd ever feel like that again, if I'd ever experience that intensity of gaze, that yearning for and from another human being.

Until Crow, the only other person I came close to discussing all of this with was, of all people, my mother. Her distance from my life, her pragmatic approach, made her, in many ways, the perfect person to turn to. And after all, she was a woman, a mother, and she'd endured a long and volatile relationship with my father.

I'd never spoken with her about wanting children, yet for so many years Mum had nagged me about when I was going to have a baby. Years back, my documentary *I Will Survive* (about the group of Melbourne drag queens who were performing shows at the

Greyhound and the Espy to fund a 'sister's' battle with lymphatic cancer) was nominated for the Foxtel Documentary prize. When I rang Mum to tell her I had some amazing news, she replied, equally excited, 'You're pregnant!' I told her about my nomination, and she didn't even try to hide her disappointment. However, for a year or so – since my parents had moved up to Queensland – Mum hadn't said a word. I'd assumed she'd given up on the idea of grandchildren.

I told her on the phone one evening that Christian and I were having 'a few difficulties'. She just made an 'mmm' sound, so I continued: 'Christian doesn't know if he wants kids.'

'That's something you should have sorted out a long time ago,' she said.

I was glad to be doing this over the phone, where I could convince myself I was revealing nothing. I took a breath, a moment to think about how to respond. 'Well, I didn't. And now I want them.'

I heard her sigh. 'Go easy on him, Lara. I know what you're like.'

I had never stopped being, in her eyes, the histrionic teen. I closed my eyes and again thought about what to say. How to defend the label without becoming it.

She added, 'You're very lucky. He's a good man.'

We left the conversation there. But for hours, and even days afterwards, I smarted when I thought of the words I'd fallen silent upon, the one line I was now dying to scream out at her (and at Christian, and anyone else who would listen):

And I'm a good woman too.

I hadn't visited Alice in months; our phone calls started to peter out too. Being around her children was hard, and it was tiring listening to her complaints about Crow, as well as maintaining the lies I'd told her about my relationship. But then I received an email from her to follow the blog of 'Alonso Magnifico'. I clicked through to a photo of a man, handsome, around thirty. His dark hair was slicked back and tied in a ponytail, and he had stubble, a moustache and a goatee. He was immediately familiar. It was Alice, dressed as a man. She was seated on one of her wooden kitchen chairs, leaning towards the camera, elbows on her knees; wearing a white T-shirt, baggy pants, pendants, an eighties-style cropped leather jacket and a backwards baseball hat. Underneath the photo was a short bio, in which Alonso announced his occupation as poet/philosopher, his religion as Buddhism, and his relationship status as 'open'.

Yes, it was Alice, the old Alice: the subversion, the humour, the playfulness. The Alice who wrote comic articles for the university magazine, *Farrago*, reimagining moments in the lives of famous men after messing with their gender (my favourite was Abraham Lincoln, sitting at his desk and composing the Gettysburg Address, the day after having miscarried a dearly wanted pregnancy); who scribed feminist, pan-racial makeovers of Shakespeare and even Hemingway. I felt like I hadn't seen this side of her in years.

I was conflicted, between wanting to call Alice and congratulate her (and inevitably get drawn into bouncing around ideas for Alonso's escapades) and thinking it was childish nonsense, and that I needed to get back to the grant acquittal document I was working on, which needed to be submitted by midday. I didn't end up calling Alice, but over the next few weeks I checked her Alonso blog regularly, to read posts with titles such as 'Ten models I'll never fuck and why', or 'Humility is the new narcissism'. When November arrived, Alonso announced from his page that he was taking part in a national men's health fundraiser called Movember, and wouldn't shave his handlebar moustache for a month. For the next four weeks, Alice added a flurry of photo-filled posts about Alonso, increasingly hirsute, firstly in recognisable surrounds, such as picking up the kids from school, or eating muffins with them at a cafe, but then there were cleverly photoshopped Alonso posters in various places, like in a busy London bus shelter, and on a billboard at Times Square. Alonso appeared with Paris Hilton on the cover of *Famous* magazine; he was photographed alongside Bono and Angelina Jolie, addressing the UN, or sitting down for an intimate chat with the Dalai Lama (with the caption, 'The only dude I'll take orders from'). In another, he was backstage at a Victoria's Secret fashion show, with 'angels' draped over him (captioned, 'Ladies, I'm here to serve'). The photos were interspersed with Alonso's philosophical quips, sleazy pick-up lines, self-aggrandisement, navel-gazing, and spiritual justification for everything from drug-taking to sex trafficking.

It turned out Alonso was a project for an online media short course Alice was doing, but she was clearly having fun with it. Every time I checked in, the visitor count to her site had grown, as had the number of comments under each post (all from unfamiliar names, and some from Europe or the US). Alice linked to other blogs in her posts, and welcomed new readers and bloggers: it was a language with which I was entirely unfamiliar. Watching the growth of this online theatrical space she'd created and the blogger community sprout up around her and applaud her efforts – who were all these people, anyway? – reminded me of her seemingly effortless slide into motherhood and that twinge of jealousy I'd felt when she'd talk about her new mothers' group friends.

On the first of December, Alonso 'shaved' his moustache back to stubble and shaved off his hair, blogging about it as his 'Samson moment'. The post, I later learnt, was linked to by a prominent American 'mommy blogger'; the day that I looked, it had already accumulated fifty-seven comments.

I sat for a few minutes, staring at the close-up black-and-white photo of Alice's shaved head on my computer. She posed with her seductive stare, looking back towards the camera's lens, cigarette smoke winding out between her suggestively just-parted lips, the stubble on her face expertly drawn. She was leaning against an outside door jamb; the daylight was bright on her face, and the sharp shadow of the door cut down across her bound chest. She had a scarf knotted around her neck, the way Crow used to wear them. Compositionally, the photo was impressive. But – maybe it was the bare skull that made it stand out from previous self-portraits – she looked gaunt: unwell.

I called her from work. 'So, Alonso.'

'What do you think?'

'You've got a nice skull.'

'That's what the mums at school say. Half of them want to date me.'

'Are you okay?'

'Having a ball. You wouldn't believe how much fun it is to be a dude.'

So then I rang Crow.

'Alice has shaved her head.'

'Yep.' His breathiness was laden with irritation. I realised that I hadn't, until now, considered how her theatrics might be affecting him and the kids.

'You bothered by this Alonso business?'

'If she wants to get her kicks by dressing like a man, that's her business.'

I thought that was quite generous of Crow. 'Is she okay?'

Crow laughed. 'She's off her fucking rocker. But she's no victim. Loving the attention she's getting, of course. All these American chicks treating her like some fucking rockstar because she's shaved her head. Hardly imaginative. So, no – I wouldn't waste my time shedding any tears for her. It's me and the kids you should be concerned about.'

I got off the phone and, again, looked closely at her face – her goading eyes, the lazy tilt of her head – trying to assess her sanity. But this concern soon passed as I thought of Crow's words. While other people were busy at work, or dealing with ageing parents, sick kids, divorce, cancer – look at her: she was at home playing dress-ups. I didn't call her again and stopped checking in to follow her blog.

How awful to remember this now, in light of her death nine weeks later.

Up until then, I'd been proficient at keeping my two worlds – work and home – separate. Or perhaps it's more that I'd never before felt such a schism within myself. But my world was changing; I was changing. I'd felt, perhaps imagined, another's heartbeat within me – experienced, although only for a few weeks, what it was to care for another's life more than my own. I often blamed myself for not being able to fall pregnant or keep a pregnancy – as if my hardness, my *male*ness – was too inhospitable for something as delicate as a new life. Now, slowly, the neuroses in my personal life started to invade my work, like damp silently rising, invisibly at first, through the ground and into the walls. I started to get forgetful. Michael noticed it – my mind being elsewhere – and asked me if I had boyfriend troubles. He seemed to think that a woman's wellbeing could always be linked to her boyfriend or her period. I wasn't about to admit that in this case he was right on both counts.

Then one day Michael and I had a meeting with an investment manager from Screen Australia, about the mental-health series that I worked on last year; the biggest job I'd ever netted. We were meeting at a cafe in Southbank, and Michael and I arrived early, around ten to eleven, to have a coffee and prepare. We were sitting inside at one of the wooden booths, and I remember feeling particularly nervous. I did, on occasion, get a little jittery before important meetings, but that day my heart was racing, and I felt so short of breath that I wasn't sure I'd be able to talk at all. As we sat with our coffees, Michael was rabbiting away inanely, going over stuff we'd already discussed several times, so I just stared down at the red-and-brown emblem on the outside of my coffee cup and concentrated on trying to calm my breath and still my mind. Then I looked up to the old railway clock on the wall to check the time and saw the strangest thing: the minute hand of the clock was moving quickly and smoothly around the face, hours clicking past every few seconds, like time-lapse footage. I turned to look back at Michael.

'Give her a sense of ownership,' he was saying, 'She'll do it if she feels like it's her idea.'

I wanted to tell him to have a look at the clock on the wall having a conniption, but he didn't pause to allow me a word in. When I glanced back, Michael still blabbing away, completely oblivious to my anxious state, the clock hands were still – well, as still as clock hands are meant to be – at three minutes to eleven. I kept staring at the clock, trying to bring back what I'd just seen, as if this perfectly working clock was the illusion, and it might break into its cartoonish sprint once more. Michael also looked up. 'Almost eleven,' he said as if interpreting it for me. 'She's never on time.'

I never told anyone about the clock incident. Quite simply, I was worried. I thought I was losing my mind. *That's what's called an hallucination,* I kept saying to myself. *You've had an hallucination. Don't pretend it was anything other than what it was.*

During an argument one night with Christian, desperate for new fodder, I told him that Alice had said ages ago I should leave him.

He just looked at me, amused. 'Yeah right, take *her* advice. She's even more nuts than you are.'

17

Caleb hasn't been around since lunch but suddenly appears, running from around the side of the house, calling for his dad, saying he has to show him something. I can barely hear him over the bleating of the crickets. His dark hair is now shoulder-length and he's shot up in height; it dawns on me how much he's beginning to look like Crow.

'Your dad's still out, honey,' I say, stepping down from the deck. 'What is it?'

His face drops. 'Nothing. Just wanted to show him something.'

'Show me! I'd love to see.' I waddle towards him, sidestepping the trenches and bits of pipe that are lying about.

He shrugs and starts walking around to the front of the house, near the driveway, then drops down on his hands and knees. I squat, then find it easier to also get onto all-fours. I'm so hot I can feel a pulsing in my temples. Looking about the baked earth, sticks and dry leaf litter, I notice red-and-green sundews with sticky dew-drop leaves, and running postman with scarlet pea-like flowers. Then Caleb says, 'It's a spider orchid,' and points out this tiny flower: lime-green with maroon-striped whisker-like petals, and a large feather-edged tongue. The flower is smaller than the pad of my thumb, and stands delicate and proud on its tall, filamentous stem.

'What a work of art,' I say.

His face is low to the ground, frozen, his eyes never averting from the flower, as if it holds some voodoo power over him. Then he says, 'Isn't it just the most beautiful thing you've ever seen?'

I feel a chill go through me; he sounds just like his dad. Crow would always say things like that about Alice. I used to be so envious of those comments. But now – I don't know why – they just make me feel uneasy.

January 2005, four weeks before the fire, Crow came to town, saying he wanted to catch up. We went to a bar in the city where he knew the manager, a woman called Cherry, who wore bright red lipstick, a red silk top, and her hair in a bun held by a carved ivory hairstick. She spoke to Crow with a strong, rapid-fire accent – I only received a cursory nod when he introduced us – before directing us onto a low leather couch in a dimly-lit room off the main bar, starkly decorated except for a framed picture of Mao, some lacquered furniture and lanterns, and a large screen against the wall, painted with a scene of ducks flying over reeds. Moments later, two red martini-like cocktails arrived.

'So how's Christian? You know I've been on his case for you. Telling him to man up and give you a baby.'

Give. Like a gift. Tied up and wrapped with a bow.

I shrugged. 'Could be better.' I didn't want to talk about it right then, though I appreciated Crow's concern. 'And how's Alice?'

'Off her medication.' He shook his head. 'But hey, some great uncle of hers – never even heard of him before – he died and left her a few thousand. So she's booking us a trip to Bali. I normally organise the holidays, but she's got the money this time. We'll see how she goes.'

He went on to tell me stories of her extravagant spending at the supermarket, and that he'd had to start rationing money into her debit card. And then the story that really saddened me. Alice had been going to her children's primary school each Tuesday at lunchtime to do knitting and craft activities in the art room with the kids. Something had happened – Crow wasn't clear about what, exactly – but Alice and Maeve were both crying and hugging each other, and according to Crow, they'd made quite a scene and upset a few of the other children; the art teacher had suggested they go home.

'I went in for a chat with the principal, just before school finished up. He's a good bloke, really understanding. I explained to him what was going on with Alice – it was just after she'd shaved her head. So he decided – and it's probably a good idea – that this year Alice won't be allowed to enter the school grounds anymore.'

'What? Was that really necessary?'

'Look, I can understand where he's coming from. They have a duty of care to a lot of kids. He could lose his job if there was any trouble and he hadn't taken precautions. She can still collect the kids from the school gates; she just can't go inside.'

It didn't seem right. Alice wasn't about to hurt anybody. Was she? Maybe I'd been in denial about how sick she really was.

'But onto other news. I've been chatting with the boys.' He paused and took a sip. 'And we're getting the band back together.' He raised his hand and clicked his fingers to a passing waiter. 'Two champagnes.'

Before I'd had a chance to digest this, and the reality of his life being in a process of growth, just as his wife's seemed to be falling apart, he continued. 'I thought I'd need a documentary team to capture it all – only the very best documentary team, of course. Access to all our archives, footage. I can organise the interviews for you. Bands that we played with at The Big Day Out and other tours. So, you know, Perry Farrell, Kim Gordon, Chris Cornell, people like that.'

A bowl of roasted melon seeds was placed on the table in front of us. I looked into the crowded main room and saw Cherry heading over with our champagne glasses on a tray.

'And I'm not the kind of boss that'd mind if my director's pregnant.' He shot me a sly grin.

I took the champagne glass from Cherry and nodded thanks. So much to think about: filming a rock'n'roll documentary, getting pregnant, Earth Monster back together; I guess my concern for Alice must have subsided within all of this. 'That's great news. Brilliant. Love to be on board.' I tipped my glass to clink with Crow's.

The last time I saw Alice – properly; alive and well – was two weeks later, the end of January. Out of the blue, she'd called me, asking if she could come up to stay the following week, bringing Tom and Maeve. She needed to take Tom to a paediatrician and a gastroenterologist, as well as visiting the Canadian Embassy – something about the kids' Canadian citizenship and passports for their trip. I said yes, of course, but felt ambivalent from the start. Christian and I had been fighting so much that we'd taken to sleeping in separate rooms; he was heading to a conference in Sydney that week and I'd been looking forward to time on my own. I realised having Alice and her kids around could be a good distraction, but I was nevertheless nervous about her stay. I'd met up with Crow several times to discuss the documentary, and hadn't yet spoken with Alice about it. And it was only now, with Alice about to arrive, that I acknowledged what I had done and felt overcome by sadness – how much I would have loved for us to hang out like in the old Greeve Street days, drinking bottomless cups of tea until three in the morning, and how unlikely it now was that that would ever happen. This feeling soon evolved into a kind of resentment towards her, as I began to suspect she may be coming to confront me.

Within half an hour of arriving, with her scruffy crew-cut hair and now rake-thin body, Alice had opened the cleanskin she'd brought, poured us both a glass and launched into a tirade about Crow being too tough on the kids, how he made Caleb practise the guitar for an hour every day, and locked the kids outside at night if they disobeyed him. Tom had even started hiding in the linen cupboard when his dad came home each night.

'Last week he started burning off around the property and all our neighbours were terrified he was going to set the bush alight,' she went on, sitting there at the kitchen table, her fingers strumming on her wine glass, her heel bouncing on the ground, while her kids, in the next room, started pulling the cushions off the couch. 'They were ringing up complaining and threatening to call the police. I tried to talk with him about it, but "Fuck 'em," was all he'd say, "I know what I'm bloody well doing."'

I just nodded, having seen Alice in this mood before, and knowing it was best to say nothing. I'd once made some derogatory comment about Crow's heavy drinking after she'd complained to me that he was so hungover on her birthday that he was outside vomiting into the bushes instead of making her breakfast. She immediately shot back with: 'Well, at least he buys me a present.' A reference, clearly, to Christian's lackadaisical approach to gift-giving.

I could feel her eyes on me as I stood and opened the fridge. 'But you'd know all this anyway, wouldn't you? Now that he spends half his life with you in Melbourne, talking about *the doco*.'

'I thought you preferred it when he wasn't around?' I pulled out some cheeses and made up a breadboard with crackers and quince paste.

'Yeah, I do.' She turned, elbow on knee, holding her wine glass near her face, and staring out the window.

'Well, that's good then. He's out of your hair.'

She turned back, grimacing, and refilled our glasses. 'You know, when I fell pregnant with Caleb, he convinced me not to return to

Canada. He promised to quit the band, saying he wanted us to raise a family together.'

I'd heard all this before. 'Listen to yourself. You don't like him at home and you don't like him away playing music. How hard is it going to be? Hanging out on your lovely farm, two kids at school, while he's away on tour making money. Aren't you being a bit selfish?'

'You have no idea what he's like! He visited the school principal and got me banned from the school. *Banned!* Because I was comforting my daughter, who was crying about her dad. He's been calling my mum in Canada, telling her how *concerned* he is about me, asking her to have a word with me and straighten me out. He's been calling my doctor too—'

'He *cares* about you.'

She lifted her hand, dropped her head into it and started laughing. 'Oh, fuck me, *he cares*! Jesus, is that what it is? He *cares* about his shitty housewife, with her fat thighs and ugly pinched-up face, the crazy whining bitch that no one else would put up with. Oh, he *cares*, does he? Silly me, I thought caring was something completely different—'

'You're being unreasonable.'

'Yes! I've been told a million goddamn times. In less uncertain terms though.' She put her wine glass down on the table so hard that it swilled up around the edges. 'Fuck it,' she said. 'Yeah, fuck you all, he can screw his way around the country for all I care.'

I cut myself a piece of cheese as she walked towards the living room and called Maeve and Tom to come eat some food. She came back in, sat down and looked at me. 'You know, there isn't even going to be a band anyway. Jason doesn't want to do it, and Mark's wife's about to have twins.'

'They've already got dates booked.'

'Have they really?' She snorted a laugh then walked back into the living room to try to draw out her kids, muttering as she left, 'Wouldn't hold my breath waiting ...'

That – on day one – was the worst of the arguments we had, but it set the tone for the rest of Alice's stay. The words hung in the air for the following five days, like prefixes and suffixes, attaching themselves to everything, even during the moments when we did chat frivolously or share a joke. Fuck you all, she'd said to me, and I'd called her selfish. Christian had called me selfish, numerous times, so I knew how difficult it was to defend against. But unlike me, she chose not to. She'd heard it though; I could tell it had stung.

That argument wasn't the only difficulty. There was also the fact that I didn't enjoy having her kids in the house. They broke things, jumped on the furniture; I couldn't help but think Crow was probably right, that she didn't discipline them enough. And Alice got drunk every night – she'd always enjoyed a drop, but this was different. She wasn't jolly, but messy: swearing, railing against anyone and anything, leaving pots burning on the stove. And bitter too. On the Wednesday, before I left for work, we went for an early-morning walk along the bike path;

Tom was tottering ahead of us, and had stopped to squat down and look at a beetle when a lycra-clad man on one of those titanium racing bikes came flying up behind us, furiously dinging his bell. 'Get off the path!' he yelled. 'Go fuck yourself,' Alice yelled back. (Was this her current mantra?) I'm not defending the behaviour of the middle-aged superhero, but, I'll admit it, Alice's aggression startled me.

Perhaps if we'd had more time to relax with our glasses of wine, we might have been able to get back onto old, familiar ground. There were glimpses – Maeve's impersonations often provided comic relief (there was Aretha Franklin's *You better think about what you saying, you better think about the consequences of your actions*, and Elvis's mumbling *Thank ya, thank ya very much*) – but they were often fleeting, quickly lost among the barking orders and domestic humdrum.

It didn't help that I was at work every day, then when I arrived home, tired, even as I was walking up the concrete path towards the house, I could hear her children screaming. The house smelled of burned toast and that fruity putrid reek of nappies. There'd be Vegemite handprints on the white hallway walls, bits of pear mashed onto the floorboards and in the rugs; hoodies, dirty socks and odd sneakers would be strewn across every room, interspersed with pieces of Lego and other miscellaneous plastic toys. The toilet was often stuffed to the brim with toilet paper – or, if not, would have a pink plastic mobile phone lying in the water, or be sprayed with diarrhoea. The living room would be filled with chairs on their sides, sheets, cushions and boxes. I'd start packing it all up, finding all manner of things inside – spoons, Tupperware, toys, a Victorian pink-china biscuit jar that had belonged to my great grandmother (thankfully unharmed) and yes, my Chanel lipsticks – only to have Maeve scream at me, 'Hey! That's our spaceship!' The kitchen would be even worse. On the second night, I found Alice around the side of the house, leaning against the cobwebbed weatherboards near the bins, smoking a cigarette, probably already half a bottle along. 'Sorry about the mess,' she said casually as she walked inside ahead of me, a leaf and a twig stuck in her hair. 'I'll clean it up when the kids are in bed.' Her ashtray breath only added to the sense of wreckage she carried with her.

On the third night, when I offered Alice a glass of wine, my head in the glass cupboard, she said no. She'd brought two bottles, which she'd mostly drunk on her own. She'd also brought some home-grown veggies, two packets of Lindt chocolate, two loaves of sandwich bread and little else other than baked beans and those liquid kid's meals that Tom sucked on all day. She felt guilty, I could tell, about the Clarines and Roquefort we'd been eating, the Tanqueray gin and the Japanese takeaway I'd shouted the previous night. She felt guilty, and I let her feel guilty. I suspected she'd already snuck away a few gins anyway. I said okay and picked out a wine glass for myself. 'Mineral water?' I asked before closing the glass cupboard.

'Tap's fine,' she said.

So I poured her some tap water, even though she was standing there at the sink, and put the glass next to her. 'Here,' I said, then sat at the kitchen table with my glass of wine, and pulled out my laptop.

She looked at my glass. 'God, I'd love a drink, but I took some diazepam earlier. Had a fight with Crow on the phone. I hardly ever take them, cos you're not allowed to drink on them.' Her face twitched, a momentary smile.

Yes, I remember her saying that, quite clearly.

'Is everything okay?' Crow phoned her every night, inconveniently, just as we were preparing dinner. She'd always leave the kitchen and talk out of earshot as Maeve pestered me for milk, chocolate biscuits or crackers. Alice often returned from the call looking rattled, but I never enquired, irritated as I was by the constant drama of their lives.

'Yeah, yeah. No, all fine now. It was nothing. I probably overreacted. Fine now.' Again, a smile quivered, not quite taking hold. 'Just wish I could have a drink.'

'Shall we get takeaway?' I asked, partly to change the topic, and partly because the kitchen was such a mess.

'Sorry,' she said. 'I'm a bit tight for cash. I don't mind cooking.'

'Sure,' I said, telling her I had a few work emails to write. Then I grew hungry, and annoyed that we'd finished the cheeses I'd only bought a few days earlier. I opened a packet of pistachios and sat back at my screen, drinking and eating nuts. She was talking to me as she prepared the kids' dinner, telling me about what a wonderful child Tom was, so much more placid than Caleb and Maeve, who she referred to as 'tearaways like their father'. She kept talking as I typed an email then checked on some boots I was bidding for on eBay.

'A woman must constantly reinvent herself; it's not quite the same for men,' Alice said at some point, making her announcement like a resolution, and I realised she'd been talking for a while.

'Yep,' I said, as I started searching eBay for handbags.

'Have you ever thought about becoming a foster parent? I'd love to foster a child one day. I reckon you'd be great at it,' she said. Was this her proving her selflessness to me? That I was in fact the selfish one? Not only incapable of having a child, but incapable of looking after anyone else's?

'No,' I said, shutting down the computer.

'You should. Really. I would if I couldn't get pregnant. You know, if I was you.'

'Well, you're not me,' I said, folding up the laptop and putting it under my arm. 'I've eaten too many pistachios; I don't want any dinner.'

'Raising kids gives you something to live for as you get older—'

'Jesus, give me a break. I've got plenty to live for. Why don't you concentrate on sorting out your own life and not worry about mine?'

I turned and left the room, but I could feel her eyes on me. I heard her mutter something as I left, and I wondered if it was 'selfish'. I really couldn't hear her, but that's what I imagined she might have said.

The following day I took an extra hour off for lunch and met Alice and the kids at the zoo. It was a mild, sunny day, with the lightest of breezes. She was standing under the pin oak near the carousel; Tom was in his pusher, sucking an icy pole, and Maeve was standing next to Alice eating a muffin and holding a zoo map.

I crouched down to say hello to Tom, but he ignored me and just kept licking his icy pole. Maeve grinned wildly, then started talking about all the animals we were going to see – lions and tigers and gorillas – and did I know there was an animal called a bongo?

'She's pretty excited,' Alice said, grinning. 'They've never been to the zoo.'

'Really?'

'Crow reckons they're cruel,' she replied, raising an eyebrow.

I smiled and said nothing. I was troubled about how poorly we'd been getting along and wanted to avoid topics such as Crow.

As we wandered around the zoo, I realised we finally had time to talk, and yet I didn't have a clue what to say. At one point Alice started telling me about the single-mothers' commune in Canada that she'd heard about through her blogging.

'I got in touch with them,' she said, staring at the handlebars of her pram as we walked. 'Thought I might write an article on them. You see, it was originally set up by single mothers, but then they started finding women were asking to move there and get pregnant with donor sperm.'

'Ha – reminds me of Harriet de Silva. Remember her matriarchal society, where men were killed in their teens?'

'Yeah, did remind me. *Men start the wars!*' She lifted a finger, evoking de Silva's vehement call to arms.

'*They're responsible for the violence! There isn't a single crime that women commit more often than men!*' I joined in.

Alice laughed, for what felt like the first time in days.

We walked to the orangutan enclosure and were leaning over the railing, watching two orangutans sitting near us on the grass. One was picking through the other's fur, which blazed in the sunshine.

'Don't they look happy,' Alice said.

'Sure do.'

'When I was a kid I used to love lying with my head in my mum's lap as she ran her fingers through my hair, looking for nits or whatever she was doing. I just loved it.'

I looked over at her.

'I need to go home,' she said, still staring ahead into the enclosure.

'I thought you had another appointment this afternoon?'

'I mean Canada. I have to go back there.'

'Well, go then.'

'Crow won't let me. He won't let me take the kids. He reckons I won't come back.' She was looking down into the gully that separated us from the orangutans. Her shoulders began to tremble. She sat down on the bench seat, her face hidden in her hands.

I stood for a moment, just watching her; no idea what to do. We'd been locked in combat mode all week; it hadn't occurred to me that she'd reach out to me in any way. I sat beside her and put my arm around her, gingerly. There were small bald patches amid her short scruffy hair; it was only now, up close, that I noticed. She seemed small, hunched over and quivering under my arm. It had been so long since I'd seen her cry: we'd been young, drunk, melodramatic twenty-year-olds, rapturously throwing our arms around each other, lapping up the other's tears. There was an awkwardness comforting her now, as a grown woman.

She lifted her head, staring forward, and said with surprising force, 'I just don't understand why motherhood has to be such a – a struggle.' She dropped her head back into her hands.

That was when I felt it, the gulf that had grown between us; a gulf that actually had nothing to do with her being a mother, and me not. A gulf that was more to do with acceptance of one another's lives and pride or shame in our own. Maeve was standing next to her mum, staring at her, frozen, and I had a sudden memory of being young, perhaps Maeve's age, and seeing my own mother cry – the only time I'd ever seen her do this – but I couldn't remember where it was. Somewhere outdoors, and there were other women gathered around, comforting her. I remembered being horrified by what I saw. I recognised the look in Maeve's eyes – of confusion, distress – and wanted to say something: that everything was okay, that Mummy was okay. But instead, I stroked her hair and pulled her stiff body in towards us. Tom, in the pram, started squealing and kicking his legs.

'I've told him I'm booking us a family trip to Bali. Got him to sign for the kids' passports.' Then she stood up, wiped her eyes with her sleeve, and in a forced upbeat tone, said, 'But sitting around crying all day isn't going to help, is it? Let's buy you kids an ice cream.' She squatted in front of Tom and stroked his head. 'How's that sound, angel?'

We walked along, Tom asleep in the pram, Maeve licking an ice cream. I was still unsure what she had told me, so I asked if she wanted me to speak to Crow. She shook her head. 'No! He'd kill me,' she whispered. I was relieved. I wanted to help her – if she'd wanted money, I'd have given it. But I didn't want her involving me in some deceptive plan. If she was going to sneak off to Canada for a holiday, it was best I didn't know. It was her doctors who needed to help her, not me. But the more I thought about it – the unpredictable, irrational behaviour Crow had told me about – the more I began to wonder if I should intervene, do something more.

It's something I haven't stopped thinking about ever since she died.

We didn't speak any further about Crow that day, and I didn't tell her about the problems Christian and I were having either. How he no longer ever looked me in the eye and how lonely that made me feel. I didn't tell her I was scared I'd end up alone with no children. We didn't talk about the documentary. No, the two of us – who had once talked about everything, no part of our lives untouched – mimed our way through the week, and didn't talk about any of those things.

The night of the zoo trip, I dreamed I had a blood nose that wouldn't stop. I had work and other things to do, but this blood was just streaming out of me. I ignored the blood and got on with what I had to do, but it was getting all over everything. I don't know what this dream had to do with anything, I just remember having it on that last night Alice stayed.

The following morning, a Saturday, I awoke grumpily to Tom and Maeve yelling, and the ingratiating patter of a children's television show. Alice and her kids had brought an ugly presence into my house, which rubbed up against my longed-for maternal world, filled with felt mobiles and string quartets, as if it might contaminate it. All week I'd watched Alice, with her snotty toddler sucking furiously on his dummy, screaming as if he were being murdered every time she changed his horrendous, composting nappy on my Persian silk rug. The smell of canned baked beans, the blaring of the TV that she turned on at 6am each morning, the crusts of toast she tossed Tom all day as if he were a farm animal, her constant harping about Crow – how he was a narcissist, a manipulator, an entitled prick. And Tom – I'm not sure I'd heard him speak, but his behaviour made me uneasy, sitting on the sofa as he did, holding his beloved plastic motorbike, spinning the wheel around and around, squealing the word 'wheel' over and over. He was large for almost two, like a baby giant, plonked on the sofa, dribbling, in his perennially dirty nappy. Alice often didn't notice – maybe she was just inured to the odour – and I grew uncomfortable mentioning it. So I was always grateful whenever Maeve walked into the room, whether or not she smelled of my face creams and wore my lipsticks, shrieking, 'Yuk! I can smell poo!' I'm afraid I couldn't have felt more relieved that the week was almost over.

But it was my fault they left a day early. I was in the kitchen that morning, making myself a coffee – the kids were watching TV in the next room – when Alice walked in and, at my shoulder, quietly spoke: 'Lara, I need to ask a couple of favours. And I need you to mind these. I'm scared he might take them. I'll just tell him I left them here accidentally if he asks—'

She had a stack of passports in her hands – her trembling hands – and she placed them on the kitchen bench.

That's the moment when I realised that she was serious: she wasn't organising a trip to Bali at all; she was leaving Crow and taking her kids back to Canada. 'Alice ...' I studied her face, her furrowed brow, her frown. 'I think you need to see someone, talk to someone about this.'

Her eyes jumped from the passports, to the kitchen table, to me, to the wall. 'Well ... I'm talking to you.'

I took a moment to find the right words. 'It's illegal, and it's—' I was about to say it again – *selfish* – but I didn't need to. She knew what I was thinking. 'You just can't do it, it's not allowed.'

At that moment, Maeve walked in with her plate of crusts and demanded more toast. Alice smiled and wiped her eyes with the back of her hand as she grabbed the bread from the fridge and chatted with Maeve about what she'd like to do on her last day.

I touched her arm with my hand as I walked past, to let her know that we'd talk about this when the kids weren't around, then went into the living room, with my coffee, and sat in the armchair. Normally I'd have sat on the sofa and read the paper, but Tom was on the sofa, spinning his motorbike wheel, and I couldn't bring myself to sit next to him. Alice walked in with Maeve and stood next to the sofa, calling Tom's name, trying to get his attention, to no avail.

I looked up at Alice and asked, 'Is he all right?'

She glared at me. 'What's that supposed to mean?'

I shook my head. 'Nothing. I mean you mentioned his bowels, but he just seems …' I could feel my eyes looking about for a place to rest.

'He seems what? Go on – say it. Jesus, you're as bad as Crow. *A retard* – that's what Crow calls him. Is that the word you're looking for?' She snatched Tom off the sofa into her arms, as if I might hurt him. 'But you wouldn't understand how that feels, would you?' She paused and her eyes narrowed in on me. 'You're not a *mother*.' She stood there, as if about to say more. Tom's back was pinned to her, his legs and arms waving furiously, and he started making that sound – the other one he made – a monotone vocal note, but flat, lifeless. She turned and took him up to her room, muttering, Maeve running behind, and shut the door. I could hear his droning from down the hallway, and some banging and thumping, but not a word from Alice. Over the week I'd often heard her in there comforting Tom or Maeve, singing or chatting to them. But not this time. She must have been packing her bags. And I didn't care in the least. I just wanted her out of my house. I stood in the living room for a moment, wringing my hands, then took the clean-clothes laundry basket to my bedroom, closed the door and started folding clothes on the bed. It was then, as I piled up Christian's T-shirts, shoving them into his drawers, that I realised my irritation with Alice must have been evident all week. For some reason, it now seemed too late to say anything, too late to ask what was really going on with Crow, or simply *How are you?* I would find out later. At the time, I was just too damn angry with her, and too damn glad they were leaving.

Ten minutes later, I heard her emerge from her room, make her kids some sandwiches, then wash up, piling the dishes high on the drying rack. She left the kitchen cleaner than she'd left it the entire time she'd stayed.

'We're going now,' she said through my bedroom door. I stepped out to see her standing in the hallway with her kids and her bags. So that was it. I could see the mood she was in, the fury in her eyes; it was best not to say any more now, in front of her kids.

'I'll call you later, okay?'

'Don't bother,' she said as she walked ahead of me, opening the front door.

'Alice,' I said, and she stopped, turned and looked at me.

'Are you okay?'

She pursed her lips tightly and closed her eyes, then she just stood there for a few seconds. She shook her head, opened her eyes and slowly, as if explaining to a child, said, 'Yes. I am, actually. That's the thing.' Then she turned and kept walking.

I wanted to say something, but didn't know what. So I just stood at the gate and watched her – her scrawny body – load their luggage in the boot, then open the car doors, buckle her children inside, and drive away. As the dusty rear of her old blue Peugeot station wagon receded up the street and disappeared around the corner, I'm not sure which was my more overwhelming emotion: sadness or relief.

Back inside, the house sat as heavy and quiet as a blanket. I made a cup of tea, perched on the edge of the sofa and sipped it slowly while gazing about the room, looking forward to putting all the sofa cushions back, sweeping the floors and scrubbing everything clean. Returning to the kitchen, I noticed the passports were no longer on the counter, and in their place was a fifty-dollar note, held down by the pepper grinder.

Over the following days, consumed with work problems, I pushed thoughts of Alice aside. Whenever she did briefly enter my mind, I'd remember that scared, twitchy look, or a haughty, defiant comment designed to inflict maximum harm.

So that was it: I'd let her down. I never called her to find out what was really going on. I wasn't *not* going to call her; I just kept putting it off, day by day, until the weekend arrived, and Crow came to town with Maeve and then invited me to stay at their house that Saturday night. My plan was to sort things out once I got down there. So I never got a chance to say sorry – or rather, I never tried. I was watching her drift away, but I realise now it wasn't just that I didn't want to see her problems, which she carried about with her like a disease: I also didn't want her seeing mine. We were not the women we once were, and we were the ones who could best bear witness to that change. Sad as it was, it was easier, simply, to look away.

18

On the Friday after Alice left, I finished in the office, signed a camera out from work, grabbed some takeaway to eat in the car, then met Crow and Maeve at a park in Carlton. Crow had just taken Maeve to see a matinee of *The Nutcracker Suite*, then out for dumplings, as an early birthday present, so it was a good opportunity to get some footage of him in town with one of his kids.

It was a hot evening at the end of a relentlessly hot week, just before dusk. The grass in the park was straw-brown and worn away in dusty patches. Several groups of parents and kids sat picnicking beneath the plane trees, others were kicking a footy or soccer ball. I found Maeve scaling the climbing wall of a tall tower and slide, and Crow sitting nearby on the top of a park bench – perched on the back rest with his feet on the seat, drinking from a styrofoam coffee cup and texting on his phone.

'Sorry I'm late.'

He forced a smile, nodded and gave me a kiss on the cheek.

I gave Maeve a quick cuddle and asked her about the show, then suggested we get started. 'I'll get set up. We can chat over a drink after.'

He shrugged and Maeve ran back towards the playground while I unscrewed the tripod legs.

We started with Maeve on the swing. She was wearing a flouncy, layered skirt, a singlet, cowboy boots and a faux-fur vest, despite the weather. Her long strawberry-blonde hair was plaited down her back. She looked the part: a real daughter of a rockstar. Her smile stretched wide across her face as her strong body arched back and forth, pushing her high in the air. Her fair, freckled skin beamed in the sunlight, which also created a halo around her hair. I walked around with the camera and the tripod, looking for the right angle without too many other children and their parents in the background, working with the long shadows and warm evening glow. Crow stood behind Maeve, absently pushing her.

'Okay, now as if you want to be here,' I called out as I started to film. I was annoyed that I'd gone to the effort of getting a camera from work and now was going to have to lift Crow out of one of his funks when I would have preferred him to be doing the same for me. I had spoken with Christian that morning; he was supposed to be flying back later today, but at the conference he'd bumped into Melanie, an ex-girlfriend and journalist, who'd invited him down to her Jervis Bay beach house, with her husband and three kids, for the weekend. As much as I enjoyed time at home alone, and could find no problem with Christian extending his stay (other than the fact that he seemed to have adoring ex-girlfriends, ever ready to extend their friendship, in every corner of the globe), it was nevertheless a reminder that, these days, he seemed to prefer to spend his time with anyone but me.

And there was something else: I was beginning to have concerns about the documentary. Crow was making it difficult for me to meet with and talk to the other band members; he'd shifted the meeting times twice, and I still hadn't heard back from two of them. He assured me tour dates had been booked but hadn't yet shown me anything official. It meant I was a long way off having anything solid to present to Michael. When I'd initially pitched the idea to him, over drinks at the pub weeks earlier, he'd shown little interest. 'Is anyone really interested in some washed up old has-been?' he'd asked. 'Why don't you just fuck the guy? Get it out of your system.' I began to wonder if that was what others were thinking, and if there was any truth to it – that it was simply infatuation driving me. Infatuation mixed with nostalgia; what a heady concoction. I'd met Crow at an age when I believed anything was possible in my life, and he'd proven it to me, and taken me, and others, along for the ride. Crow once joked that men hang on to the haircut they had when they were at their peak – their most sexually potent. I was beginning to wonder if I'd done that with Crow. He'd been my talisman for power and success.

Crow grunted a laugh then perked up, and started chatting to Maeve. Her response was immediate, and she started arching her head back to catch a glimpse of her dad as her suede, tasselled boots rose in the air. I took several shots from different directions, aware, in between takes, of people shifting around us, mindful of not interrupting our activity. Some of them would have recognised Crow. Many would have assumed it was our child: a couple, blissfully in love with their daughter; that's how we would have seemed. I concentrated on the light and the sound to avoid the awkward questions that such role-playing raises, but it was impossible not to consider the issue. As I leaned in, my face shielded by the camera once more, I began to imagine it was my child I was filming. I imagined her jumping off the swing and running into my arms, just as she had earlier run to his.

Maeve jumped off the swing, taking a tumble into the tanbark. Aware that the camera was rolling, she got up, brushed off, and took off towards the tower. I stopped filming, stepped back from the camera and looked over to Crow, who was walking towards me. Two women with prams were smiling at him as they pushed their buggies out of his path.

'Good?' he asked.

'Yeah, fine. Good.' I didn't want to have to remind him that these kinds of shots wouldn't necessarily be used, and if they were they'd be brief cutaways. Crow kicked the tanbark around with one of his boots as I started to explain the kinds of shots I'd need: footage of him practising and working on new songs, and I'd need something else, another story. 'You can't get any more work with the CFA can you?'

'Those bastards?'

Then, from the direction where Maeve had run, there was a scream – frightened, falling – abruptly cut short. We turned to see a child – not Maeve, but a young boy, a motionless pile of flesh, T-shirt and shorts – lying on the tanbark at the base of the climbing tower.

There were several other kids on the tower, staring over at him, and a few parents running over. I looked about for others, for Crow, but he was already on his way there, the first to be crouched at the boy's side, even quicker than the mother: long black hair, floppy hat and sundress, screaming out, 'Will!'

When I got there, lugging the camera and our bags, the mother was on the ground next to Crow, leaning over the boy's unresponsive face, holding his hand, stroking his cheek, and looking up and around. 'Help! Someone help!'

I was standing on the other side of Crow. He looked up to me, 'Call an ambulance. Then look after the mother. I'll check the boy.'

A voice called out that an ambulance was on its way, so I went and sat next to the mother, near Will's skinny, pale legs, which lay limp, one knee sporting a *Ben 10* bandaid. The boy was yet to respond, but I could see his chest rising and falling. The mother, bent low, started kissing his face, but also seemed nervous to touch him. She pleaded for him to wake up, to say something, her dark hair trailing over his skin. I couldn't even bring myself to look at her, let alone speak.

'Excuse me, I'm medically trained,' Crow said, hand on her shoulder, 'Do you mind if I help?'

As soon as Crow spoke, the boy's mother calmed and, though heaving and sobbing, she was able to tell Crow her name and the boy's name and age.

It was as if Crow's voice had an effect on Will too. His eyes squinted open, then his face screwed up into a howl. He was lying on his left side, and with his right hand he clutched his left upper arm, then retracted his knees inwards, as if enveloping pain.

As Crow got down low and spoke to Will – eliciting a small, pained voice in reply – I watched the mother, who was behind Will's head, stroking his hair, pulling out bits of tanbark.

Crow looked up at her. 'Maybe a few broken bones, and he'll need a CT scan to be on the safe side, but I'm pretty sure he'll be just fine.' Crow tried to entertain the boy with some jokes, but Will appeared unable to listen. 'I think he just needs his mum. And for everyone else to piss off,' Crow whispered to the mother. 'Get going, nothing to see here!' he said, as he stood, to the few other parents who stood around.

From the side street alongside the park, two ambulance officers jogged towards us. Crow went to greet them, and the mother turned to me and said, 'Your husband's wonderful.'

'He's good with kids.'

'Your daughter's very lucky.' She was stroking Will's forehead but looking over to where Maeve stood, next to Crow, chatting with the two paramedics.

'He's a good man,' I said to the woman, watching Crow pull Maeve in front of him, strapping his arms over her chest.

I thought about this time at the park during the second police interview – the one after Alice had died. I told Hafley how Crow had sprung into action and dealt with both mother and child in such a calm and caring way. That was when Hafley asked me if Crow and I were having an affair. I gave a laugh of disbelief and shook my head, unsure why the questioning had taken this turn, and tried to provide the reaction most likely to dissuade this line of investigation. But I could tell my response was too much – too much for someone with nothing to hide – and that puzzled me. I had to question myself at the time, while under Hafley's unwavering stare: why did I feel I was protecting a lie when I wasn't? I kept shaking my head and looking from him to Detective Vella, feigning a kind of laughter as I waited for the seconds to pass, for them to stop staring at me in that way, for Hafley to put me out of my misery and ask his next question.

'Were you in love with Mr Crowley?' he then asked, with the same emotionless gaze that told me he wasn't going anywhere until I'd given him something. And again, I didn't know what to say or do: it was as if my entire being were working against me. I kept shaking my head, saying no. I didn't know how to convincingly go about denying any wrongdoing. Was I in love with Crow? It's a question that keeps bothering me, even now. I don't believe I was, yet I'll admit there was something there, some unshakable force that drew me towards him, that made everything he did seem right and good. I felt like I could see the world through his eyes. And I needed, I realise, to be liked by him. Is that love? Or something else entirely? I still, really don't know.

There'd been weather warnings all week. Fires were burning out of control in Kinglake, the Grampians, Moondarra and the Brisbane

Ranges, and the outer suburbs of Melbourne were on bushfire alert. Even in the inner city, far from that crackling, bone-dry bush, the heat felt ominous, unnatural.

Crow texted me early in the morning, around seven, checking that I would be coming down that night with my camera gear. We'd decided, the evening before at the park, that I would drive down after a screening I had to go to, and that I'd spend most of Sunday filming around their house. I replied that I wouldn't be there until after one in the morning. 'That's fine,' he texted back. 'Let me know when you're on your way.'

Crow and I had parted ways at the park on a bad note. We'd talked about Alice, and Crow had sunk into one of his dark moods and stormed off. So I took the fact that he still wanted me to come down that night as good news – presumably, he'd calmed down.

I was driving over the Westgate Bridge at ten o'clock – I remember because the news had just come on: they were talking about sending more firefighters to the Kinglake fires, which were moving closer to transmission lines. There was also something about a northern bottlenose whale that had died after days of swimming up the Thames. I was thinking that Alice was probably already in bed. Yes, I remember thinking this, relieved that I wouldn't have to face her until the morning.

Other than those occasional guilt-ridden thoughts, it was an uneventful drive. In fact, I have no clear memory of any of it until I was five minutes from their house.

It was only as I got close that I started thinking, again, about Alice. Worrying, actually. Would she be awake when I arrived?

Unlikely, but still. Was she angry with me? I had to trust that Crow would have let me know if it wasn't a good idea to come down.

I turned right, onto their road, and that's when I first noticed anything: they looked like some kind of insect floating about in my headlights, except that these things – tiny, like fireflies – lacked any real animation, and were falling, ever so slowly, to the ground. Could I smell anything at this stage? My window was down, so I must have been able to smell something, but it all moved so quickly from that moment onwards that I'm not sure what order things happened in, what I noticed first. I had music playing – Radiohead or Nick Cave, some morose male – so I wouldn't have heard any sirens.

The road curved around to the right. Up ahead I should have only seen the darkness of the trees screening Crow and Alice's house from the road – with possibly, upon approach, the faint glow of the porch light. Instead, I saw a bright orange flickering. As I drew closer, the light intensified, silhouetting the manna gums that stood along that section of the road. There were half a dozen figures and some vehicles too, black against the spectacle, and a couple of cars pulled over on the other side of the road. Up above the horizon of bush, billowing clouds of orangey grey blanketed the stars.

Their house was on fire. I couldn't see it clearly through the trees, but I knew it, as though I'd lit the thing myself. Their house was on fire; I was breathing the scratchy ash of it into my throat, and the reality and scale of it kept magnifying the closer I got. I pulled over behind a ute in the ditch on the opposite side of the road, stepped out into the heat and started running towards the house. I wanted to run right into it, to scream into it, to do something, but the heat was like a wall, and so I stood there, in the middle of the dirt road, screaming out for Alice.

The house was visible through the trees as a black carapace. The side of the house was alight, and the roof was fully engulfed in flames, with wads of embers dripping down the sides like golden icing. The windows glowed like macabre, hellish eyes. There were two police officers nearby, and four silhouetted figures – firefighters – moving around the front; three of them hosing into the house, and one working between the bushes, the wooden bench seat, and the spot fires that took hold as wads of flame leaped off the roof and onto the ground like sprites.

I ran over to a group of people – there were seven – who stood watching, faces glowing orange.

'There are people inside!' I yelled.

'There's no one there,' a young bearded man replied – George Kovak, I later learned. 'Ambulances took 'em away.' His voice was a slow, marvelling drawl. He spoke looking straight ahead, his face lit up as if by the midday sun. I could see the fire flickering about on his eyes. 'I was driving past. On me way back from Sara's.' He nodded towards the woman next to him, in a white cotton beach dress and thongs, who was filming the fire on her phone while smoking a cigarette. 'Saw the flames, called the CFA, but they were already on their way.' He turned away, spat on the ground then had a sip of beer.

'The dad was over at the letterbox,' he nodded to the top of the driveway, 'with two kids – boy and a girl. They were screaming and all. I ran over and asked if there was anyone else inside and he told me to stay with the kids, said he was going to get 'em. He came back out carrying a woman. Her whole bloody chest was on fire. He grabbed a hose and started hosing her down.' George shook his head. 'She had fucking smoke coming out of her mouth.'

I couldn't feel my legs, and my brain was whirring, revving like an engine. I grabbed his upper arm and lowered myself onto the ground.

'Hey,' he said, leaning over. 'She was alive but.'

'And the boy? The little boy?'

'A toddler? CFA guys got him out. Put him straight in the back of the ambo, put a mask on him. Think he must have been okay, though. They had to peel him off the fireman, he was clinging on so hard.'

The right side of the house – the kitchen, kids' rooms and the study, where I would have slept – was fully alight. Flames spewed out of the windows, then the roof above the window in the living room collapsed, and the left-hand third of the house crumbled. So violent, yet so slow and incontestable; an almighty power calmly, lazily, having its way. And hypnotic. It was like staring into the devilish face of an actual being.

I would have expected a roar from a fire this intense; there was occasionally the sound of a gusting wind, but otherwise all I could hear above the shuddering noise of the fire truck pumps was a crackling, like a slow greedy feasting: the magnified sound of a colony of ants munching away. There were also voices, yelling out orders, talking through radios or speakers. Then a small explosion, a shattering of glass, and a slow cascading and crashing sound as a wedge of roof above the kitchen crumbled away and fell gently, flaming, to the ground.

Something cold nudged my shoulder. I looked up from the dirt. Another man, who looked a little like George, was holding a can of beer towards me. In his other hand, he held the plastic ring of the six-pack, where four other cans dangled. I opened the beer, took a sip, then gulped the rest down in one.

I imagined Alice in the ambulance, oxygen mask on her face, paramedics hunched over her, hurtling along the dark rural roads. But there, my thoughts stopped, as if the darkness she sped into was in my mind too. I couldn't conceive of her going to Colac, Geelong or Melbourne, nor how to find out where she was. The question of where I might now go dawned on me. I didn't know, but it also didn't seem to matter.

My chest was tight, breathing was difficult and my eyes stung. More beers were produced from someone's car, more fire trucks arrived, more people turned up, pulled out their phones and filmed, and we all just stood about watching and listening as the moon rose above us, through the smoke. Apparently the police spoke to me – that's what they said when they interviewed me later on during the day – but to be honest, I really can't remember. I just sat there on the dirt, drank beer and watched their house burn down.

19

After a restless nap on the daybed, I've spent the last hour with Tom and Maeve in the garden. Tom, with his stub nose, freckles and big blue eyes, has still barely spoken, preferring to shake his head or nod when I talk to him. I can feel his gentle step lightly padding through the bracken right behind me, wherever I walk, always within arm's reach. Earlier, when we retreated into the shade and picked dandelions to make daisy chains, he sat cross-legged and rested his knee ever-so-softly against mine. Before long, his entire body was leaning into me; I could feel the rise and fall of his chest with each breath. After I'd helped him finish his chain, he silently placed it on my head, and his dimpled little hands tracked down my hair to my shoulder, where one gingerly rested. I had an urge to scoop him up in my arms and nurse him, but given how his body suddenly stiffens when I reciprocate his touch, I decided against it. It might take a while for him to trust me. Maeve, on the other hand, has barely stopped talking, all the while holding my hand or stroking my hair.

We're now harvesting tomatoes for our pasta tonight, and

strawberries for the jelly dessert. Maeve tells me the tomato sauce recipe – called 'crazy sauce' – was given to them by Abby, who lives up the road. I presume she's the same Abby Alice used to complain about. Maeve tells me that these days Abby stays most nights.

'So will we be seeing Abby this weekend?' I ask Maeve as she pops a cherry tomato into her mouth. Tom, watching his sister, does the same.

'Don't think so.'

'Why?'

Maeve shrugs. ''Cos you're here.' She sucks the insides out of another cherry tomato. 'Dad's probably at her place now,' she says, grinning cleverly, flashing her mother's dimples.

Back in the house, Tom wanders off to his room and Maeve and I embark upon dinner. She makes the pasta dough amid a cloud of flour and a trail of eggshells, and directs me on how to cook the sauce. She also tells me about the scrapbook she's making, how each page is for a different endangered animal. She's up to number fourteen, the Sumatran rhinoceros. If I like I can help her after dinner, she says.

'I want to be a zookeeper when I grow up,' she continues, wiping the hair out of her eyes with her shoulder. Her hands are deep in dough.

'That would be fun.'

'Or a scientist. Or be in a rock band.'

'You could do all three.'

'Dad says I have a voice like a dying galah.'

'I'm sure you can sing.'

'Caleb's the only one who's got Dad's voice,' she says firmly.

I want to tell her that her mum had a beautiful voice and that sometimes her dad can be a real shit, but I restrain myself. Besides, Maeve is now frowning as she stands staring at her splayed fingers, watching the clay-like dough slowly drop from each digit into the bowl. I imagine she's thinking about her mum anyway, here in the kitchen, cooking.

'You know that concert Dad did, when we were all camping, and there was that big jumpy castle?'

'Byron Bay festival, yeah?' One of the few 'comeback' gigs Jason and Mark agreed to do with Crow, out of sympathy, I think, in the months after Alice's death.

'Why were all those people crying when Dad sang?'

I take a moment to think about how to answer. 'Your mother was a wonderful woman, and her death made a lot of people very sad.'

She doesn't say anything for a while, but she seems to be thinking as she stares at her hands, kneading the dough.

'Dad says it was Tom's fault.' She rolls her hands together and picks off the scrolls of dough.

'What was Tom's fault?'

'That Mum died. Dad says he saved Mum. He says that she was standing with us, and she should have stayed there, but Tom was hiding in a cupboard and Mum went back in to look for him.' She's still picking at her hand.

'That's not true at all,' I say, even though I knew that the facts were possibly correct – or so I'd heard. 'Not at all, Maeve; you mustn't believe that at all. Your mother's death was a very tragic accident; it was no one's fault at all.' I hear myself quoting my counsellor. 'No, no, sweetheart, you mustn't think that!'

She looks at me momentarily, right into me, eyes narrowing – just like her mum's. She doesn't look convinced though. I stand staring at her, still angry, but aware that I mustn't let her think this anger is directed at her. I grab her hand, soft and curled in a ball, and cup it in mine. I want to say more, so much more, but I also recognise that I'm just another perplexing adult, smudging the truth, bound to disappoint her. What's more, Maeve isn't my child: she's Crow's. And at the end of the day, I will go back to my life – my new life, my baby – and maybe even forget about Maeve for a time, and she will go back to her dad. But I will speak with him. I must speak with him about the fire, about what happened between Alice and me, and about what he should or shouldn't be telling the kids.

'I've had enough of cooking,' says Maeve, pulling her hand from mine. She walks, and then runs, to her room.

A fly lands on my cheek and I brush it away with the floury back of my hand. It buzzes insistently around my face, its back now white with flour.

Flies. Fireflies. The ash was floating about like fireflies.

He's a good guy – that's what I'd said to Hafley when he asked if I thought Crow could have lit the fire. Crow wouldn't hurt a fly.

My phone, over near the sink, beeps. It's another text from Christian, and I realise I never replied to him earlier: 'Is everything ok? I really think you should leave.'

Crow doesn't return, nor does he answer my texts, so I end up serving up the pasta and eating with the kids. After dinner and dessert, I wash up, looking out through the kitchen window at the darkening sky to the west. The clouds have been low, sitting just above the treetops all afternoon, trapping in the heat. The wind has picked up in the last five minutes and now seems to be rushing about from all directions, great gusts blowing through the open windows and doors, hitting the black plastic in the bedrooms, making it crack and shake. The air, so dense earlier in the day, is now lifting. There's going to be a storm. I'm gripped momentarily by a painful clenching cramp – a Braxton Hicks – and my legs are weary. I empty the grey-water bucket outside, and carry the camp chairs in from the deck, and collect the various toys, shoes and other bits of clothing that are lying about on the grass – time to batten down the hatches. Where's Crow? He should be here.

As I wipe down the butcher's block to the sound of the kids in the bath, I think of my mum, cleaning the kitchen each night, sozzled on gin-and-tonic, my dad out lord knows where. My fabulous dad, off being fabulous elsewhere, only ever around long enough to tell us what disappointments we'd turned out to be.

It's eight o'clock. Crow still hasn't replied to any of my texts or calls. Is this how he's always behaved?

After the kids finish their bath, clean their teeth and get into their pyjamas, I read them some Spike Milligan and put them to bed. None of them asks after their dad. I kiss Maeve and Tom goodnight; Caleb, lying on a camp stretcher and curled away from me in a ball, pulls his covers tight around his ears. I gently squeeze his shoulder and then watch them for a moment, all three of them, from the door before switching off the light. I imagine Alice that final evening, kissing her kids goodnight for the very last time. Apparently Crow had cooked a curry for dinner as well as a lemon meringue pie – Alice's favourite dessert. Hours later, at four o'clock in the morning, she still had an alcohol level of 0.03 per cent and approximately 3 milligrams of diazepam per litre in her blood. I never understood that. I still don't understand.

The house is silent now except for the rush and rattle of the wind. I climb into bed, turn out the light and lie there listening for the familiar sound of the bush. But nothing can be heard above the wind whipping about in the trees, from afar at first, and then approaching steadily from the west. The plastic tacked to the window frame flaps so hard I'm sure it will be shredded. I pull the doona up around me, as if that might protect me. But I can't sleep – I've come all this way to speak with Crow, and he isn't even here. The wind eventually dies down enough for me to hear the thud of fat raindrops on the roof.

The rain grows to a downpour of such weight that I no longer hear individual drops, but a blaring white noise. Then comes thunder, right above me, and snatches of lightning illuminating the room. The kids must be terrified. I bet they're thinking about their mum. Bloody Crow.

The last time I saw Alice was in hospital, two days after the fire. Her scalp and much of her body bandaged, her swollen face covered in a shiny yellow ointment; IV drips, monitors, and a plastic tube that came out of her throat and connected to a ventilator at the side of her bed. Pictures drawn by the kids – the house and chooks by Maeve, a fox padding through a dark forest by Caleb – were stuck on the bedhead and around the walls of the room.

Alice had burns, they said, to sixty per cent of her body, and carbon monoxide saturation of forty-six per cent. She was extremely lucky to have survived. People said that Crow had done all the right things. He carried her out, hosed her down and kept her alive until the ambulance arrived; his actions had been commended. It was Alice who'd disobeyed. The four of them – Crow, Alice, Caleb and Maeve were on the back deck. Caleb can remember his dad yelling to his mum that he couldn't find Tom anywhere, and that they would have to wait until the trucks arrived. Alice – she must have been so groggy, so beside herself – told Caleb to take his sister to the letterbox, then went back inside. At some point George Kovak turned up; then Crow went back inside too, and reappeared carrying out Alice. It wasn't until the CFA turned up that Tom was found, curled in a ball, hiding in the bottom of the linen cupboard. Alice would have known he was there – but so would've Crow. Even I knew he hid in that cupboard when he was scared.

It was the Wednesday after the fire, early afternoon; I was working from home when Colette, Alice's mum, who'd flown in – finally, after all these years – from Canada, telephoned me from the hospital to tell me that Alice had died. She'd contracted a blood infection during the night, and had a heart attack in the late morning. Crow and the children had been by her side. The rest of the conversation is a blank to me now, although I believe we said little. Before I knew it, I was staring back at the blinking cursor on my computer screen, wondering what to do next. Sun streamed through the window onto my desk, which was strewn with doctor's bills, bank statements, my notepad and diary, and a half-drunk cup of tea. Blu-Tacked to the edge of my monitor was a photo of Alice sitting outside a Queensland pub, pot of beer in hand, packet of chips on the table next to her, wearing denim shorts, RM Williams boots, a floral cheesecloth shirt and a suede hat. A young, sunburned, freckled face. She looked just like Maeve. From outside my window, I could hear Indian mynas chirping in the flowering gum and the metal drag and clang of someone closing a corrugated-iron gate in the side laneway. I remember thinking how strange it is that we spend so much of our lives creating these big displays to showcase our creative endeavours, our material success, but then the really significant moments – the arrival or departure of life – often occur so quietly: a sky-blue line writing itself across a pregnancy stick, or a final exhale as a head sinks into a pillow. While I was thinking this, a breeze blew outside, lifting a drift of thistle seeds from the back garden, spinning several around in the air and sucking them up and away over the back fence. And that was it. With that, I told myself that Alice was now gone.

I've never spoken with Crow about the fire. He didn't want to talk about it at the time, and I was uncomfortable phoning him after that first afternoon. As soon as the police had left my house, I'd called him and left a message on his phone, saying I hoped Alice was doing okay, and that I'd head in to the hospital soon, but I'd been held up by the police. I added that – about the police – to let him know that I was in this too: he wasn't alone. But later on at the hospital, when I did get a moment to speak with him, he didn't want to talk – wouldn't even look at me with those bloodshot eyes. He just kept walking off, saying he needed to find the doctor or feed the kids, carrying around an empty coffee cup in his hand. Then later, when I was standing alone in the hallway, having just come out from the toilets, he walked right up to me, close. 'Don't go leaving messages on my phone,' he said quietly. 'You trying to get me arrested? You think they're not listening to everything you say?' And then he leaned in closer again, gripping my upper arm. 'Don't call me again,' he said, then turned and took off down the hall. I was mortified that I'd done the wrong thing. So I didn't call him again, all through that time. And now, a year later, I've come down to see him, weeks before having my baby, and he still doesn't want to talk.

He's not talking with Christian either, after twenty-odd years of friendship. I'm not sure what happened; Christian just stopped visiting Crow soon after helping him get set up in the rental house in Deans Marsh. I assumed at the time that it had just become too draining. I never really asked, with everything else going on: the police investigation finishing up, Christian and me breaking up, and then, a week later, finding out I was pregnant. My God, what a month. And Christian didn't say anything. He barely said anything about my pregnancy either; he just hugged me, and his eyes – which, in all those years, I'd never seen cry – were all tired and watery. I'm really happy for you, he said. You'll be an awesome parent – I'd have been useless. Maybe he was just feeling as exhausted and flummoxed by life as I was. He said he'd come to the birth if I wanted, which I said I did, but I doubt that will happen now. A week later he told me he'd decided to accept a position that had been offered to him at the University of Sydney. Within two weeks of setting himself up in a Bronte apartment, he was going out with a twenty-five-year-old model-slash-publicist whose father owns a small hotel chain. And now he's in Dubai. So I doubt very much I'll see him at the birth.

People keep telling me that having a child will be the best thing that's ever happened to me. I mostly feel good about it, and I'm even looking forward to us being on our own. The two of us will have each other. We'll be a team; we'll be fine.

Occasionally though, I wake up at night, always around 3am, my bed sheets soaked through with sweat and my heart hammering with this overwhelming sense of dread. I also keep dropping things – it's as if my grip has weakened. Keys, coffee cups, pens: I'll pick them up off a bench and just feel them slide against the pads of my thumb and fingers, before hearing them hit the ground. And I've become much jumpier. I've never liked railway crossings, especially those country ones without boom gates, where I almost feel compelled to come to a complete stop before I'm satisfied that it's safe to cross. But now even city train tracks fill me with terror. At first it was only if the bell started ringing and lights flashed as I approached that I'd feel a quickening in my chest. Now, even when it's all clear, with traffic flowing back and forth over the lines, I feel myself start to panic, and I have to close my eyes for the half-second it takes to make the crossing. Christ, my fear's grown so severe that even *waiting* in line, first car in front of the boom gates, makes me anxious. I worry that a car will drive into me from behind, pushing me onto the tracks.

I also have dreams of the fire. But in these dreams, it's not Alice but *me* in the house, fumbling along the walls, screaming for help. I can see people – Christian, Crow, my mum and dad, Michael – outside, through the flames. But no one's helping. They're all just standing there, watching and filming it on their phones.

I've always had trouble sleeping. As a kid, I remember lying in bed on stormy nights – nights like these – with the double-sash wooden windows above my bed rattling in their frame. I would lie there frozen, my blankets in fists around my chin, sure it was a kidnapper trying to get in, trying to steal me away, just like they did to that girl – Eloise Wachtell – who was the same age as me, and who disappeared from out her bedroom window one night and was never found. She used to live just around the corner from my grandma. Gran used to see her playing at the park.

Then I remember learning of something else, something even more frightening than the disappearance of Eloise Wachtell.

I remember one evening walking into the living room as my mum was watching the news and seeing the footage of the Jonestown mass suicide on TV. I can still see the images: it looked like hundreds of sleeping bodies, everywhere, almost entirely covering the floor. There was no blood, no sign of harm; they almost seemed peaceful. But it was just so strange to see them there, lined up in approximate rows, face-down. I don't know if it was real footage or whether the camera was panning over still photos– it didn't seem to matter; the entire scene was motionless. The people were mostly wearing jeans – I remember that – and T-shirts. And within their lines, they were arranged in small groups. There was a mother with her arm draped over a child, tucked in at her side. There was an aerial shot from a helicopter too: the grassy outdoor area was also dotted with the bright colours of people's clothing. I had no idea what I was looking at, but it just looked so wrong for all these adults to be sleeping like this, not in their own beds; I knew that something very terrible must have happened. I asked my mum what the people were doing. Without taking her eyes off the screen she told me they were all dead. I had little understanding of what death really meant at that age; I just knew to be very, very scared. That night, I was still upset by what I'd seen, and Mum tried to comfort me by saying I needn't worry because something like that could never happen to us. The people from Jonestown had actually chosen to die – no one had killed them – and they had chosen to die because the man that they lived with, their leader, had told them that was the best thing for them to do, and they had believed him. So I really had nothing to worry about.

But I think that actually made me worry more, because sometimes it was hard to know what to believe, and you had to listen to others and believe them. What's more, up until then I'd only ever known of terror coming from outside, somehow managing to break into the safety of the home – like the kidnapper who took Eloise Wachtell. This was the first time I had seen that terror could live *within* a home. And when it did live within – who did you believe then? There was really nothing you could do.

I've just remembered where it was: the one and only time I saw my mother cry. I was almost twelve, and it was at our family friends' annual cricket day, up at Umina Beach. It was one of those rare occasions when we came together – made an appearance – as a family. Mum and Dad would get drunk: she would do it in the kitchen with the other mums while buttering bread, tossing salads and unwrapping sausages and chops from the butchers-paper packages. He would do it at the barbecue or over at the cricket field while regaling his audience with marvellous stories, like the one I'd heard a million times about spearfishing off Kangaroo Island and being charged by a great white, who took the kingfish off his spear as if it were picking an olive off a toothpick.

I'd recently started my period and was all too aware of how my body had changed over recent months. I had stood, witnessing it at my bedroom mirror, in a kind of excited horror. My breasts were swollen and sore, and I'd put on extra weight around my stomach and hips. Dad had bought me a set of bathroom scales because girls my age had a tendency, so he said, to 'pile it on'. I dressed in a loose

T-shirt and long, baggy linen shorts, and resolved to get through the day playing cricket.

I was called up for my first over against Harry and Richard, brothers a year older and younger than myself. My first four balls travelled straight towards the wicket, and Harry and Richard managed to score a run off each. I wasn't being humiliated though, and that's all that counted. My fifth ball, against Richard, had a bit of topspin on it. It curved between his bat and his leg and shaved the outer edge of the wicket. The fielders, all bent down in concentration, rose up, their cheer ascending and falling like they were floating over the crest of a wave. Afterwards, Richard looked around and shook his limbs amid the nervous titter of a close call.

'Jesus, Dick,' my dad yelled out. He was half-tanked, standing mid-field, wearing a terry towelling hat and zinc cream across his nose and cheeks. 'You're not gonna get bowled out by a girl, are you?' Dad and I were on the same team.

The next ball was so wide it bounced outside the pitch. Richard was courteous about it and stood relaxed at the crease, waiting for the next ball. There were probably other responses, but all I heard was my dad whoop with laughter. My last ball was straight down the wicket but so slow that Richard smashed it for a six. Dad – I knew it was him without turning to look – slowly, loudly, clapped his hands.

I walked from the crease, eyes to the ground. I should have stayed on to field, but waved my hand towards the house, over the road, and mumbled over to Don, our captain behind the wickets, that I was going to the toilet. As I passed twenty metres from where my father stood with one of his mates, Dad called out: 'We're getting hungry here. Bring out some sandwiches, that's a good girl.'

I didn't even lift my head to reply, just kept walking. 'Fucking useless,' he said to his friend, followed by his boyish guffawing.

Once past the white paling front fence, the Norfolk pine and monstera-covered palms, the house came into view – a double-storey fibro cement sheet beach shack, with wooden steps up the side – and that's when I saw Mum. I didn't realise it was her at first; I just saw a scrum of women hunched over, fussing around something. Mum had tripped and twisted her ankle down on the bottom steps, and someone had carried her onto a folding deck chair, metres from the landing. Half a dozen of her friends now encircled her: one held a tea towel of ice on her ankle; another was fixing a chair for her foot to rest on; others were checking if she wanted an aspirin, a doctor, a drink. It was only as I joined the group that I saw that my mum, in her watermelon-coloured top and white shorts, had her head in her hands and was loudly sobbing, like a child. Her face was contorted as if in a howl, the thick foundation dripping from underneath her eye, like flesh-coloured paint, down one of her cheeks, revealing the mottled purplish-red of the bruise on her cheekbone. Dad. I felt a sharp pain in my chest, watching her. So many things: that it should have been me comforting her now – not these other women – and also that I had lost her. She was no longer the mum that I knew; she was broken now; she would never be okay again. And there was nothing for me to do but stand there, mortified, and watch.

But then we all heard the rowdy voice of my father – among several of the other cricketers' – heading up the driveway; they must have been stopping for lunch. And these women – they moved so quickly. Two on each side of my mum's chair, another on the chair that carried her foot; like a many-legged creature, they lifted her up, scuttled around the side of the house and put her down about twenty metres away, but out of view, on the grass in the shade of a tree. Although I didn't see my mum for the rest of the day, I kept imagining that I would. That she'd tap me on the shoulder and whisper for me to follow, and we'd get in the car with Miriam. We were going to run away. We were going far, far away and never coming back.

There's been no thunder for a while, just a steady shower. It's quite comforting now, like I'm on a boat and waves are washing all around me. I think about my mum quite a bit, now I'm about to become a mother myself – trying to better understand her life. It's been many years since I last confronted her about why she's stayed with Dad all these years. I was up visiting at their apartment, where they'd recently moved, near Noosa: Dad has been mellowed by age and a triple bypass, and spends his days drinking whiskey in front of the sport channel, with the paper open on his lap, and Mum plays golf, and lawn bowls, and lunches with the other female retirees. She's the happiest I've ever seen her. So I shouldn't have been surprised when she snapped in reply, 'I've had a very good life – I've got nothing to complain about!' Maybe I should just believe it too.

My belly, swollen and melony, rests next to me on the bed. I feel a jab just below my right rib and a mound briefly protrudes – a miniature elbow? A knee? Then I get that wriggling-fish feeling of something – some*one* – shifting its position inside me. My dear little girl, I'll be meeting you soon. I promise I'll always love you; I promise I'll look after you. I promise.

I fall asleep eventually, thinking about all these things, and at 4.15am, I rouse enough to hear the soothing patter of light rain, the front door creaking open and then closing, and Crow walking down the hall to his room.

20

I wake again, later in the morning, to an insistent single-note *peep-peep-peep* birdcall, and the laconic cry of ravens flying overhead. I step out through the kitchen and onto the back deck to see Crow drinking coffee from a ceramic cup and eating banana bread as the kids run around on the grass just past Crow's trenches, thwacking the metre-high thistles with sticks. The damp grass is glistening, and the air smells of eucalypt and moss.

'G'morning, Glory,' says Crow, standing. He gives me a smile and a peck on the cheek, and even holds my forearm and guides me into a camp chair, then goes into the kitchen to fetch me a coffee.

I cradle my mug and stare down at my lap as Crow settles back into a chair beside me.

'Beautiful morning,' he says then takes a sip. 'All my bloody trenches are full of water, though. Have to pump them out.'

A few quiet moments pass, a magpie sings from a nearby tree.

'Why didn't you come home yesterday?' I say.

'Oh, I dropped in on a friend. She was pretty upset, been going through a bit of shit lately. Ended up having a few drinks and—' he laughs '—you know how it is, before I knew it ... I really shouldn't have been driving.'

'You could have called.'

'Phone died.'

'She didn't have a charger?'

'Nah, different phone. Samsung or something.'

I can feel my fury, bubbling up inside. Not just fury at him, but at me, at my ineptitude, my inability to deal with this calmly.

'So I just crashed, slept it off a bit. Then when I'd sobered up, I headed home. Kids were good, yeah? I mean it was them you came to see anyway, hey?'

I look up at him. 'Maeve said you blame Tom for Alice's death.' I feel hot, fat and bloated.

He scoffs and looks away. 'Yeah, right. Why the fuck would I say that?'

'You tell me.'

'Jesus. Why would she make that shit up?'

'You told her about Tom hiding in the cupboard.' I'm an angry, red-faced toad. He must hate me, I think. But I don't care, I really don't.

He's beginning to turn, his brow furrowing, his eyes squinting. A taunting, sarcastic look. 'So you've decided to believe some confused little kid whose mum's just died. And you're going to blame me – turn me into the bad guy, the evil father. I'm the one who's here, looking after these poor kids, day in day fucking out—'

'No, no—'

'And you're just going to swan in like Lady fucking Muck and tell me what a shit job I'm doing as a single dad, a widower, then go back to your house – that Christian is probably paying for. Am I reading this right? What would you know about anything, Lara?'

'I'm not saying—'

'What *are* you saying? What would you even know? You weren't here when I was trying to save Alice, you weren't bloody here when I was struggling with three kids who'd just lost their mother—'

'Crow, can I just—'

'You weren't even here when Alice was alive! You were never here; you didn't give a shit.'

That's when I start crying.

'That's what Alice said. She said it all the time. You looked down on her 'cos she was just a mother. Her life wasn't important enough for you – she used to say that. You just didn't. Give. A shit.'

He keeps at me, blow after blow, even though I'm sobbing, head in hands, curled over my baby, shaking. He just keeps at it, delighting in my state.

'You couldn't have given a flying fuck about her so, yeah, it's interesting that all of a sudden you care.'

He pauses, then stands, feet firmly planted, staring out towards the bush. 'I mean what kind of person betrays their friend?' he says, more calmly now, as if asking the land. 'That's what Alice wanted to know. She asked me that the day of the fire. Yeah – what kind of person betrays their best friend?' He turns to look at me, his eyes sharp.

I feel cold, shivery, all over.

'Anyway, don't know about you, but I've got shit to do. Got a house to build and kids to look after.' He swigs the rest of his coffee, walks to the edge of the deck, skips down the steps and disappears around the side of the house, leaving me to sit here and cry.

I try to stand, but my whole body is trembling. It feels like the inaudible rumble you feel when a train is on its way. From deep inside, low in my bowels, I can feel a roar rising up in me, the chasm of my body shaking to contain it. Alice, dear God, Alice. I'm sorry, I'm so sorry. My abdomen tightens and aches, holding in this bellow. I walk towards the house – I need to get out of here, I need to get home. The tendons in my inner thighs spasm and my legs feel wobbly, as if I might fall.

I shove my bag in the passenger seat of the car and am about to open the driver's door when I hear crying. It sounds like Maeve, yelling out for her dad. Then she appears, clutching her right hand out in front of her. 'Where's Dad?'

'I don't know.'

'I've got a splinter!' She runs towards me.

I take the small, dirty fingers in mine and see the long black splinter, running across the top crease of her second finger.

'Come inside, I'll look in the bathroom.' There is nothing else to be done.

We go inside together, but there's nowhere to even look in the bathroom; it's just a sink and a toilet in a small vestibule next to the shower tank.

'Where else might your dad keep first-aid stuff?'

'In his studio? I know where he keeps the key.' She turns and runs into the kitchen.

We walk across the grass to the studio. Maeve hands me the key, and I slide open the glass door, push aside a heavy maroon curtain and step into the cool, musty darkness. I haven't been inside before, so fumble around for the light and turn it on. The walls are a sand-coloured render. There's a desk against one wall, with a monitor, mixing board and a tangle of black boxes, cords and powerboards. There are mike stands, an acoustic guitar, a bass guitar, amps and various drums strewn about the room – even a small pair of bongos on the purple velvet sofa against the opposite wall. There's also a tall antique wardrobe.

'Maybe in here.' Maeve opens the top drawer of the desk. I join her and look down, then run my hand through a mess of pens, cords, batteries, allen keys. I'm about to close it when I see some tweezers.

I usher Maeve to the sofa, where we both sit, in the strip of light coming through the half-curtained window. Her body clenches as I tweezer out the piece of wood lodged under her skin, withdrawing it in one go. 'Right. Run up to the bathroom and give it a good wash. Ask your dad for some antiseptic later.' Maeve runs out the door. I return the tweezers and close the drawer.

I take a last look around then, for some reason, walk over to the wardrobe and open the door. Inside, on hangers, are an array of leather and vintage jackets that I recognise. I've seen them on Crow over the years. On the floor of the wardrobe are some Dr Martens, and several other pairs of his shoes – brothel creepers, those handmade Italian brogues he loved, and a few others. Against the right-hand-side, behind the shoes, I can see something wrapped in a black cloth. I squat down, pull it out and unwrap it. It's a tall, silver pyramid: Earth Monster's ARIA award. I can now also see a postage cylinder and a shoebox, right at the back. I don't know why – my heart is pummelling against my chest – but I pull them out and lift the lid of the box, which is filled with photos and clippings: Crow and the band collecting their ARIA; that one of Robert Plant with his arms around Alice, with Crow and the rest of the band; Crow and Angus Young, both doing a thumbs up; the newspaper clipping of Crow in his old firefighter uniform, that used to be on their fridge. My hands are shaking as I replace the lid and return the box to the wardrobe, then pull the red plastic stopper out of the postage cylinder. The paper inside is soft and almost furry in my fingers. It unfurls in front of me: Alice's watercolour picture, the one she painted after Caleb was born, with its large purply-red weeping heart, and those words: 'How can there be so much love?'

There's a clamouring in my chest. My heart is beating so hard I can feel it through my body, in my ears. My God, Crow. No, no, no.

I'm shaking so much I can only just manage to roll up the picture, stuff it in the cylinder and toss it in over the shoes. I try to close the wardrobe, but the large wooden door won't shut properly and springs back open. I just leave it and get out of the room, slamming the door behind me. The key is in the door but I have no idea where it goes. There's no one around, not even the kids. I can see my car in the driveway, across the grass, past all the trenches. I run up the slope as fast as my heavy, trembling body can go.

The car keys are on the driver's seat, thank God. I start the car and slowly reverse in an arc. My leg is shaking violently and I stall the car. I start up again, and as I shift into drive I look around and see him down the hill. Heading towards the old chook house. That skulking strut: shoulders slightly raised and hunched, scapulae sticking out, feet almost kicking the dirt with each step. I put my foot down to accelerate, my tyres spinning on the gravel, then I edge out onto the road.

You lit the fire, didn't you. You saved your stuff and left Alice and Tom to burn. You monster. Tears are now pouring down my face.

My chest feels tight, as if it's being squeezed. With one hand on the steering wheel, I push my finger just near my sternum, between two ribs, to relieve the pain. The car rattles loudly over the stones and corrugations of the road, and throws up a cloud of dust in my wake. The petrol light flickers on; I'm just above empty.

I asked Detective Hafley once, what happens if they can't work out how the fire started, and he said, 'Fires don't just start on their own. And if someone's committed a crime, they usually tell someone eventually, or they do something stupid to give themselves away.' Then, the closest I ever saw to a smile. 'They can't help it,' he said. 'It's human nature.'

There's something else I've been trying not to think about. Something I didn't mention to the police, that I couldn't even tell

Lisa. Because history is made not through events but through their retelling. And I couldn't tell, I just couldn't. I thought it'd disappear. But Hafley's right. And it's been eating at me, Alice. Alice – I'm so sorry I didn't listen.

The Friday before the fire, after Crow had helped that kid in the park, Crow said he'd nip to the pub for some beers and an ice cream for Maeve.

We sat on a bench seat on the edge of the park, near the car. Crow cracked a beer, handed it to me, then cracked another for himself, and Maeve sat next to him, her lips working like a lathe on her rainbow ice cream as she twirled it in her hands. It was about seven-thirty, and the softest warm evening breeze washed across us. It had hit that time of day when everything is suddenly pinging with a warm luminosity.

'Fuck. Still hot, hey?' he said, swigging at his beer.

'Yep. You reckon the boy'll be okay?'

'Yeah, fine. Broken collarbone, probably.'

'Well, anyway, I got a bit of footage before that happened.'

'Shame you didn't film me with the boy.' Crow huffed a laugh.

We then sat for a moment in silence, enjoying the late afternoon sun on our faces and the tinny taste of warm beer.

'So how are things going with Christian?' Crow said. 'Has he given in to fatherhood yet? I've been on his case for you.'

I let out a short laugh, giving the answer some thought. 'Have you ever heard of Waller's principle of least interest?'

He shook his head after gulping down more beer. 'Nup.'

'In any relationship, every party holds some power, but the person who holds the most power is the one who's least interested in the relationship, the one with the best 'walk-away' strategy. Relationships, economics, politics: it's all the same. It all comes down to power, supply and demand. Christian could walk away from our relationship at any moment; I can't. He holds all the power. And that's a really shitty feeling.'

We sat there gazing out towards the plane trees at the edge of the park, the terraces and shops behind them, and the sun setting in the distance, casting a dusty pink-orange over the buildings and the treetops. I was surprised, myself, by what I had said, how it had suddenly crystallised for me; I hadn't seen my relationship in such simple terms until now. The fragments of lives I'd glimpsed at the playground an hour ago – the panicked, grieving mother, holding her child; the dutiful father, there at the time of need – had reiterated all I felt was missing in my life. I could feel my throat tighten, as if being twisted. But despite the pain of acknowledging my thoughts – that I may never be a mother, that I may never experience the doting attention of a man like Crow – there was also some comfort sitting there, giving voice to it, confessing my grief to a person I knew would understand. That's how I saw Crow and me: two people being left, sitting there, contemplating our own impotence, our inability to hang onto the things we wanted. The sadness – the powerlessness – in knowing we had lost all control.

I'm almost at the main highway now, just outside of Colac. There's a petrol station just ahead on the left, so I pull in.

I pay for the petrol, return to my car and think about calling Christian – but he's in bloody Dubai – or Nadia, Freya, anyone, to come and get me. My body feels cold and I'm shaking. I don't think I'm able to drive. I call Nadia, and as the phone rings out I look out onto the road and see an old blue Peugeot station wagon, sailing past, towards Geelong.

Crow didn't even look at me as he spoke, that day at the park. He was leaning forward, forearms on his knees, beer clasped in both hands out front. 'So who's got the best walk-away strategy in my relationship? Me or my mad fucking wife?'

I'd been so absorbed in thoughts of Christian and me that I wasn't prepared for this turn. I looked behind us; Maeve had slunk off and was sitting in the shade of a tree, digging in the ground with a stick. I decided to answer, not just to prove my loyalty and honesty, but to strengthen our union – our sameness.

'You know the answer to that,' I said. 'She does.'

He didn't move or say anything for a few moments. He sniffed as he wiped the back of his wrist against his nose, then leaned back into the wooden seat, stretching his legs out in front and resting his beer on his thigh. My pitch at closeness had fallen flat. He was thinking about her, not me. I told myself that I hadn't meant to bring the conversation here.

'So what did she say to you last week?' Again he didn't look at me, and I gazed ahead, parallel, in sympathy. I could appreciate the humiliation of asking another person about something held close, something that *you* should know about, not them.

I shook my head and shrugged my shoulders. 'Nothing.' But even as I spoke, I was contemplating what to tell him.

'Just tell me,' he said, his voice quiet and firm. 'You know I'd always tell you anything. About Christian.'

I paused, steeling myself for what I was about to do, looking out at the reddening sky. 'She hasn't booked for Bali. She's taking the kids back to Canada.'

He remained still. Those penetrating blue eyes stared straight ahead, blinking. Then he lurched forward, leaning onto his thighs again, one of his knees jiggling up and down.

'You can't tell her I told you. I just thought you needed to know.'

I could see the bones moving around in his jaw like marbles.

'So I'll come down to your place tomorrow night? I'll get there around midnight, or one.' That was my attempt at deactivating whatever I'd set off, letting him know it wasn't that serious, just one of Alice's crazy throwaway lines. But it was too late, anyway. I'd said it. I'd told him what she had planned.

The colours above the horizon had dialled up in the last few moments: yellows, orange, peach, pink; a garish watercolour smeared across the sky. Drifts of cloud, deep mauve on top, hot pink on the underbelly, gathered near the skyline, near the sun. I sat there on the park bench, watching the celestial show; I felt like it was needling some distant memory but I couldn't work out what. I just had this sense – of overwhelm, of timelessness. And despite the fiery sky, despite the warm breeze, I could feel – just like now – a chill coming over me, a prickling of skin: a creeping, simmering dread.

Crow got to his feet and stood, facing towards the sunset. He seemed to be quivering, like a newly emerged dragonfly, drying its wings before launch. Then he started walking towards Maeve. He mumbled something; I thought I'd misheard him at the time, and I find it hard to even trust my own memory. That's why I never said anything to anyone. To Hafley, to Lisa or Christian. But at the time it sounded like, 'I'm going to fucking kill her.'

I sat there watching him, watching the sky, telling myself it would all be okay; I wondered if I should yell out goodbye. Then he reached down, grabbed his daughter's hand, and they walked off together, into the blaze of the setting sun.

Acknowledgements

I only recently remembered that back in 2002, when I was studying at RMIT, I started a novel with four main characters who bore remarkable resemblance to the four main characters who inhabit *Into the Fire*. The manuscript was called 'The Bee Farm'; it was set on the Victorian Surf Coast; the main character was called Lara; and somewhere, within a plot I can no longer remember, there was a fire. I say this only as a means of explaining that elements of this story have been marinating inside me for a long time, and too many people to mention have supported and inspired me, and the writing of this story, along the way.

I started on the manuscript that would eventually become *Into the Fire* in 2011, when I was pregnant with my youngest child. Since then, many readers, to whom I'm incredibly grateful, have given valuable feedback on various drafts: Jacinta Halloran, Ellie Nielsen, Janine Mikosza, Julienne van Loon, Jenny Darling, Fran Bryson, Nadine Davidoff, Sally Rippin, and especially Cassandra Austin, whose Skype workshops, friendship and support were, and still are, priceless. Thank you also to Antoni Jach's masterclass group; my fabulous writer dinner buddies: Jacinta, Ellie, Rosalie Ham and Tali Lavi; and to all my early motherhood friends, with whom I spent many hours on our back deck in the northern burbs, drinking tea, coffee or wine, while all our kids ran amok. Your lives and stories have permeated this book.

In 2016, I received a Victorian Government grant through Creative Victoria, and also a Varuna Affirm Press mentorship. These were very timely – both practically and emotionally. Thank you to Varuna and the Victorian Government.

Thank you also to everyone at Affirm Press, especially Martin and Ruby. Martin's passion and Ruby's patience and generosity are a magnificent combination. Also many thanks to Jane Novak, my new agent. I feel like I'm in great hands with the three of you.

Finally, thanks to my mum, for looking after my kids while I tapped away on a manuscript that for many years seemed to be going nowhere. And the biggest thank you goes to James, who knows these characters almost as well as I do. This story would never have made it this far without your insight, love and support.